Between Heroes and Villains

A Superpower Anthology

The display type was set in Goudy Bookletter 1911.
The text type was set in Garamond.

Published by Rowanwood Publishing, LLC.
www.rowanwoodpublishing.com

First Edition

Introduction

We are the Just-Us League, a group of friends dedicated to the craft of telling stories.

We come from all over the world. We all have different backgrounds and different styles of writing. But we all have storytelling in common. We bonded over our writing, and our love of putting words onto a page to entertain is what makes us truly happy.

For our second anthology, we have each created an original superhero—or, in a couple cases, supervillain—story. To us, a superhero is someone who has the ability to do something others cannot in order to achieve something important, whether that is world peace, protecting a planet, or something less dramatic such as saving a cat stuck in a tree. Our superheroes encompass a variety of different abilities, from teleportation to ice generation, and face many different adversaries, but at the heart of each story lies the age-old question: What is the difference between a hero and a villain?

Without further ado, we present to you the *Just-Us League Anthology: Volume Two*. Please enjoy.

Sincerely,
The Just-Us League

Table of Contents

ANTI POWER
TASK
FORCE
DETECTIVE
RANCE

Like You

Sam Waterhouse

Jorge Rance hated superpowers. Give an ordinary person an unnatural ability, and sooner or later they lost their humanity. It didn't matter a person's intentions, the power always went to their heads. When that happened, others got hurt.

His train of thought was broken as the tires lost purchase and his police car skated over a section of road that had been turned to glass. The steering wheel spun uselessly in his hands. For a terrifying moment, the car slid out of control at fifty miles per hour.

He slammed down on the brake, causing the car to fishtail. A parked van flashed by only inches away. As quickly as it had happened, the tires regained traction, squealing loud enough to drown out the blaring siren. He hit the accelerator, and the engine roared in response, lurching the car forward.

"What are you doing?" Lillie Alders, his partner, shouted, bracing herself against the dashboard as if her life depended on it.

"The road," Jorge replied over the cacophony of the high-pitched siren and deep-throated growl of the engine. "He's turned it to glass. Hang on, we're almost at the bank."

"Then go faster," she hissed through gritted teeth.

A flicker of movement drew his eyes up to the rearview mirror. Not far behind, two cars lost control on the glass road, slamming into each other. Their frames crumpled on impact in a metallic embrace.

He turned the steering wheel sharply to the left, whipping around a corner. The cars and their unfortunate occupants were lost from sight.

"There it is." Lillie chanced lifting a hand to point. "Global Mercantile Bank. He's going to beat us."

Glass cars and streetlights lined the road. Their target was running along the road, bursts of power changing everything to glass around him. Walter Gomez was easy to spot in his yellow high-visibility jacket.

"No, you don't." Jorge floored the accelerator.

They hurtled forward, across the next glass strip. Jorge was ready for it this time, letting the car drift across. Lillie shouted wordlessly beside him.

He regained control on the other side, only a hundred meters behind Walter. The Unnatural raised his hands over his head. Jorge ground his teeth together, anger boiling up from inside.

Walter glanced over his shoulder and their eyes locked for the briefest of moments. An understanding passed between them, that together they stood on the precipice of a decision that couldn't be taken back.

Jorge hit the brake, the car screeching as it fought against its own momentum. Walter turned away and thrust his hands forward toward the bank.

Jorge yelled, his voice lost amidst the rising noise. Even as the car ground to a halt a handful of meters behind Walter, the stone facade of Global Mercantile Bank changed.

Too late. He was too late.

The transformation started at the ornate wooden doors. They crystallized from dark mahogany to thick glass within moments. From there, Walter's power drove the glass out across the carved stone with an unstoppable momentum.

Sunlight bounced off the glass, blinding Jorge. He winced and raised a hand to shield his eyes, scrambling blindly to find the door handle to exit the car. He drew his sidearm and took aim in Walter's general direction.

"Hands down, Walter! Make it stop or I'll shoot."

Through blurry vision, he saw Walter turn around. The man lowered his hands to his sides; the bank's glass transformation continued.

"Make it stop," Jorge bellowed, moving his finger onto the trigger.

Walter opened his mouth, but whatever he was going to say was lost in a deafening *crack*. Above them, the glass walls of Global Mercantile Bank exploded into a billion shards.

Jorge dove for cover behind the open car door. He curled into a tight ball as glass rained down, hammering into the pavement like an endless rolling crash of thunder. He raised an arm over his face, wincing as piece after piece found its way past the sheltering door, leaving behind stinging wounds as they passed through fabric and flesh.

He lifted his head when he felt the glass rain stop. His ears were ringing. Luckily, the wounds on his arms were superficial. He pushed himself unsteadily to his feet, glass fragments falling from his clothes to tinkle on the ground.

Carnage greeted him. Glimmering fragments coated the road like stars in the night sky. Nearby vehicles were pitted and still. The windows of other buildings added to the crystalline carpet, shattered teeth left behind in the window panes.

As the ringing in his ears cleared, car alarms and panicked cries rose to replace it. Hapless pedestrians clutched at wounds. Splashes of blood stained clothes. Faces stared through new holes in buildings and vehicles. This was what happened when Unnaturals wielded their power.

The painful memory of his daughter constricted his throat. It had been a scene like this, brought about by the hands of an Unnatural. With a snarl, he used that memory to lift him to his feet. He had a job to do.

Turning around, he looked over the dented remains of the car door. Walter Gomez's remains lay smeared across the ground. Nothing had protected him from the full brunt of the explosion. The glass had been traveling at such a high speed that it had carved straight through Walter's flesh and bone without slowing. Jorge couldn't bring himself to feel sorry. The Unnatural had brought it upon himself.

Beyond Walter, a new hole had opened in the cityscape where Global Mercantile Bank had once stood. The bank, one of the city's oldest buildings and a historic landmark, had been reduced to a pile of glinting shards. Jorge flinched away from the dazzling, reflected sunlight.

"Lillie, are you okay?" Jorge turned toward the passenger side, glass crunching beneath his shoes.

Her red hair poked above the dented roof of the car. "I'm still alive. You?"

"The weight of the building must have been too much for the glass," he said, ignoring her question. "It exploded under its own pressure."

Lillie stood up. "Not much chance for anyone inside…"

His anger at failing to stop yet another catastrophe turned outward. He pointed a finger at his partner. "You Unnaturals have no regard for others."

Lillie averted her eyes and didn't reply. He'd made it clear from the very start of their partnership how he felt about working with an Unnatural. Her kind, created by the Gifter, had started a war against normal humans. Jorge understood that every tool had to be used, and Lillie had proved herself valuable. Yet she was still one of them.

He took a deep breath, trying to find focus. He didn't have to like her, but he could use her. "Can you do your thing?"

"My thing…oh." She glanced around nervously before moving over to Walter's remains. She knelt down to gingerly touch his shredded body and closed her eyes.

Jorge waited, uncomfortable being so close to an Unnatural who was using her ability. Only a handful had ever turned their "gifts" to the higher purpose of tracking down their own kind. When he'd been told that his partner could read a dead person's past just by touching the body, he'd done everything to be reassigned. Each attempt had been knocked back, put off, or just straight out denied, leaving Jorge with no choice but to work with a person he despised.

During their years working together, Lillie never showed an urge to kill or spread mayhem. Sometimes, he even had to remind himself what she truly was. Jorge believed that it was inevitable she would snap and show her true Unnatural nature.

Despite this, he couldn't deny that her gift, as she called it, had proven useful. The physical description of the Gifter had come from Lillie's abilities. Somehow, he'd managed to evade all other attempts to identify him through conventional means. Perhaps today she'd be able to use Walter's remains to give them the vital clue to stopping the Gifter once and for all.

At the edge of the disaster zone, gawkers and reporters had started to gather. They pointed fingers and cameras, their voices merging and swelling into a dense wall of sound as more and more people appeared.

Good Samaritans broke from the crowd to kneel beside the unlucky individuals who had walked by at the wrong time. Wounds were bound with makeshift bandages and comfort was given.

He wanted to help. The least he could do was ease those suffering because of his failure. He balled his hands into fists at his side, clenching them so hard that his knuckles turned white. It would be irresponsible to leave Lillie alone, not only for the potential information she might glean, but also because of what she was. All he could do was watch and listen, the sound of approaching sirens reassuring him that more help was on its way.

Minutes ticked by slowly. By the time Lillie opened her eyes, Jorge was pacing back and forth in frustration. He'd waved off two EMTs with reassurance that he was fine.

He stopped in his tracks and watched as her huge pupils began to shrink back to normal, revealing the red lines of blood vessels. Gore coated her hands. She wiped it on the ground, leaving a red smear beside what was left of Walter.

"What'd you see?" he demanded.

Lillie raised a red hand to shade her eyes from the reflected light. "Walter was scared and very alone. His wife had been sick for a long time with a disease that left her bedridden. They had to mortgage their house to pay for the medical bills. Eventually, he couldn't make the repayments." Lillie wiped a tear from her eye.

Jorge kept his disapproval to himself. Walter had just murdered an unknown number of people and didn't deserve an ounce of sympathy. Lillie always became too emotionally invested in the deceased after a reading.

"His wife died and then the bank took his house," Lillie continued. "He's been living on the streets since then. He came here most days just to look at the bank. I don't think he ever went back in. He became obsessed, blaming the bank for what had happened to his wife. That's when the Gifter approached him."

Walter's story was sad and all too familiar. The Gifter always targeted those who were vulnerable, at a low enough point in their lives to consider taking up his offer. Jorge couldn't imagine what it would take for a person to trade away their humanity.

"What did he know about the Gifter?"

Lillie's brow furrowed. "They only ever met once. They talked for quite a while, right down this road, outside St. Vincent Children's Hospital. The Gifter kept saying that name, even when it was out of context. After that, just the same words the Gifter used with all the others."

Jorge noticed Lillie's cheeks redden slightly. Perhaps she was remembering when she'd been convinced by those same, smooth words.

"Is there any clue as to where the Gifter could have gone? Anything at all?"

Lillie shook her head. "Nothing. They just shook hands and parted ways."

"Useless," Jorge growled. "Call HQ and tell Captain Basara we're on the scene and awaiting backup. I couldn't stop Walter, so the least I can do is help."

He left Lillie to make the unpleasant call and hurried toward the nearest injured bystander, glass crunching beneath his shoes.

***

Jorge did what he could. He reassured those who'd witnessed the catastrophe, helped those with injuries, and herded reporters away from the crime scene. When the ambulances and police reinforcements arrived, he finally took a step back to get his breath and assess the situation.

Sweat and blood covered his clothes. The most seriously hurt had been taken away, leaving behind bloodied glass. It painfully reminded him of another such scene, one he strove not to think about even after so many years.

A wave of activity caught Jorge's attention. Captain Avil Basara, leader of the Anti-Power Taskforce, had arrived with the second wave of police and paramedics. A circle of calm energy radiated outward as she took control of the situation. She directed people here and there, handing out orders and banishing any useless individual beyond the yellow crime scene tape. Captain Basara was a towering authority, despite only being five feet tall.

Lillie rejoined Jorge. He noticed how she refused to look his way and how she kept her eyes down. A flicker of angry heat returned to his heart. She should be sorry. Her kind had caused this tragedy.

They waited together, knowing that Captain Basara would demand their report when she was ready for it. Neither of them spoke.

Jorge watched as the firefighters began to search for survivors under the ruins of Global Mercantile Bank. They lifted meter-long glass shards, straining to stack them out of the way. Jorge wished them luck but held little hope for success.

At the last moment, he saw a man hustle toward him. The man, dressed in a dark suit with short, gray hair, knocked into Jorge as he headed toward the sizeable crowd of onlookers.

"Watch where you're going," Jorge called after the black-suited man.

The man glanced over his shoulder, showing an old, worn face. A smile flashed across his lips before the man turned away.

"Detectives Rance and Alders, give me your report now."

Jorge jumped around to see Captain Basara approaching. She strode toward them, a scowl etched deep on her face. She came to a stop, folded her arms across her chest, and glared up at them.

"Yes, Captain," Jorge and Lillie said in unison.

He looked toward his partner and gestured for her to continue. He didn't want to be the one to deliver the bad news. He was happy to direct the captain's infamous temper at Lillie.

"We were on our way to apprehend the target, one Walter Gomez," Lillie started, keeping all emotion out of her voice. "Electronic intelligence and surveillance linked him to possible unnatural events that had been occurring over the last week. This was all in the briefing a couple of days ago."

Captain Basra continued to pierce Lillie with unblinking eyes.

"We...ah...were following standard capture procedure when a report came in that the target's car was seen parked in the city center. Detective Rance drove to intercept, but we were too late to stop...the incident."

Captain Basara's glare transferred from Lillie to Jorge. "There was nothing else you could have done to prevent this almighty mess, Detective Rance?"

"I would have driven faster if I could, Captain."

Despite the constant dissatisfied attitude she projected toward her subordinates, Jorge knew that they shared a hatred for Unnaturals. Captain Basara had lost as much as Jorge to Unnatural attacks.

"We've got dozens of injured and who knows how many dead and all you can tell me is you weren't bloody fast enough?" Captain Basara's tone of voice didn't change, making her accusation all the more ominous.

"Yes, Captain," he replied.

Captain Basara looked away. "Yet again, the Gifter has outplayed the entire law enforcement apparatus of an entire damn country!"

Jorge opened his mouth to suggest that it wasn't his fault when a phone started to ring. That in itself wasn't unusual. The fact that the sound was coming from his back pocket was. He never kept his phone there.

The ringtone was jolly and upbeat in a way ill-suited to the current situation. Both Captain Basara and Lillie frowned at him.

He never kept his phone there. That wasn't even his ringtone. Reaching around, he pulled out the phone and frowned at the unfamiliar device.

"This isn't mine," he tried to explain. "I don't know how it got there…"

His voice faded away. Did the old man put it there?

"Answer it," commanded Captain Basara.

He looked at the caller ID. It read *For Jorge Rance.* He held the phone up to his ear.

"Who is this?"

"Good afternoon, Detective Rance. It is nice to finally have the chance to speak with you." The voice on the phone was silky and pleasant.

"Who *is* this?" Jorge demanded again.

"Watch your temper, Detective. You seem to like calling me the Gifter, so let's go with that."

"The Gifter," Jorge said breathlessly. "Wait, you were right here, that old man who bumped into me."

Basara pointed at Lillie and mimed a phone with her hand. Lillie nodded in understanding and got her cell phone. Basara pointed at Jorge and rolled her finger, urging him to keep the conversation going. A trace on this call could lead them straight to the heart of the Unnatural epidemic.

Jorge took the briefest of moments to absorb what was happening. The Gifter was calling *him*. This was the first time that the Gifter had ever directly contacted the authorities. They didn't even have a picture of him. The only reason they knew what he looked like was because of Lillie's ability.

"It was good to finally see you in person, Detective."

"Why did you do it?" Jorge asked. There were other things he knew he should be saying, but the words just came tumbling out. "People died today because of you. What do you even want?"

Basara shook her head, motioning Jorge to lower his voice. He had to keep the Gifter on the phone until a trace was established.

"I don't force people to do anything, Detective," came the reply, smooth as butter. "I merely provide people with another choice, to either have the ability to take control of their own lives or to live as sheep under the grinding control of society. Am I to blame for how they react to the gifts I give?"

"You gave a grieving man the power to kill. What did you think would happen? What about that opera singer who could scream so loud blood would pour from your ears, or the abusive husband who could punch through brick walls? Anyone would've been able to predict things would end badly."

"You're upset. It's understandable. Any time a life is lost is a tragedy, but who was caring for those people when they lost their loved ones, when they were in the darkness of despair? This is about creating a better world for everyone, not just those who already hold the reins of power."

But what about my daughter? Why did she have to die?

He stopped himself before the words came out, taking a moment to calm himself.

"How do you want to create this better world?" he asked steadily. "You need to start talking to us so that we know what you want. How can we work with you if there is no communication?"

"What I want? I don't want anything from you. At least, not yet. You're not ready. For now, if I may change the subject, did your dear partner use her gift to find the clue I left her? I'm heading there now. I hope to see you soon, Detective."

The line clicked and then went silent. Jorge lowered the phone.

"Did you get a location?" he asked Lillie.

She listened for a second then shook her head. "He hung up too soon."

"Tell me what he said," Captain Basara ordered.

"He wanted to gloat, but there seemed to be something more. As if he wanted us to find him." Jorge paused then pointed a finger at Lillie. "He said that he left a clue for you from Walter's past. Something that only you would have seen."

"Do you think he means…"

"The hospital."

Captain Basara looked between them. "What on earth are you two talking about?"

Jorge turned to the captain. "The Gifter's going to St. Vincent Children's Hospital."

***

They sprinted toward St. Vincent's, leaving Captain Basara to gather reinforcements. The hospital was only a couple of blocks away. The thought of the Gifter preying on vulnerable kids, changing even one of them into an Unnatural, was horrifying. Jorge put his head down and willed himself to go even faster.

Despite his effort, Lillie took the lead.

His chest burned as he bullied his way through the gathered crowd. He wheezed as he dashed down the traffic-filled street.

With each moment, he fell another step behind Lillie. When the sculpted gardens in front of St. Vincent's came into view, he could barely keep himself moving at more than a fast walk. How had he ever become this unfit? It was like his chest was being squeezed from the inside.

Lillie slowed down to let him catch up. As he came up beside her, the pain in his chest dissipated as quickly as it had started. He rubbed his chest in relief. She gave him a concerned look, perhaps wondering why he was out of breath from the short run.

"Did he…give any clue…as to where he'd be?" Jorge panted.

Even as he voiced the question, Jorge caught a glimpse of a suited figure amid the patients, families, and health professionals moving in and out of St. Vincent's main door. The old man looked in their direction and Jorge thought he caught a hint of a smile. The Gifter turned away and disappeared into the hospital.

"There…did you see him?"

"He was waiting for us." She sounded suspicious.

He broke into a run again, Lillie at his side. The press of people increased as they entered the hospital atrium. Whether this was a normal day or the nearby Unnatural attack had brought out the crazies, Jorge didn't know. The large room was so crowded he could barely move without jostling someone. He stood on his toes and scanned the crowd.

"Can you see him?" Lillie asked.

He held back a curse. "No luck. Someone has to have. You talk to the people here. I'll head that way." He nodded toward the central reception desk, where a long line of people waited to harass a single male nurse.

"Excuse me," Jorge said, pushing his way through the crowd and to the front of the line. He knocked into a woman clutching at her arm, causing her to yelp in pain.

"Sorry, this is urgent," he said in way of an apology.

He ignored the disgruntled murmurs and baleful glares from those in the queue and flashed his badge at the nurse. "Hi, did you happen to see an older man pass through here? He was wearing a black suit, came in just now?"

The nurse didn't seem impressed by the badge. "A man in a suit? There's been dozens. Now, if you don't need medical assistance, please step out of line."

"I'm with the Taskforce," Jorge insisted. "This man is a potentially dangerous Unnatural."

A pocket of silence formed around him at the mention of an Unnatural, as if he had said a lion was loose in the hospital.

"An…Unnatural?" the nurse stammered, blood draining from his face.

"Can you help or not?" Jorge asked.

"I think I saw him," said a voice from behind.

He turned. It was the woman with the injured arm who'd spoken, eyes wide with fear. "I saw him," she repeated.

"Where'd he go?"

"I saw an old man," she stammered, now seeming less sure. "He pushed his way past me toward the elevators." She pointed with her chin. "Are…are we going to be alright?"

"Everything will be fine," Jorge said, mustering every ounce of reassurance he could, while pushing his way in the indicated direction. He shouted for Lillie, raising his voice over the dozens of conversations.

Lillie's head snapped toward him, and she hustled over, leaving behind her own enquiries.

"Did someone see him?" she asked.

"He took the elevators. We need to hurry."

There were half a dozen elevators, filling up as quickly as their doors opened. Turning in a slow circle, he watched as dozens of people went up and down the many levels of the hospital. His stomach sank. How was he going to find the Gifter, just one man among hundreds?

"Look!"

Lillie was pointing toward a sign listing the hospital floors. Floor three had been circled in black pen and Jorge's name written next to it.

It was a near certainty that they were walking into a trap, but he couldn't afford to wait for backup. He squared his shoulders and pushed through the crowd, flashing his badge to clear space.

An elevator door *dinged* and rolled open.

They entered, Lillie keeping others out while Jorge bashed the 'close' button. The door clanged shut and the elevator lurched into motion. Jorge watched as the screen above the door showed their agonizingly slow process, taking a half-dozen seconds to ascend to floor two.

"Should have taken the stairs," muttered Lillie.

Pain blossomed behind his eyes. He squeezed them shut, mouth stretching in a grimace. As quickly as it had come, the pain faded away. Jorge opened his eyes, passing a hand over his face. There was something wrong. He'd have to get checked out after today was over.

"Are you okay?" Lillie asked.

"I'm fine," he snapped back. He didn't need an Unnatural's concern.

The elevator finally shuddered to a halt and the door slid open to a silent and sterile white corridor. To the left was a window that showed the concrete wall of the neighboring building. To the right, Jorge could see identical, closed doors marching along both sides of the corridor. Disinfectant permeated the air.

"He can't have gone far." Jorge stepped out first. "You take the rooms on the left. I'll take the right."

The first door opened to a dark interior filled with shadowy objects. It took a moment for his eyesight to adjust and for him to make out hospital beds and IV stands. He gave the room a cursory glance, making sure no one was lurking within, before moving on.

The next door opened silently to a brightly lit room. Two people, a man in a hoodie and a woman in jeans and a t-shirt, stood next to a bed. They were talking to the young girl tucked under the covers. Her eyes were huge, emphasized further by her bald head.

He swallowed a sudden lump in his throat. He remembered standing in a similar room, looking down at his own daughter.

The conversation drew to a jagged stop as they became aware of his presence. The girl watched him with curious eyes. The two adults, presumably the girl's parents, turned, annoyance on their faces at the interruption.

Jorge held up an apologetic hand, inadvertently flashing them his badge. "Sorry, wrong room."

He shut the door quickly before they could ask any questions, blinking rapidly to fight back the tears. It wasn't productive for him to think of his daughter. He would fall apart if he dwelt on it for long.

Across the hall, Lillie was backing out of a room. She looked his way, shaking her head. "Not there."

They checked each room, one by one. Some were occupied, but most were empty. The ward felt strangely desolate for such a busy hospital. It sent silent alarm bells ringing in the back of his head.

When Jorge shut the door of the last room, he found Lillie waiting by the occupied nurse's station at the end of the corridor. A locked security door blocked further access to the hospital.

A nurse watched them from behind her desk, twirling strands of gray-speckled hair between fingers.

"Anything?" Lillie asked.

He shook his head. "I doubt he even came here. We've been played so that he could escape. You should call Captain Basara and tell her the Gifter isn't here."

"How come I always have to deliver the bad news?"

"Because I told you," he snapped.

From the corner of his eye, he saw the nurse stand up from the desk and start walking toward them. Jorge wouldn't have paid her any mind, except for the beads of sweat on her forehead, the intense way she stared at him, and how she clenched and unclenched her hands.

Jorge took a step forward, raising an open hand. "Excuse me…"

Before he could say more, the nurse split down the middle. Like an amoeba reproducing, she created an identical copy of herself. The division was accompanied by a loud sucking sound.

One second, Jorge had been facing a single middle-aged nurse, the next, two pairs of malevolent eyes stared back at him.

His hand fell to his gun. With another wet sound, two became four.

"Lillie!"

He heard her phone hit the ground. He drew his weapon and aimed it at the closest nurse. There was no way of knowing which one was the original, or if it even mattered. This time, he gave the Unnatural no warning and pulled the trigger.

The bullet punched through the nurse's blue scrubs with a spray of clear liquid. Jorge flinched as sticky droplets splattered his face. The nurse fell back and her body dissolved, her liquid remains pooling at his feet.

He didn't have time to adjust his aim before a nurse clone grabbed his arm. He yanked it back, knocking her off balance, and took a step back.

Three nurses became six.

Lillie's gun *cracked*, and a second nurse clone fell, clear liquid pooling on the ground. Behind them, people started shouting.

Jorge pulled the trigger again, spinning his assailant away with a wound to her shoulder. He shot her again. The nurse crumpled.

Four became eight.

"Get back," he shouted. This situation was literally growing out of control. There was no way they could take out the nurse clones fast enough.

Lillie shot two clones in quick succession and Jorge put down a third.

The clones split again.

The shouts from down the corridor turned into screams. Jorge backed up slowly with Lillie right beside him, unsure which target to take down next. The nurse clones seemed content to herd them. If the Unnatural clones attacked as one, they wouldn't stand a chance.

"He said you would come," ten identical voices said in unison. "He wants to talk to you, Jorge Rance."

"Get to the elevator," Lillie shouted. "It's the only way out. I'll cover you."

"Only you, Jorge Rance," the nurse clones said.

Jorge turned and ran. A quick succession of gunshots followed as Lillie covered his retreat.

He reached the elevator door and hammered the call button. He turned just in time to see clones rush forward like a wave, trampling over their fallen to wash over Lillie. Hands grabbed at her, knocking her gun to the ground. Jorge aimed his weapon but hesitated, not wanting to hit his partner. Clones seized Lillie's legs and arms, pulling her down.

Jorge's eyes locked with Lillie's. He could see her terror, written large on her face. She might be an Unnatural, but she was *his* Unnatural. He took a step forward, wanting to help, but froze as dozens of eyes locked onto him.

Lillie disappeared from view, dragged back into the still growing mass of clones.

The clones ceased their advance, as if they were satisfied with their prize.

His partner was gone. There was no way he could counter this…thing. Even if the nurses didn't continue to multiply so swiftly, he doubted he had enough ammunition.

"He's waiting for you," the crowd of clones called. "Go to your house. He wants to talk to you, Jorge Rance."

The elevator dinged and opened behind him. He hesitated for a moment, weighing his next move. His home? Was the Gifter on his way there now? Could he trust anything an Unnatural said? It would undoubtedly be another trap.

He made his decision and took a couple of steps backward, keeping his weapon up. The nurse clones made no move toward him.

"Don't call for backup or we'll kill her."

The elevator door closed.

***

Jorge pushed his way through St. Vincent's crowded atrium. Subconsciously, he had already decided what to do. Lillie was his partner. No one had the right to hurt her.

He looked up as reinforcements finally arrived. A dozen police officers made a beeline toward him, their uniformed figures parting the crowd in a ripple of hushed whispers.

"Where do you want us, detective?" the lead policewoman asked.

"Block off the elevators and stairs," he ordered. "No one is to get on or off floor three. There's another Unnatural up there."

"Where's your partner, detective?"

He didn't answer, quickening his pace toward the hospital's entranceway. Now that Lillie wasn't by his side, he finally understood how much she meant to him. They'd worked together for years. They had a connection, one that he couldn't deny.

"Detective, where are you going?"

Ignoring the police officer, he ran outside and toward the nearest taxi stand. Jumping into the first cab, he barked his home address.

"14 Rowsphorn Court. Hurry!"

As the taxi pulled out into the slow-moving traffic, the pain behind Jorge's eyes returned, more deep and intense than before. He curled in on himself, pressing a hand to his forehead.

"You alright? Should I go back to the hospital?"

The pain passed. Jorge straightened in his seat, wiping the beads of sweat from his brow. The driver's dark eyes studied him in the rearview mirror, corners creased with concern.

"I'm fine. Just drive."

The driver turned his eyes back toward the road. No doubt he'd seen a lot of strange things.

The traffic was heavy due to the lane closure near Mercantile Global Bank, and it took several long, anxious minutes before they pulled onto the freeway. Once there, the taxi quickly pulled away from the high-rise buildings of the central city district.

Jorge was reassessing his decision when his phone rang.

"Jorge here."

"Detective Rance, where are you?" demanded Captain Basara.

"I'm tracking down a lead, Captain." Jorge winced at how unconvincing he sounded.

"And what lead would this be?" She didn't give him time to answer. "This is not the day to go off by yourself. The incident at the bank still has to be dealt with, and I've been told you left the hospital without your partner. She hasn't been responding to phone calls, and the officers onsite haven't seen her. Care to elaborate? The press are circling around me like frenzied sharks with blood in their noses. Someone needs to give me answers so I don't look like a freaking idiot."

The taxi pulled off the freeway. He was only a few streets away from his house. "Yes, Captain, I'm on my way to get answers now."

"And what would those answers be?"

"I'm sorry, Captain, but it's best I tell you afterward. I need all the facts first."

There was silence while she digested this lie.

"I'd better hear back from you soon." Captain Basara hung up.

Jorge threw the phone onto the seat next to him. There was no way she'd swallowed what he said. She was giving him enough time to come clean, but Captain Basara's leniency wouldn't stretch far. Not under the current circumstances.

By the time the taxi rolled up to the curb outside his house, he'd gone over every detail from today, wondering if he could have prevented the current situation. Every decision had seemed logical, and his actions all made sense. They still did. Perhaps he'd made a mistake a week ago, a month or a year? How did he come to be on this path where everything just kept going wrong?

He paid the driver and got out, waiting for the vehicle to roll away before drawing his weapon. Tall weeds obscured the few remaining bushes and white paint flaking off the weathered walls, unlike the pristine houses and well-manicured yards of his neighbors. He never had enough time away from work to properly care for his home. It used to look much nicer before...

Clenching his jaw, he forced himself to concentrate. He jogged silently across the lawn, the long grass whispering against his ankles.

The doorknob turned in his hand.

Unlocked.

A bead of sweat ran down Jorge's neck, and his hands were sticky on his gun's grip.

He inched the door open enough to squeeze through. The interior was dark, the blinds still closed. Jorge moved slowly down the hall, weapon raised, avoiding the squeaky floorboards. The first door led to the living room. He listened intently before entering, but could only hear the ticking of the old wall clock.

A few quick steps took him into the next room, gun leading the way. He scanned behind the couches and coffee table, peering into every dark corner. Empty.

He edged into the kitchen as doubts crept in. Had he not locked the door when he left for work? He had been in a rush, eager to confront Walter.

He tracked his gun over the darkened kitchen. Slight movement from the deepest of shadows drew his attention. His heart skipped a beat.

"Don't move," he shouted, pointing his weapon toward the shadow.

Jorge waited, body tensed, ready to spring into action. Nothing happened for several long seconds. Slowly, he took one hand off the gun and reached out to flick on the light switch. He squinted against the sudden illumination as it revealed the now-familiar figure of the Gifter.

The Gifter held a framed picture in his thin hands. It was the last one Jorge had taken of his daughter. The one that sat on his bedside table. To see this man, this *monster*, holding it pulled a strangled cry from Jorge's lips. How dare he even touch it, after what he'd done, after killing her? Jorge gritted his teeth. One bullet and it'd be over.

"Hello, Detective." The Gifter looked up and gave a faint smile. "I've been looking forward to having this little chat."

Jorge suddenly found that he couldn't pull the trigger. Doubts wormed their way past his rage. Could he justify killing this man if it would lead to his partner's death? She was his partner, even if he didn't like what she was. Her near-certain death weighed heavy on him.

He tried to convince himself that it would be the right thing to do, but his trigger finger refused to move.

The Gifter gave a long sigh. He put down the photo frame, tapping a finger on its filigreed edge. Again, Jorge resisted his first urge, this time to rush forward and snatch it out of the Gifter's reach.

"As you might have guessed, I'm changing the way I do things. I feel like I can be honest with you. My plan is taking too long to come to fruition. When I started down this path, my whole life lay before me. I was going to save the world." He shook his head, sadness turning down his mouth. "But it's going so slowly. I need another way to bring about the new age, a way of finding those deserving of my gifts."

The Gifter pointed a finger at Jorge. "That's why I'm bringing you into the fold. The work will continue, but no longer in the shadows." There was iron in the Gifter's voice, as if this future would become fact by his will alone.

Jorge finally found his voice. "I don't bloody care about what you want or what plans you have. What you're going to do is call that nurse, the one you infected with your vileness, and tell her to let my partner go."

"Lillie," said the Gifter, dragging out each syllable. "It was her role in your Taskforce that gave me this idea. Imagine dozens, or even hundreds, of gifted working openly in the very government that wants to destroy us? If they come to rely upon us, then how can they get rid of us? Reliance is just the first step toward acceptance. From there, it's a short distance toward directing humanity's next evolutionary step."

Jorge gave a dry laugh. "Are you wanting me to volunteer to become a monster? The only reason I haven't killed you is to save my partner's life. You will comply or you will die. I lost everything to you and your kind."

The Gifter glanced down at the photo. "I did some research on you. I am deeply sorry for your loss. No parent should suffer the death of a child." He looked back up. "But all wars have casualties. I did not start this war, but I will end it so that no more innocents suffer."

Jorge took a step forward and jabbed his gun at the Gifter's face. "Call the nurse and tell her to let Lillie go," he shouted. "After that, I'll make you understand what it is to suffer."

The Gifter raised both hands. "Calm down, Detective. I'll call her as soon as I leave. Tell me, are you getting the headaches yet? Easily exhausted? It takes longer for some people."

"Headaches?" Jorge's eyes widened. "How did you know? What have you done?"

"I made you one of us." A smile spread over the Gifter's face, filled with genuine warmth. "A gentle tap of a finger while I put the phone into your pocket. That's all it takes. You're on my side of the war now. I'm really looking forward to seeing what you can do. Powers are always a reflection of the person. Like Walter, the glazier. Like Grace, the nurse who never had enough hands."

"No…I'd never…"

As if brought on by the Gifter's words, the headache returned with a vengeance. The pain stabbed behind his eyes, growing and spreading until it felt like someone trying to jackhammer their way out of his skull.

"No, no, no!" He doubled over in pain, gun falling from his hands. He clutched at his head as he fell to his knees.

"You'll thank me later, Jorge. Make me proud."

The pain grew worse. He squeezed his eyes closed, felt bile rise up his throat. He bit down on his tongue, filling his mouth with blood. A million strobing lights burned through his eyelids. When he thought he couldn't take anymore, that he was at the edge of all endurance, the lights vanished, and the pain was gone.

Jorge found himself curled on the ground. He wiped tears from his eyes. He swallowed and found that his throat was dry, as if he'd been screaming. The room was empty. A second or an hour could have passed. He felt numb inside, the knowledge of what had been done to him holding his emotions captive.

Why hadn't he just shot the Gifter? He'd been pointing his gun, ready to take the shot, when that monster had started talking. Understanding flooded in. The Gifter must have done something, used his voice to stop Jorge from ending him.

Pushing himself to his feet, Jorge staggered over to the photo. Picking it up gently with shaking hands, he stared into his daughter's brown eyes, examining the half-smile that hinted at mischief. She sat in the grass wearing a blue and white dress, hair in pigtails. It had been the day after this photo had been taken that he'd lost her.

His most precious possession, a mere reflection of his precious girl. It was how he reminded himself every day that Unnaturals were evil. What was he going to do now he was one? How was he to keep going, knowing what he was?

Lillie! She lived like this. She could tell him.

The world spun around him, and yet didn't. It was like he was on a merry-go-round, stationary and spinning at the same time. His eyes told him the first, but his mind said the second.

Just before the nausea of non-movement made him throw up, everything came back into focus with a *snap*. He found himself standing in front of Lillie. She was sitting on a hospital bed, surrounded by nurse clones. Everyone jumped at his sudden appearance.

"You… Jorge… What…" Lillie managed to stammer.

He was an Unnatural. Looking down, he saw he still held the photo of his daughter.

Raising his eyes, he saw one of the nurse clones had recovered with extraordinary swiftness, pulling out a phone and punching in a number. "He's here," she told the call recipient. "He teleported right into the room."

Jorge turned his gaze toward Lillie. There was a strange combination of expressions flashing over her face, like she was both relieved and distressed to see him.

"Did he…the Gifter…" She didn't appear to have the words to finish a full sentence.

The nurse clone on the phone nodded in acknowledgement of whatever was being said. She hung up and looked straight at Jorge. "Welcome, brother. You're free to go."

One by one, the clones filed past Jorge until he was left standing silently before Lillie. He noticed a purple bruise painted on her cheek and the slight trembling of her hands.

He clutched the photo frame tighter. He would be strong.

"We need to go," he said, proud at the steadiness of his voice. "We can't stay here and wait to be apprehended. I need time to think. I can't tell the captain what's happened to me." His voice started cracking, the enormity of what had happened threatening to overwhelm him.

Lillie could only shake her head, no words coming out of her open mouth.

He cleared his throat and took a step forward, pulling her gently to her feet. "Come on, I need to understand how you live like this. I'm like you now, Lillie. I'm just like you."

Super Love

Louise Ross

Long had I suffered at the side of the most gorgeous and graceful woman in history. For my lady, Madame Pain, the fear-inspiring and all-powerful, no bank vault is too secure, no victim too innocent, no torture too great.

In great service to my lady, I crammed myself in the industrial paper shredding bin within sight of my lady's desk, to support and protect her alter ego Stacey Schumm. On a bed of yesterday's paper and blanketed in financial readouts, I waited for her to need me.

"Jerad," my lady called.

How I wished she would call my name instead. Alas! She called to her coworker, the one with the square jaw who never misses a deadline, no matter how many emails I delete from his computer.

"Yes, Stacey?"

How dare he say her name so—so—well, plainly. Her name should be caressed and glorified. But not by him. How dare he say her name at all!

Leaning over her cubicle wall, she held up a flier. Bamboo shoots and red writing surrounded the picture. In the picture, a man with a white chef's hat stood in front of a flaming table surrounded by couples with surprised but happy faces.

"Are you free Friday night? I thought we could grab dinner together. There's a fun Japanese steakhouse downtown."

With those words, she crushed my heart again, and I squeezed the voodoo doll in my pocket, wishing I had my lady's power to crush the man's bones to powder.

"You mean, like a date?" Jerad rubbed his square jaw, but the angles failed to slice his fingers. He plucked the flier from my lady's fingers and flipped it over.

Was that curiosity? Would I be flame-broiled as I hid in the rafters, watching them eat chicken teriyaki?

"Yes." My lady's blond curls bounced up and down like the strings yanking on my heart. If only he'd say no.

Please let an anvil drop on the man's head. Let an emergency email demand that he work late. Let someone splash hot coffee on him and melt his face.

"I'm sorry. I can't." He stabbed the flier through the paper slot, cutting my forehead. I ripped it out of the way.

My lady sighed. "Maybe another time, then?"

Blood oozed from my brow, but I stayed focused on my lady and the pain in her voice. How dare this man upset her! How dare he say no! But hallelujah, he said no. I stuck my fingers in the slot and readjusted for a better view of my lady.

"Sorry, Stacey, but there's a woman I'm seeing right now." He glanced at the shredding bin, eyes narrowing.

I shrank back into the dark.

"Okay. I got it." Her voice held all the disappointment of her eighth birthday when she got a bike instead of a pony.

The agony! I should jump out of my hiding spot and rip him into strips. If only the door was not locked. If only my mistress commanded me.

I stewed in my mistress's pain and discarded paper until the other henchmen rolled me away. My bones ached, and my back wouldn't straighten, but there was no time for rehabilitative yoga. I needed to be home, prepared for my lady's return. I needed to be where she might use me. Nothing mattered outside of her wishes.

My lady's mansion was everything the magazines told her it should be, with a manicured lawn, shaped hedges, and decorator lighting. My brothers and I waited in the front foyer. Subdued white marble and light gray walls reflected the evening light so brightly no lighting was needed, but an iron-worked chandelier danced across the entrance anyway. Along the walls, we stood in our white button-down shirts and black dress pants. She had chosen us for our sameness—dark hair, broad shoulders, and bright blue eyes.

My henchman brothers and I waited in the entryway like pillars of my lady's perfection. When my lady entered, she stormed into the house in a wave of anger and destruction that made me want to bow down and kiss the ground she crushed beneath her heels. So I did, and I pocketed a piece of the broken tile as a souvenir of the awe-inspiring sight.

"You, you, and you." She pointed at me. I swallowed my squee and scrambled after her. "We need a plan. I need to destroy a woman."

Chasing after my love, I closed the distance between us, coming within inches of her back. Inches I craved to erase but dared not. I followed her toward her lair in the sparse concrete basement.

The doors stood open to the storage rooms of seasonal decorations and feed sacks. Stopping in the hallway between two rooms, she turned on her heel fast. "Well?"

It was too late. I could not stop. My body collided with hers. I pushed my hands out as if that would help, but it didn't. My hands landed flat against her, pressing against her shoulders. Then my chest bumped her breast, and our bodies moved together. I reveled in the moment of our contact. We bumped into the wall.

I touched her! A bolt of lightning slammed into my brain and powered my whole body. I could jump for joy, run a marathon, provide her with anything she wanted.

She slapped my hand away, and I stared at it, the hand that grabbed my lady. I'd gild it, take a picture, let my brothers stare in amazement at it.

"Imbecile! Go to the back of the group."

Grinning, I moved where she told me. I held my hand where it would not be touched by my brothers.

"Now. Who has a plan?"

I looked to the others, but they stared at me. We could shoot the woman, but if my lady agreed, I'd need to use my hand, the precious hand. It was too soon to cover this gift. I needed a suggestion that required no hands. "Send zombies to rip her apart?" My brothers and I looked back to our lady for approval.

"No good. I have nothing of hers to anchor the curse." She turned again. The lair door was a metal one with ragged strips of blue and red paint. An electronic keypad controlled the seven-bolt locking system. Her fingers caressed the keypad. The lair's door opened.

Inside these rooms, my lady was free to be who she wanted to be. She walked across the tattered brown rug to a rough wooden table so unlike the polished glass in the upstairs. Framed newspaper clippings and magazine articles of Madame Pain covered the stone walls with as much care and design as the oil paintings in the chambers above us.

As we entered, the head henchman returned to brewing the chemicals. His assistant threw feed into a pen, and the chickens clucked and pecked at it. The doll maker sewed a seam and tightened the stitches. The torturer selected a butcher knife from his table and ran its edge on a whetstone. My brothers took their stations, leaving me at my lady's side. Alone. Our few private moments. Together.

My lady yanked off her blond wig, the curls giving way to her smooth, shiny scalp. She thrust it at me, and I resisted the urge to smell the wig and the sweet sweat of my lady's skin. A patchwork cloak replaced her work blazer, and I tucked the discarded items under my arms. She slipped out of her heels and I knelt at her feet to collect the shoes. I set fur-lined boots in front of her and she stepped into them.

When I stood, Madame Pain, the love of my life, shoved me against the wall where I took my official guard post at the bathroom door. I hung her blazer on a hook under the magazine cover of Madame Pain and Volcano in battle at the Grand River Bank. Volcano may have stopped us breaching the main vault, but my lady distracted him long enough for my brothers and I to empty the lockboxes. I positioned myself between the picture of Madame Pain as villain boardroom director with Dr. Blood and the Freak as her executives and the cover of Madame Pain with her hands marionetting a cemetery of rising zombies. As Madame Pain, she was more powerful than any villain and scarier than any movie monster. She was perfect.

"I'm not hearing many ideas, boys." She dropped back into an oversized wood-backed chair with leather cushions and feather adornments. From her throne, she surveyed us. "Well, hurry up. I need a way to get rid of Jerad's girlfriend. I don't know her, don't have anything of her to anchor a spell, and know nothing about her. Ideas?"

"Ask him her identity?"

My lady growled. "Is there a newbie in the lair? Who said that?"

The photographer stepped forward. He wasn't new, and just last week she had complimented him on his shot of her dancing around a burning warehouse. "We could, um, investigate her identity?" His voice quaked, and I winced. It was never pleasant to watch one of my brothers die, but maybe it would lighten my love's mood. That was the most important thing after all.

"Dear boy." Madame Pain smoothed her hand over her bald head. "I have a secret identity for a purpose. I can't ask him her name and then have her die by zombie attack hours later. I would never keep the secret that way." She flipped open the armrest on her throne, and her fingers caressed the needles she kept there.

"You could have him followed?" the photographer suggested.

"You are not understanding." She frowned, and I cringed at her displeasure. She pulled out a needle and twisted it through her fingers. "He can't have any clue Stacey and I are connected." Her fingers flicked the needle, and it stabbed into the eye of the Volcano poster, increasing the collection of pins protruding from his face. My lady had such perfect aim. "Someone feed this one to the dogs."

Two of my brothers grabbed the man and dragged him out of the room. His legs kicked and his body jerked, but a third brother covered his mouth so he could not further anger our mistress.

"The dogs." I gasped it under my breath. She had not fed a henchman to the dogs in a decade. Her wrath was mighty today.

"What about my dogs?" Her head turned slowly toward me. Our gazes locked. The blood drained from my face, and I tried to grab at a thought so I would not be another hunk of meat for the hounds. "Use the dogs to find the woman. We can get her scent from his apartment when he's not home and sic the dogs on her."

Her eyes narrowed, and she glanced up and down my body.

I stood a little straighter.

"It's not a horrible idea. Anyone else?" She turned back to the room.

The head henchman stepped forward. "If the woman likes him back, then we could use him for the spell. Or a piece of him."

She leaned forward, placing her elbows on her knees. "Go on."

"If we have a piece of him, we can set two curses: one to attack the woman he loves, then a second for him to fall in love with you. When she dies, he'll turn to you."

"Zombie attack and a love spell. I've never tried it before." My lady's grin spread slowly, creating sweet dimples more appropriate to her alter ego. "This is why you are the head henchman. Someone make this plan happen. You." She pointed at me.

I wanted to swoon. Blood rushed to my cheeks. The rapid blood flow change left me swaying on my feet.

"Get something of Jerad. Hair, blood, spit. Something from Jerad's body, not clothing. Got it?"

I nodded. My lady entrusted me, and I would succeed.

The next day, I disguised myself as a janitor. Hiding beneath Jerad's desk, I sorted through his trash, looking for snotty rags or strands of hair. There was only paper. When I checked an hour later, it was the same.

The trip-wire strung across his office doorway failed to topple him onto the waiting glass table. When he spotted the tack in his chair before he sat down, drastic measures had to be taken. Then he bypassed the alley where I waited to mug him and evaded the football thrown at his head. If only my mistress didn't want him alive!

I followed him into the restroom with a pipe wrench from the maintenance shop, planning to bash in his head at the urinal, but he used the stall instead. Grunting came from the stall, and I moved to strike him as he exited. I waited, pipe at the ready.

The health food nut from the corner cubicle came in. We nodded at each other. "Is there a plumbing issue?" He tipped his head at the wrench I held.

If only there was a plumbing problem, but there didn't have to be. I bobbed my head and searched the wall for the water shut off. I found one on a pipe running along the wall and turned it off. I waited. The health food guy left in search of a better bathroom. Jerad stopped grunting, and I grinned. Soon, I would complete my task.

Then the toilet flushed. No water started to refill the tank, but it was too late. My piece of Jerad had already flushed down the pipes. How did he miss every trick, every attack? He exited the stall, and I ran at him with the wrench.

His grip stopped the heavy metal and held it stationary in the air. I leaned into it and it did not move.

He spat. "Stop following me."

The spit landed on my cheek. It was done. I had my sample. "Okay."

He let the wrench go and stormed out of the bathroom.

I smiled and carefully collected the spit on my cheek. My lady would be pleased.

Back at the lair, the head henchman waited at a table made from the door of the first business my mistress robbed. The company's voodoo and occult logo still decorated the door. On the table, a bowl-sized cauldron boiled on a gas burner and a voodoo doll dressed like Jerad lay next to a box of pins. On a bended knee, I presented my lady with the spit. She cackled, opened the box, and sniffed. If only it was my spit she wanted to smell. I would donate to her anytime.

My lady chanted, her voice filling the room. The cauldron bubbled louder. She spat into it. Then Jerad's spit rose out of the container and divided. Part dropped into the cauldron. The liquid bubbled and frothed a bright pink color that smelled of strawberries. Madame Pain twisted in a dance. Her fingers pulled a pin from the box as she stomped in a circle. The second part of the spit landed on the doll and was absorbed. In a second, she stabbed the doll in the heart then poured the strawberry froth on it.

Then we waited. The liquid seeped into the material.

And waited.

Eventually, the head henchman cleaned up the table. There was nothing more to do.

Stacey went to work the next day.

I followed her and hid beneath her desk in a cardboard box, peeking out through the handle hole.

"Jerad?" Stacey called out to him at lunch. Her voice was bright and matched her pink blouse and blond curls.

"Yes, Stacey?" He sounded chipper.

"Hey. I wanted to let you know that even if you are dating someone, I'd still like to be your friend. I think we'd get along great outside of work." She fluttered her lashes.

He turned his head to the right, displaying his perfectly developed jawline. It was good that he did not have blue eyes or she might have collected him as a henchman. "Well, my woman is the jealous type. I don't think it would be a good idea."

"Oh. Okay. Sorry." Stacey dropped into her chair and kicked my ribs through the box. It hurt, but that didn't matter. If my pain could ease hers, she could stomp me in the eye and feed me to the dogs. She kicked my box again and again in a steady drum. Bruises blossomed on my arm, ribs, and leg.

We waited. Work ended.

Jerad never came to confess his love. The news never reported a horde of zombies shambling down the street. No hysterical calls came through the office, and no sympathy flowers were delivered. The spells had failed.

My lady threw open the doors to her lair, stripped her wig off, and tore it in two.

"Plan B. You." She stabbed her finger into my chest. It would leave a bruise and mark the spot where she touched me. No one could ever deny that she touched me. I'd show my brothers. "Go to Jerad's house. Get me something with this woman's scent for the dogs."

I nodded. Anything for her.

His house was not far away. Using his address from the personnel file, I found the mansion in a neighboring estate. A sign on the gate announced the home as part of the Better Homes Tour.

I crept onto the mansion lawn and duck-walked behind the hedges lining the grounds until I could peek into the windows. The front rooms looked much like my lady's, staged tables and unused chairs. Oil paintings of forests hung on the walls, and a large flame sculpture waited in one room's corner. Like my lady, he probably had an alarm system.

I needed a way in, and his house had decorative stonework at each corner. Protruding red stones created a zipper effect that staggered back and forth and provided half-inch finger holds. I climbed the stones. At the top, I tore through the clay tiles into the attic, leaving my fingers bleeding and raw. All remained quiet. Not a single alarm.

The top floor was uninteresting. Cracking open doors along the hallway, I found bedrooms: cream, beige, and blue rooms. Utterly forgettable. On the second floor, the rooms were accented in greens. Swampy, homey greens that my mistress would love. The last door was not off to the side but square in the hallway. Instead of a linen closet, a spiral of stairs went back up to the top floor. I grinned.

I found a lair, the kind only my lady and her super rivals might need. Pillowy, white insulation and concrete panels of fire proofing lined the room, and only one of my lady's rivals used fire. On a hook behind the door hung a red and yellow suit with an atomic cloud exploding in the center of the chest. It was the emblem of my love's arch nemesis, Volcano. Jerad was the Volcano.

The need to tell my lady warred with her command to bring back something of his love interest. With this knowledge, she could attack and defeat her greatest rival. How could she ever love him after finding this out? And I would be there to console her. I could make her happy.

Destroying the life of his love would make her happy too. The death of his love would be the teriyaki glaze on his downfall. For my lady, for her happiness, for her love, I'd find the Volcano's love.

I searched his lair, finding nothing but ashes and exercise equipment. No henchmen waited for him. No décor decorated the walls. It was unimpressive, proving how amazing my mistress was in comparison to her rivals.

Down on the main level, I found his bedroom. The en suite bathroom probably had a hidden camera to record razor commercials, but the bedroom was perfection; every inch of carpet and detail was devoted to my lady. A collage of her posters hung on the wall with her as the boardroom executive in the center. A collectible figurine still in its box sat on the bedside stand. A decorator pillow with her logo lay in a chair. It was a pillow I had never seen before, and it had twisty fringe around the edge. I took it for my collection, and I grabbed the figurine for my lady to see.

I returned to the lab.

As I bowed with the figurine on display, her squeals of delight tore me to pieces. A henchman could never compete with a superhero love. My torture in my lady's name would continue, and the man who had already thwarted all attempts to injure him would be the object of my lady's attention.

"I have to let him know I love him back. He loves me!" Madame Pain doubled over laughing. "So glad the curse to kill his love didn't work. Ideas, guys? How do I confess my love without upsetting the balance, ruining my secret identity, or destroying my marketing?"

"You can't. Madame Pain doesn't love. She hates and attacks. She's vicious."

"Who said that?" She scanned the room.

The photographer stepped into the center of the lair again.

"Didn't we feed him to the dogs?"

The man cringed. "They tried, but I climbed the fence and escaped. No matter how you confess, Madame Pain, you will hurt your image. We must confine the damage as best we can."

"Fine." She dropped into her throne and waved him forward. "What's your plan for damage control?"

"Location. It has to be somewhere remote. I don't have to take pictures, but unless we disable his marketing team, they will be actively capturing every moment of this meeting. It needs to look like an epic battle, even if you only talk. I'm envisioning hordes of zombies, freshly raised from the grave, with dirt clinging to their skin. Early night with just enough moonlight to illuminate the scene. Maybe a storm brewing on the horizon."

"And why would I be raising a zombie horde in a storm at a distant graveyard? How will that accomplish my goal?"

The photographer stepped back. "Um. Because Volcano always tries to stop you when there is a big event happening. The zombie horde will get his attention. You can say you were about to take over the National Bank or take control of the newspaper. Or you could wait until he arrived and confess your love and never give a reason at all."

My lady nodded her head. "No one feed him to the dogs. Your punishment is waived. This time. Okay, boys. Let's go raise a cemetery."

And she did.

The waning moonlight bounced off the gravestones. Some shone with polish while the older ones faded into the darkness. The head henchman built a fire in the oldest part of the cemetery, and his assistant stacked cages of birds along an outer circle. Squawking and ruffling feathers lent the graveyard a sense of foreboding. The drummer pounded out a fast heartbeat, and my lady chanted, cutting into the sacrifices. Blood pooled around the dead birds and decorated her skin. Power swirled around her and into the sky like a beacon.

From the sky, a streak of fire zoomed into the graveyard and hovered among the newer graves.

"Madame Pain," Volcano called through the power.

She stopped chanting and stared at him. Her feet pranced a few times to the drum before she stood still. "Volcano."

Two SUVs pulled up along the cemetery road, and Volcano's entourage set up next to our marketing team. Tripods and men with cameras huddled together, fighting for the best angle.

"What is your dastardly plan?" Volcano challenged.

"To steal your heart." She released her energy. A wave of pink pulsing light shot across the graves and collided with Volcano, his entourage, and my lady's. It wasn't her usual magic. No zombies climbed out of the ground. It hit me with everything I loved about my lady, like her stripped down bald head and her decisiveness. The magic tasted of fur-lined boots, smelled of sweaty wig, and felt like bits of crushed tiles and decorator pillows.

Volcano fell to his knees. He crawled across the ground to my lady's feet and kissed her boots. Looking up, he confessed, "I love you."

The magic shifted. An opposing power from outside the graveyard locked around me. Invisible ropes tightened around my body. This power tasted of strawberries and frothed against my skin. It shoved me forward. I knew without a doubt, I had only one purpose in life. To kill the woman this man loved.

The magic pushed and stabbed, pointing me toward his love. I could feel her close by. With each step toward her, the magic caressed me. It tugged my hand and felt like my brothers helping me crawl into boxes. It smelled like tile dust and a golden hand.

It pushed me forward, and I followed the need until I found the target. I ripped into her. Her blood coated my skin. She tasted of hope at the end of long torture and life. I ate. Sweet, metallic blood. I would share this moment with my lady later, and she would laugh. Beside me, my brothers ripped into the target. Then it was done. The ropes released me. My brothers and I stopped and waited.

A man laughed. No, *Volcano* laughed. "Madame Pain is dead." He pumped his fist in the air. "And all it took was my love." Clapping and cheers from the SUVs filled the silence.

On the ground around my feet, Madame Pain's ripped clothes and gnawed bones lay about. My lady was dead. Her murderer was here. I had to take revenge.

I growled and ran after Volcano. My left leg stopped working and dragged along behind me. Then the right leg fell out from under me and I pulled myself along by my arms.

"Don't try, zombie. Without your creator, you can't survive. You're done." Volcano threw his head back and laughed. A fiery glow illuminated him in a magazine-perfect moment.

For my lady, I crawled toward him.

"She thought I wouldn't notice her zombies at the office. Who hides in the trash? Really. So sloppy." He walked off toward the SUVs where he high-fived his marketing team. Our team followed in their vehicles.

I worked my way across the ground until my arms gave out. For my lady, I tried to pull myself across the ground with my chin, but all too soon that ended.

Lying there with no way to move forward, I smiled. Volcano thought he'd won, but he couldn't get her in death. She was free of him, and I'd soon be at my lady's side again.

The In-League

LB Garrison

Amayah leaned against the cold brick exterior of the high school band hall. The olive-colored windscreen surrounding the rebuilt tennis courts rippled in the chill morning wind that cut through her sweats. She slipped her cell phone out of her back pocket. Her stomach churned. What would it be? A dragon? Two years ago, Jackie fought a dragon for her initiation. Predictably, that had turned ugly.

A green glow faded the stars along the horizon. Thumbing through her messages, she found the In-League invitation. Her finger hesitated above the olive branch icon. Was this what she wanted?

It had only been three years ago when the Ange Noir slammed into the tennis courts and gave superpowers to all the kids at the school, plus a few random teachers. That's when the fights with Mom started. Stupid hunk of black metal. Amayah didn't ask to have her life jacked up.

And where did Mom get off? Yeah, Amayah hadn't done as much good as some had. What's wrong with wanting to be normal? She hadn't gone villain either. No credit for that.

Amayah tapped the In-League icon. "I'm not useless."

Someone answered. "Change your mind?"

"Stacy? Yeah. I'm at school."

Static crackled on the other end. "Use my hero name, pumpkin."

Amayah rolled her eyes. "Okay, Gravity Jinn, what do I do?"

"You have Dr. Chronomancer's app installed?"

"Yes."

"Get to the Nether-Maze. A traitor sold Yin the map. Stop her from getting inside. You have about thirty minutes. Screw up and you'll have to use the app to beat her to the heart of the maze."

Amayah trudged down the shaded sidewalk along the building. Yin was part of the Outcast League. "Is she alone?"

Gravity Jinn paused. "There are no other Outcasts with her, but you have to stop her. She is going for the Janus and plans to use it to bust her brother from Timeout lockup."

Amayah stopped. Her breath turned to mist in the autumn dawn. "The Janus. As in half the adults disappeared because someone wished for a cheaper house price, Janus?"

Gravity Jinn sighed. "Yes, and supply and demand drove the prices down. We all know the story."

Amayah's grip on her phone tightened. "I lost my Dad that day. This is too big for me to handle on my first mission. On an initiation, even."

"Is it unfair, Amayah? Fair is for games with rules and referees. Life has neither. This isn't the chess club. It's the In-League. If the big girl panties don't fit, there's always the minor leagues. In or out?"

If she was ever going to prove herself to Mom, she had to do something that mattered, and heroes didn't get to choose. "In."

The line went dead.

There would be no backup. She pulled the self-adhesive wrap tight on both hands. A splotch of blood had already wept through, staining the new bandages. Nerves always made it hard to control the blood flow from her stigmata, which was why she stopped dating.

Her phone chimed. She fumbled but managed to save it, inches from the sidewalk. One more broken screen and Mom would send her to Timeout. The text was from Brooke.

> Sorry for the late notice.
> Have to reschedule. :)

Between waking to find Mom gone and the In-League, she had forgotten about the weekly piano lesson. Her little student usually spent more time talking than practicing, anyways. Brooke was an interesting kid for her age. So inquisitive. Amayah had canceled so many times on Brooke that she hardly saw her anymore, but she needed to practice her powers in secret for the initiation, didn't she? Things would change after today. Probably. She texted back.

> I'm sorry too. I'll make the
> next one, promise.

Amayah sent the message and zipped her gray track jacket to the top. The band nerds would be here soon and future superheroes didn't procrastinate. She hurried to the alley.

The gate to the Nether-Maze was in the back of the school, hidden under the west dumpster by the cafeteria.

The congealed smear of a popped ketchup packet marked the place the dumpster had been. No sign of the dumpster itself. The hexagonal glow of the gate shimmered like a watery reflection on the concrete. If being early was good and tardy inherently bad, didn't it follow that supervillains should be habitually late? And yet, Yin had gotten there first.

She had to go in. Anticipation sat in her stomach like a cold stone. Amayah opened Dr. Chronomancer's app.

"Netherworld Navigator wants to know your location," the phone's female voice crooned.

"Yeah, yeah. Accept."

An unwinding ball of twine rolled across the phone. "Getting route…"

Through the purple sheen, a well of glossy onyx stretched away into the darkness. Once she crossed the threshold, the sides of the well would become the floor. Because it was the Netherworld.

She grabbed the smooth edge of the gate and swung her legs around, crawling onto the maze's floor. Stones gnashed together as the walls shifted. The maze changed every few minutes.

The first part was easy enough. A second tunnel of mismatched stones crossed her passageway. She checked her phone and took the path to the right. Amber lanterns attached to the walls provided some light, but only about a tenth of them worked. They weren't much better than a guide to where the walls were. Once the light from the entrance faded, she shuffled through the darkness, feeling her way along the bumpy stone.

The maze grumbled and shifted again. Whispers echoed through the tunnels.

"Hope Yin talks to herself," Amayah mumbled.

Flickering pink light came from a new opening to the left, along with the taste of acrid smoke. Her shadow stood on the opposite wall. It turned its head when she didn't. A prickly cold slithered down her spine. Yin knew what the shadows knew.

Showtime.

Amayah had never hurt anyone before. Not on purpose.

That would probably change today.

She unwound the dressing on her hands and let it drop. In the unbroken skin of her palms, blood pooled. Nerves.

She crept to the entrance. A short passage made of massive stones opened into a large chamber. A road flare lay on the floor near the doorway. More light sputtered. The room must be littered with flares. Gloom crowded the flames. Yin was ready for a fight.

Amayah curled her right hand into a fist. Her stigmata burned as the blood flowed, warm and sticky, onto her cold fingers. She pressed her palm against the stone. A wave of dizziness passed through her as the greedy rock drank her life.

Her blood took whatever form she asked and animated whatever it touched, but it only obeyed her because it needed her to live. Her gift from the Ange Noir.

Faint red veins pulsed across the rock's surface as it woke. The stone was granite tribe. It spoke of sorrow. Of agonizing eons, slowly traveling through the heat to the surface, longing for the light, only to be cleaved from a mountain and laid low in this tomb by humans.

I beg your forgiveness, ancient one. Please, be my shield, and I'll lend you a moment of life, like your brothers have never known.

The rock slurped and agreed.

Yin's lithe form stepped onto the gray and pink shadows cast by the flare. Her high neck halter bodysuit was white, except for the curved black teardrop shape across her chest. "You can't hide from me here. I am ally of the darkness and child of the night."

And too into the villain thing. Amayah stepped into the light and, without intending to, glanced down at her own off-the-rack gray sweat suit. She could have totally worn a leotard, but who wanted to live with wedgies?

Yin touched her lips. "Amayah? You're a villain, right? When you were a freshman, you wore that black lipstick and those funeral clothes."

Amayah rolled her eyes. "It's called Goth and it was a phase. I go by Sangue Rose now."

Yin snatched one of the pinkish shadows from the floor and snapped pieces off it, like a stale cookie. "Hero, then. You know, the thinner the blade, the sharper. Most don't realize shadows are very thin indeed." She paused. "Monologuing was always Yang's passion. I miss Brother so."

Amayah clenched her fist. Blood filled the gaps between her fingers. At lunch, Yin and Yang had always sat at their own table. Alone. "I know you miss him, but he isn't coming back. You need to think about yourself and your life."

Yin's brown eyes narrowed, glistening in the dark. "What gives them the right to judge and to sentence people to Timeout for eternity? What gives you the right to keep us apart?"

"I'm not trying to keep you apart. Janus isn't the way. It's too dangerous. I know."

"Without it, I'll never see him again." She broke the last bit of shadow. The pieces fluttered from her hand, circling above her head.

The walls rumbled. A passageway opened.

Yin pulled a yellowed page from her pocket. The map. "The only way out, is in."

Shards of darkness swarmed across the space between them.

Amayah slung her fistful of blood at Yin, willing the droplets into crystalline needles. Blood splintered shadow fragments, but some got through.

The awakened stone wall flowed like water. Fast as lightning, it splashed against the floor and ceiling, hardening into a web of rock. Shadow fragments thumped against the stone. It cracked but held. Scarlet threads pulsed across its dark surface. The cracks healed. Amayah's darts popped against the far wall, somewhere beyond the circles of light.

A tuft of Yin's raven hair drifted down onto her shoulder. She brushed it off. "Deadly force, no conviction. Hero."

Amayah squeezed more blood into her hand. The copper smell filled the air. She needed to end this before she ran out of ammo, which would be bad for several reasons. "Give up or I will hurt you."

Shadows flowed, forming a block like tinted glass between them. It would be hard to break.

Yin turned away. "I brought you a playmate."

Amayah scanned the room. The inky blackness and bright flares made it impossible to even judge the size of the space. *A trick?*

Yin laughed as the passage closed. The shadow shield evaporated.

Amayah willed the blood on her hand to crawl back into her palm. It stung, but she couldn't afford to waste any. She pulled out her phone. Yin's static map showed the path to the Infinity Hollow. Amayah had the builder's blueprint and there were shortcuts through the maze. She touched the stone web. "Come on, Grant, we're leaving."

The web condensed into a ball five feet across and ground against the floor, following Amayah like a grumpy puppy. She stayed away from the flares, tracing a path to the northeast corner of the room. She stopped and waited. Nothing moved in the dark.

"What are you doing?" echoed a child's voice. The voice had an odd bass quality, as if she were trying to disguise it or sound older.

"I'm waiting for the next opening." Amayah slipped her phone into her back pocket. A team of third grade gymnasts had visited her high school the day the world changed. The kid was probably just twelve or thirteen. "You're one of the Cupcake girls, aren't you?"

A sigh echoed in the darkness. "Yeah. We were supposed to watch the cheerleaders, then this happened."

"Who are you?"

"I'm still deciding on a name. It's hard."

"Why did you join Outcast?"

Feet shuffled beyond the fires. "Didn't exactly join, okay?"

The maze grumbled. The wall beside Amayah slid open.

"Is that where you're going?" The girl had snuck closer. But she had lowered her voice as she approached, making it hard to tell how close she was.

"No. The next one. Grant."

The stone pivoted toward Amayah.

"Protect."

The stone splattered into a mesh of stalagmites that walled Amayah off from the rest of the room. Only seconds remained until the way opened. Cupcakes weren't known for their power or utility. The wall would be enough to stop her and Amayah might need her blood later.

She touched the smooth stone. "Thank you."

The passage to her right began to close, while the one in front opened.

Blood streamed from the cold stone, through her stigmata, and into her arm, chilling her as it mixed in her veins. She shuddered. Grant turned to dead rock again.

A figure dodged between the flares and struck Grant. The stalagmites shattered. Stone fragments thumped off the wall. Small hands and strawberry-scented curls hit Amayah's midsection and swept her through the closing aperture.

She landed on her butt with a jarring thump and sickening crunch, a masked girl's face inches from her own. Blood oozed from the girl's knuckles. The smell of her blood made Amayah's stomach churn. The girl was strong and tough, but not invulnerable. It was a common superpower mash-up.

"Recalculating," her phone murmured.

The glimmer of the flares dwindled as the door closed.

"Sorry, about the phone," the girl whispered, scrambling to her feet. She turned to slip through the narrowing doorway.

Amayah slammed her hand against the floor and let her blood flow. Warm breezes, chilly water, and bright sunlight gushed through her soul. The sandstone floor giggled to life.

Help me, friend.

Tentacles of stone tripped the girl. She squeaked and clawed furrows in the floor. "No fair!"

The tentacles surged up her body, growing thicker until they fused. The girl's strength would have shattered ordinary stone, but Amayah's blood reinforced it. More sandstone flowed into the bonds, pulling the girl upright and encasing her in a block three feet thick.

The door closed with an echoing thud, sealing them in darkness. The girl's muffled struggles stopped.

Amayah drew her phone. A crack ran from the top of the screen to the bottom. "Outstanding."

She used the phone's light to find her way to the stone-bound girl. She was up to the neckline of her black jumpsuit in twisted appendages. A small black mask and waves of brunette hair surrounded her brown eyes.

Amayah brushed the hair away. Her heart thumped against her ribs. "Brooke?"

"Aw, how'd you know?"

"The mask barely covers your eyes."

"Well, it's my first costume, isn't it?" Brooke's eyes traveled over Amayah. "At least I put in some effort."

"I picked a name."

Brooke wiggled her nose. "Oh, touché. Beat up on a little girl, why don't you?"

Amayah pursed her lips. "This is serious, Brooke. You're working with an Outcast freelancer. Why?"

Brooke blinked in the phone's glare. She turned her head to the side, nose up. "I don't think you would understand."

Amayah walked around Brooke to the closed door and touched the stone. The walls were interconnected. Reopening the passage would necessitate moving several stones and would take a lot of blood all at once. "You never even mentioned Yin?"

Brooke sighed. "We don't talk anymore. You didn't tell me you were a hero."

"Not yet. I'm trying out for the In-League." And it was getting harder. Brooke wouldn't turn villain, not if she understood what that meant. Maybe it would be worth opening the way back to get Brooke out before the In-League saw her. If she did that, Yin might get away and do real damage with the Janus. Amayah's stomach knotted up. *Would being a hero always be so hard?*

Brooke clicked her tongue. "In-League? Not sure that's right for you."

"That's what I told Mom," Amayah mumbled.

"What?"

"This isn't about my choices." Amayah's phone chirped, like a baby sparrow. It had found a new route that would get her to the Infinity Hollow ahead of Yin. She had to hurry.

Dust trickled from the ceiling. A rumble vibrated the floor.

Amayah shined the phone toward the sound. A black opening yawned across from them. "I have to go. I'll be back for you later."

She ran to the opening. A line of widely spaced amber lanterns stretched into the distance. This passage angled downward.

Brooke sniffed. "I'll just wait in the dark, then. Alone."

"I won't be long." Amayah walked into the tunnel.

"Well, I'm sure nothing bad will happen to me."

Amayah slowed. With all the pieces of the maze moving around, she wasn't sure that the room wouldn't disappear or Brooke wouldn't be crushed.

"Even if something bad does happen, I'm sure you'll be able to live with yourself."

Amayah stopped.

"Eventually." Brooke sighed.

Amayah spun around. "Really? You're going to try to guilt-trip me?"

Brooke's curly head was just a dark outline against the gray walls. "How am I doing?"

"Pretty good, actually."

Sandy. Follow.

The tentacle mass squirmed with joy. It broke loose and trotted next to Amayah on six mini-elephant legs.

Amayah employed her best scowl. "You better behave."

"I don't have much of a choice. And, Amayah, I really didn't want to be alone."

"Yeah, I know." Amayah took a couple of steps and faltered. She lit the way with her phone. Steps littered the descending slope at irregular intervals.

"Careful," Brooke said. She sounded sincere.

"Thanks." The phone was down to seventy-eight percent already. If Dr. Chronomancer, aka no-thumbs Murphy the shop teacher, could build things that work, she wouldn't need the light.

Amayah turned her screen brightness all the way down to conserve battery life and felt her way down the treacherous route. Her eyes adjusted and she only needed the light occasionally. Brooke seemed content in her stone straight-jacket, mumbling to herself now and then.

The next opening lay between two crooked steps. Amayah held the dim screen close to her face to scroll through the path. It showed Yin's progress and they were still ahead, but just barely. If they got there first—then what? Could she beat Yin? And if she didn't, what would happen to Brooke and how many people would be harmed by Yin's wish? Even if she won, the In-League might find out about Brooke and charge her as a villain.

Brooke blew a wayward curl away from her face. "Are you okay?"

Amayah was breathing too fast. She swallowed and let the screen fade to black. "I'm just strategizing."

"Oh. I thought…I know your mom left again. I saw her this morning. She looked like she was packed for a long trip."

Amayah ran her thumb over the crack in her phone. "Two months. I found out by catching her taping a note on the fridge door."

"Cute. You know, Daddy leaves me alone a lot too. It helped me grow up, a little."

The corridor closed and the wall opened. Amayah started down a new path. "Your dad has to work. Mom has a trust fund."

Brooke's head bobbed as her stone prison trotted down the steps. "Just saying, people have their reasons for doing stuff. Sometimes we don't know what they are."

The school counselors wanted her to open up. Like that would fix anything. It only made her angry. But in the darkness, the anger didn't come. Just a sort of numb weariness. "She went to save some weird tadpoles in South America, because the ones with two stripes were endangered."

"Tadpoles?"

"Last time, it was blue moss. If there's a problem, she feels it's her responsibility to solve it. This all started when I got my powers." And got worse when Dad disappeared, but no point in mentioning that. Maybe Mom was right and she should have gotten the powers instead, or maybe Amayah hadn't found the right cause. "I just don't know."

"Don't know what?"

"I need to concentrate on where we're going."

"Take your time. I'll be here."

They traveled in silence for several minutes.

"Yin's not so different from us. All she has is her brother," Brooke whispered, as if to herself.

"Sounds like you two spent some time together."

Silence.

Amayah paused at a lantern where the next opening would appear. "Yin and Yang are bank robbers. They never hurt anybody, but that's mostly due to Yang's influence."

"She told me he was a political prisoner back in her home country." Brooke looked away. Her tawny skin had a deep amber cast in the dim orange light. "If Yang helps her make better choices, don't you want him back?"

The hall lurched. A brick wall slid past, sealing the way forward for a moment, then a different passage connected with theirs. One more door and they would be in the Hollow.

Amayah glanced back at Brooke. "Do you remember Kyla Moore?"

Brooke looked up and to the left a moment. "That's random, but no, I don't know many high schoolers."

Amayah's mouth went dry. Kyla's story was too close to her own. "Almost no one remembers her. I do because I was on a tour of Timeout that was supposed to scare me onto the right path. It exists outside reality. Kyla's parents weren't right for each other. They always fought. So, she wished happiness for them. They never met and she was never born."

"God," Brooke whispered.

"The Janus blurs probability and blends world lines. The results are unpredictable. Even when used with good intentions, it's dangerous."

"I didn't know Yin could hurt someone by mistake. Sorry. We were supposed to sneak in, she would make her wish, and we would sneak out. I'm just here to delay anyone who tried to prevent her from making her wish. I didn't know it would be you."

Amayah turned on Brooke. "Even if she didn't take the Janus, did you ever think about what would happen if you were caught?"

"Well…no. I wanted to help Yin. Are you mad? Please don't be mad."

"Mad?" Amayah threw her arms up. "Pieces of the Ange Noir have been made into all kinds of dangerous things. The most powerful are sealed in the maze for a reason. How did you think the In-League would react to you breaking in?"

"I didn't think," Brooke whispered. "We weren't supposed to get caught."

"But you did."

Brooke bit her lower lip. "What will happen?"

"There's only one punishment for people with superpowers. Timeout. It's a hypercube that sits between universes with no star. The prisoners shovel coal all day to keep from freezing to death. And time doesn't pass the same way there. You'll literally be shoveling the same coal forever."

Brooke's eyes widened. "But we didn't hurt anyone. You'll tell them that, right?"

Amayah leaned against the cool brick. "The In-League doesn't care. Why did you do it, Brooke?"

Tears darkened the stone tentacles. "Because she paid attention to me. Okay? And it was just one favor. When I changed…my friends were all weirded out. Normans aren't friends with exonormans, unless they want something. High schoolers look down on Cupcakes. Mommy—my mom left because of me. Daddy is alone because of me. God, I thought you'd understand. You were alone too…an exonorman."

"Is…is that why you wanted lessons from me? As a way to just spend time together?"

Brooke sniffled. "It took all the money I had, but I couldn't even pay you to be my…my friend." She sobbed. "I just wanted…to get Yin's brother out…for her."

Amayah leaned back and let her head bump against the wall. She had watched Brooke grow up. Even babysat her. With her mother gone and her father always working, Brooke was vulnerable and villains recruited young kids. Amayah knew that and still she let it happen right next door. Mom was right about one thing, Amayah was too self-absorbed. She made a mental note never to tell Mom.

The tentacles loosened, allowing Brooke to wipe her eyes.

Outstanding. Even a rock has a higher EQ than me.

Usually, Amayah ignored the impulse that tugged her toward other people. It never ended well. Maybe, just this once, she could make an exception.

The stone flowed away and Amayah wrapped an arm around Brooke's shoulders, pulling her in. She hadn't been this close to another person in a long time. "We both messed up, but most of this is my fault. The In-League may not even know you're here. You weren't mentioned in the briefing. If there is any way, I will get you out."

Brooke looked up at Amayah. "What about Yin?"

Amayah's phone chirped. The wall grumbled open, spilling mist onto the floor. Beyond the door, a marble floor stretched to the horizon. This was the Infinite Hollow, the eye of a storm where conflicting realities met. Thousands of bright orange Chinese sky-lanterns hung stationary in the raging wind. Churning clouds formed the walls. Lightning splintered the darkness.

Amayah pulled away from Brooke. "I can't let her get the Janus, but I promise, I'll try my best not to hurt her. Stay here."

Brooke wiped her eyes and nodded.

Amayah stepped onto the marble plain. In the distance, an assortment of gears ground against each other. A turquoise glow glittered between the gnashing teeth of the spinning cogs, sending flickering beams of light into the darkness.

Each step ate up the distance, moving her impossibly fast. In a few strides, she stood before the interlocking gears of the maze's heart. A gear the size of Amayah's house rolled by, rumbling the marble floor. She slipped inside.

The clacking gears drowned out the thunder and veiled the tumbling clouds. In the darkness, a shimmering turquoise glow brightened. Amayah took one last look at her phone. Yin had been right. The way out lay in the center. The heart of the maze not only held the Janus, but the exit. The idea being that if they ever needed the Janus, it would be an emergency and they would need to get back out fast. Stupid design.

The marble ended at a platform hundreds of feet across. Massive gears turned, their teeth slotted in the notches along the platform's edge, rotating it slowly. A shimmering pool occupied the center with four walkways leading to the middle where a jewel in a glass cube sparkled with every color. Every possibility. The Janus.

Amayah hopped across the gap to the platform.

Shadows wavered, ripping from the objects casting them. They tore into fragments and swirled in the still air, like fall leaves driven by wild winds. Amayah stepped to the edge of the shimmering pool. "I know you're here, Yin."

One of the fragments brushed by her cheek. It stung. Warmth seeped down to her chin. She touched her face and her hand came back with a bright red smear on her fingertips.

Yin watched from the far side of the revolving stage. She stepped into one shadow, only to reappear from another, closer to the Janus. Swirling bits of darkness formed a silent cyclone around her.

Yin smiled. "You shouldn't leave precious things lying about."

Amayah clenched her fists. Blood flowed. "I won't let you take the Janus."

Yin's gaze shifted over Amayah's shoulder. "I wasn't speaking of the Janus."

"Sorry, Amayah," Brooke said.

Amayah stepped to the side, so she could see them both. Multiple versions of Brooke's shadow held the girl with her arms behind her back. Their two-dimensional fingers wrapped snakelike around her skin.

Amayah turned to Yin. "She's your friend."

Yin smirked. "The Cupcake? This is one of the few people you care about, or hadn't you considered that? She is a diversion. Nothing more."

Brooke's expression didn't change, but she made a slight "umpf", like she had been hit in the stomach.

Yin laughed. "I'll not hurt her, but will you let her die?"

The shadows tossed Brooke into one of the deep platform slots. She grabbed the edge. The gear teeth rolled down. One of Brooke's shadows jumped into the slot, pulling her into the pit and the path of the gear's teeth. She held on to the edge.

Amayah's next breath didn't come. She tensed and shifted toward Brooke.

Brooke swallowed and locked eyes with Amayah. "It's my fault you didn't stop her before. Do what you have to. I got this." The shadows pulled her in. The gear turned. Brooke was brave, but as the gear sealed the notch and rolled down to crush her, she finally screamed.

Yin seized the Janus. The walls shifted and opened a path to their Earth.

Amayah couldn't stop Yin and save Brooke. The whole Outcast Legion would have the Janus and the power to shape reality. Some of them were psychopaths. With potentially millions of lives at stake, one little girl didn't matter so much and a true hero made the tough choices. Amayah made hers.

She ran, blood already dripping from both stigmata. She slammed her palms against the unyielding metal. It drank so much, so quickly, her knees betrayed her. She slid to the floor, dizzy and tired. So tired.

The smeared colors and flowing shapes of the Netherworld seeped through her.

Please. She's just a child.

The infinite maze shuddered to a halt.

Slowly, the gear reversed.

"Brooke? Brooke!"

God, no.

"Amayah? It's okay. I'm alright."

Amayah bowed and rested her forehead on the cold metal. "Can you get yourself out?"

"Uh, I think so."

Amayah grabbed the gear's teeth and pulled up. She leaned against it a moment, until the world stopped wobbling. "Don't leave this room."

Amayah stumbled. Her heart thumped in her chest. She had done it this time. Used up her reserves. She held her arms out for balance and stumbled to the pool. And all this for what? The love of an emotionally distant mother? The respect of people she barely knew? To be honest with herself, she only wanted peace at home and to fit in enough to be invited to the In-League party, so she could say no. Then she would be the one doing the rejecting for once.

She dropped to the damp tile by the pool's edge. Blood oozed from the cut on her face, sending ripples through her pale reflection. In the darkness, Brooke huffed as she climbed out of the hole.

It all got out of control somehow.

Brooke could have died. Amayah could have been a friend, a big sister to her. She hadn't. So many people were at stake and the In-League was willing to risk them to test her. She gripped the edge of the pool. Blood oozed between her fingers. Red drops unfurled into ringlets and faded into the water.

Amayah didn't remember Dad. Didn't even have a picture. She hadn't been in Timeout when someone wished they could afford their dream home and taken him away. She never wanted the attention of being a hero, but she knew what responsibility was. There might still be enough time, enough of her left to keep the Janus from hurting anyone else. Blood ran from her hands and into the water.

Hydrogen had the oldest memories of all. Fiery dreams from the beginning of time, dinosaur spit, and Cleopatra's bath. Amayah spread out on the ripples.

The maze shook. Tons of water awoke, rose from the pool, and stretched like an ancient glass willow.

Amayah held her arms up. "Take me with you."

The water swept her into its icy grip, and they gushed into the human world. Amayah and the water surged high into the morning air.

Like a child at Christmas, Yin hadn't waited. She sat on the grass behind the cafeteria with the open box and Janus. She stared wide-eyed at Amayah.

Amayah's new body spun and opened like a flower into hundreds of arms with translucent fingers.

Yin snatched the glittering Janus and stumbled back. Shadows tore loose from the buildings and whirled around her, thickening into a shield.

Amayah swung her watery fists up and brought her wrath down. Water slammed into the darkness with a sound like thunder. The cafeteria windows shattered. Gray cracks spread across the shield. The water surged into the fissures, prying the barrier apart like the shell of a boiled egg.

The shadows of the chain-link fence slashed at the water, cutting dozens of arms loose. Amayah screamed at the ripping pain. Chucks of water splashed on the asphalt. Her sight went fuzzy at the edges.

Amayah had left too much behind in the maze. Yin had to be stopped now, before Amayah lost consciousness or worse. No time to hold back. No mercy.

Amayah punched through the shield and struck Yin, knocking her to the ground. Yin scrambled away but couldn't escape. Amayah forced water through Yin's clenched teeth and down her throat. Fingers stretched into needle-sharp spikes and plunged toward Yin's body. The shield crumbled. Frothy bubbles escaped Yin's mouth as she screamed her last breath.

No!

Water rippled in the light breeze. This wasn't—couldn't be who she was. The In-League might justify any level of force in the war on supervillains, but Amayah wouldn't. Even Yin's life mattered. She pulled the water from Yin's lungs and released her hold.

Yin gagged and clutched the fabric of her bodysuit at her chest. She coughed and rolled into the damaged school's shadow, vanishing. The Janus lay on the yellow grass.

Lightheaded euphoria flooded Amayah. She could wait no longer. Her blood streamed into crimson threads that wound together to reenter her hands. The water peeled away. Amayah fell to the ground, soaked and shivering. The wind stole more warmth than the weak sunlight gave.

Hands seized her shoulders. Shadows surged around her and slammed her back against a brick wall, punching the air from her lungs.

Clothed in vines of darkness, Yin's one-handed grip tightened on Amayah's throat. Amayah's feet dangled above the sidewalk that ran along the building. Yin held the Janus in the other hand. Dark filaments twisted in her eyes.

"What is the secret? How does it work?" Yin screamed.

"I...I don't know," Amayah gasped. Her hands slipped along Yin's arms, leaving bloody trails. Fireflies danced at the edges of her vision as Yin's gloom-reinforced grip squeezed. The world turned gray. Yin's memories surged through Amayah. Smoke from cooking fires and bland rice. Family. Tradition. Overwhelming loss.

On a frozen river, they had tried to cross in search of a better life. Soldiers hid along the banks. The crack of rifles echoed through the valley and Yin's mother dropped. Her father too. Yin laid very still on the ice beside her mother, feigning death and holding her younger brother still until the sun set. Her wish wasn't to break her brother out of prison. She meant to bring her family back.

Amayah fell to the concrete, the connection broken. She gasped cold air that burned her lungs. The corners of her eyes stung with tears and the world blurred.

Yin stumbled back and collapsed. She sobbed so hard, she couldn't catch her breath.

Amayah's stomach clenched. Memories she never had threatened to crush her. It must be so much worse for Yin. She wiped tears from her eyes. The Janus glittered on the dead grass, forgotten. There was only one thing left to do.

She crawled past it and held Yin, rocking her gently. "I am so sorry."

Yin slipped her arms around Amayah and wept. Time passed, though Amayah couldn't tell how much. Yin's sobs ebbed.

"The shadows would have teleported Brooke from danger, but I knew you would save her," Yin whispered.

Amayah wiped the tears from her eyes and sniffled. "You couldn't have. It was the wrong choice."

"It was the only choice for you."

Two superheroes in white leotards with blue capes jogged across the asphalt. One carried a bracelet of woven barbed wire. A power-neutralizing cuff for Yin. They were White Knights, members of a minor hero league and the In-League's garbage collectors.

"Yin, they're coming for you. The shadows. You can escape."

"No." Yin pulled away and shook her head. A smile played along her lips. "Don't you see? I shall be with my brother again. Either way, I win." Yin leaned closer. "They aren't your friends. They used us both."

The Knights power-cuffed Yin and dragged her to her feet. She didn't resist, but they handled her roughly all the same as they took her away.

Amayah willed herself to stay awake against the weariness. Focusing on every breath. She was so cold inside.

A shadow fell across her. She slipped closer to the yellow lawn, but it wasn't fatigue. She actually weighed more in the shadow. A plastic bottle of orange juice bounced on the grass.

She missed it the first time but managed to grab it on the second try. The top was already loose. She gulped it down, cold, tart, and thick with a hint of iron. They had mixed it with some kind of body building supplement. She let the empty bottle slip from her fingers.

A bundle of gauze dropped to the ground and rolled.

"Cover up, pumpkin. You're disgusting."

It hurt too much to think, let alone protest. Amayah took the gauze and wound it around her right hand. She tore it off with her teeth and began binding her left hand.

A soft whistle cut through the chill air. Vox, the ex-quarterback, stood resplendent in a black and gold body suit, surveying damage to the school. It wasn't often that the prom king and queen of the In-League were seen together.

Amayah set the gauze on the ground. The back half of the building was a pile of loose bricks and twisted mauve beams. Amayah had been so intent on fighting Yin, she hadn't noticed the collateral damage. "If you had helped, this wouldn't have happened."

Gravity Jinn's hair fluttered slowly, floating in a blonde halo around her head. Her silver tights sparkled in the yellow morning light. "What's the point of an initiation trial if you have help?"

Amayah snatched the Janus from the grass. "Yin had this in her hand. If she figured out how—"

The Janus oozed the smell of ancient plankton, rotting away in the dark. Plastic. It wasn't a piece of Ange Noir. She should take care in her weakened state, but warmth flushed her face. "What the hell is this?"

Gravity Jinn smiled. "Villain bait. Dr. Chronomancer had a fit and destroyed the Janus after Kyla went poof and the housing glut."

"Who's Kyla?" Vox asked.

Gravity Jinn checked her nails. "Don't worry about it, Rick."

Amayah gathered her legs beneath her, but they trembled instead of lifting her to grab Gravity Jinn by the neck. "I almost left someone to die for this. I almost killed for this."

"But you didn't and that's what's important. When our agent sold Yin the map, we let her know you would be there. Brooke was part of your test. A test for you and for Brooke. She failed," Gravity Jinn said.

The new bandages turned crimson. Tentacles of blood wrapped around the Janus prop, cracking it.

Gravity Jinn put her fists on her hips. Light rippled in her gravity field. "Don't make me chip a nail, pumpkin pie."

Vox put his hands out. "Girls, please. We're on the same side."

Gravity Jinn stared into the distance. Vox wasn't much in a fight, but with a few words, he could convince the President to launch a nuclear strike on his own family. He was the architect of the new world and the most dangerous hero of all. Only his ex-girlfriends were immune and fortunately for this situation, Amayah was one of those.

"Amayah's power is growing," Vox said. "Most exonormans are only as strong as five normans, but she is going to be a walking nuke, maybe a hurricane. We need her."

"Power growing…" Gravity Jinn blinked. They must be fighting, close to breaking up, or she couldn't have resisted. "Cut it out, Rick," she huffed and knelt so she was eye level with Amayah. "I have reservations about this one."

Two more Knights roughly pulled Brooke from the Nether-Maze backdoor.

Brooke glanced quickly at Amayah. *Help me*, she mouthed. With a yank, they turned her around and slipped a pair of power-binding cuffs over her wrists.

Amayah took a deep breath. The orange juice worked and the dizziness faded. She needed to focus on the present. "What will happen to Brooke?"

Gravity Jinn shook her head. "We saw what she did. The Pan-League Counsel will decide her fate, but there is no juvie hall for their kind. A villain's a villain, no matter how small."

The Knights finished securing Brooke and half-dragged her away to the waiting police cars, her little feet flicking up bits of grass as they trailed across the ground.

Amayah clenched her jaw. "She doesn't deserve that. Yin took advantage of her kind nature and you tricked them both. I'm not even sure Yin deserves Timeout."

Gravity Jinn turned to Vox. "That's what I'm talking 'bout. Can we trust her to follow orders?"

Vox shrugged. "Suggestions?"

"One," Gravity Jinn said, holding out her hand to Amayah. A golden ring sat in her palm. "You still want this. Right?"

The emeralds in the ring's olive branch symbol were rendered black in Gravity Jinn's shadow. This was prestige. Amayah had played the good girl and the bad to no effect, but the hero, even Mom couldn't ignore that. She reached for the ring. Her gaze slid to Brooke's small form being hauled away. She hesitated.

"The girl is below the In-League's notice," Gravity Jinn said. "I'll give you a choice, the ring or her."

"Take the ring," Vox advised. "How many people have the quarterback and head cheerleader in their contacts?"

Gravity Jinn never took her eyes off Amayah. "This isn't about social status. The In-League is the best of the best. It's about the power to do good."

They shoved Brooke against one of the police cars. Her sobs shook her whole body. She must know she was going to Timeout. Real eternal damnation.

Amayah struggled to stand. Vox took her arm to help, but she pushed him away. She stood tall in front of Gravity Jinn, meeting her blue eyes. "It's all power. And after everything that's happened, it's still just high school, isn't it? I want Brooke. Charges dropped. In my custody."

Gravity Jinn closed her fist on the ring. "Done. The invitation is withdrawn for now. I doubt you'll ever be ready for us."

Witty threats filtered through Amayah's mind, but her ego wasn't important enough to risk Brooke's freedom by fighting. She walked past them.

"Sangue Rose," Gravity Jinn called.

Amayah paused but didn't turn. Gravity Jinn rarely used people's hero names and she had never used Amayah's.

"You're seventeen with no league affiliation," Gravity Jinn said. "Statistically, that puts you at risk of going villain. When you turn eighteen, the Pan-League Counsel stops looking the other way."

Amayah started walking. "I've made enough choices today. Let them know to release Brooke."

"Already done," Vox said.

Red and blue lights played across the tennis courts. Ordinary cops worked crowd control to keep the gathering people away. The Knights' armored containment wagon perched on six tractor tires with its back hatch open, like a drawbridge. Yin must already be sealed away inside. Brooke stood at the ramp's base, staring into the dark interior. The light wind tossed her dark curls.

Amayah took a deep breath and let it out slowly. Brooke was safe and maybe Amayah's life could get back to what passed for normal these days. She wouldn't take that for granted again.

The Knights were talking to the cops and gesturing toward the crowd. Apparently, they wanted the crowd parted so they could move the wagon out into the street.

"I'm taking the young one with me," Amayah said.

When the Knights hesitated, Amayah gave them her best icy stare. One of the Knights raised her hands. "We got the word. Take her."

Amayah walked up behind Brooke. She placed her hand on the heavy black chain between the thorny cuffs.

Brooke gasped.

"Brooke, it's me."

Brooke glanced over her shoulder and half-smiled. "Oh, hey, Amayah." Her gaze shifted forward to the wagon. "I guess I've been pretty stupid, huh? I'm sorry. Daddy will be all alone, won't he?"

"I've been the fool, Brooke, and you'll see him tonight." Amayah focused on the Ange Noir material of the power cuffs. Within the metal lay a deep nothingness. Every material on Earth talked to her through her blood, but the

Ange Noir was always silent. Its darkness swallowed Amayah.

The world snapped back into place. Brooke was wrapped around Amayah's waist, holding on tight. "I don't know how you did it, but thank you. I, uh, I don't have to be your sidekick now, do I?"

The cuffs had become a black sphere in Amayah's hand. She let it splatter on the asphalt, where it reformed into cuffs. Amayah ran her fingers through Brooke's messy hair. "No. But I've been wondering something. Do you think your dad would let you spend the night? We can just talk, about anything you want."

"Really?"

"Really, and I make wicked hot chocolate, with real cocoa, cream, and a little vanilla bean."

Brooke stared up at Amiyah for a moment. "Marshmallows?"

Lord Chimera

Matthew Dewar

Nanobots whirred to life in my bloodstream as the tattoo faded from my wrist. It took two seconds for the triskele symbol—three spirals with a central connected point—to completely vanish. After mentally syncing with the bots, I prepared myself for the change.

Agonizing pain ripped through me from deep within my core. I clenched my jaw, steeling myself against it. It was a price I willingly paid for the freedom the bots gave me. Bones hollowed as the excess calcium and connective tissues flowed to my shoulder blades. Two large falcon wings unfurled and grew through the wing slots on my Kevlar bodysuit. After a minute's recovery, I threw myself off the balcony of my penthouse apartment into the warm afternoon sky.

Windows flashed past and the pavement neared with each pounding heartbeat. My wings spread wide and caught a warm updraft, lifting me higher as wind buffeted me about.

The thrill of flying, of being the only man on Earth capable of such a feat, paled in comparison to the rush of seeing the parade dedicated to me.

From my vantage point in the heavens, the people below me resembled ants. Thousands of them gathered along the cordoned-off streets to cheer singers, dancers, acrobats, and performers on as they marched.

With a ripple effect, a comical Mexican wave, heads and hands turned to the sky and a chant reached me with growing fervor.

"Lord Chimera! Lord Chimera! Lord Chimera!"

Smiling and waving, I flew above the parade. Hearing my name shouted over and over filled me with pride and a sense of purpose like nothing else in my life ever had. Over a decade of isolated research, trial and error, and more failed attempts than I care to remember, had led me to this moment. The days of watching the world slowly rot and suffocate from greed and pollution were almost over.

In the middle of the local high school's sports field, a large stage had been erected for my acceptance ceremony. Cameramen and news presenters jostled for the best position as I glided down to them.

My feet touched the wooden decking and my wings folded behind me, ready for use in a few moments' time. Extending my arms wide, I beamed at my fans. Without my nanobots, these people wouldn't cast me a second glance. But behind my mask and Kevlar suit, with my nanobots, I meant something to these people.

The mayor waddled over, his multiple chins jiggling about with every shuffling step. He embraced me in a warm, sweaty hug.

I kept my smile plastered on my face and clapped him heartily on the back. "Dylan, you've outdone yourself."

"I am so thrilled you suggested a celebration such as this," the mayor exclaimed in my ear as we embraced. The hug ended but he remained close. "This is exactly what the people need after those attacks on the city. This has lifted their spirits," he paused for a moment, then continued in a much lower voice, "and has almost guaranteed my next term."

I shook his hand cordially. "You have my full support, Dylan. Brunning City doesn't deserve a man as generous as you. We are so grateful for all you do for our glorious city."

Dylan positively drooled at the praise. With the pleasantries aside, he ushered me over to the podium to address the thronging crowd.

Silence blanketed the crowd as the mayor tapped the microphone. "People of Brunning City, we have been blessed with a savior." Dylan's voice droned on as he read the speech I had prepared for him. I took a minute to scan the sea of reverent faces staring back at me. I imagined this was how the Pharaohs felt looking down on their people, or the Roman Caesars.

Dylan turned to face me, waking me from my daydream. "…to thank Lord Chimera for all he has done for us over the last few weeks, we would like to present him with the key to the city." Beaming like a Cheshire cat, he handed me a large golden key on a shiny wooden plaque.

Posing in front of the flashing cameras, I noticed several reporters from major national networks. My good deeds would spread far and wide, and soon, it wouldn't just be Brunning City that needed rescuing.

As the flashes subsided, I took my place in front of the microphone to address the people. "Thank you for your kind words, Mayor." I held up the key for all to see. "I did not become a hero for the fame or glory. I became a hero because you needed one. I will not rest until the evil mastermind behind these attacks is defeated."

A roar of applause pleased my ears, and I waited for calm before finishing my acceptance speech. "I am your Lord Chimera, and I am your hero!"

My words ignited hysteria. Like putty, they had begun to soften and bend to my will. Soon, I'd be able to mold them into thinking like me, into taking charge of caring for one another and the planet.

As the crowd hushed once more, I spied a young mother with a small child, perhaps eight or nine years old, and beckoned them on stage.

The mother's face reddened to a deep crimson, and she patted down her blouse and adjusted her mop of blonde hair, flashing a very bare ring finger at me several times.

Her son bounded up on stage in a blue soccer shirt and grass-stained pants. His shoes had more holes than a hunk of Swiss cheese, and ketchup stained the corner of his mouth and the front of his top.

"What is your name?"

His eyes were as wide as saucers as he answered, "Conner."

"And I'm Karen," the boy's mother said, placing both her manicured hands on her son's shoulders.

"Well, Conner, you're in for a treat."

A lithe woman in her early thirties stood off to the side of the stage. At my nod, she straightened her shoulders. The trousers of her beige pantsuit swished as she marched on stage to stand beside me, holding a briefcase in front of her.

I spoke into the microphone. "Toyland and I have been working hard this past week to deliver you a range of Lord Chimera action figures, costumes, and merchandise. All products will officially hit the shelves tomorrow. Conner here will be the first boy in the world to receive his very own toy version of me."

Immediately, a wave of childish pleas rose above the applause.

"I want one, mummy!"

"When can I get one?"

Conner bounced up and down on the spot.

With a flick of the locking mechanism, the briefcase lid opened, and I withdrew a colorful box with a clear plastic screen.

He was the perfect idol of me. 3D imaging was used to create my exact dimensions to scale, immortalized forever in biodegradable plastic. The doll's suit had my red, blue, and gold coloring, with my chimera logo on the chest: a lion, ram, and dragon-headed beast with a python for a tail and two large wings protruding from its back. A golden mask covered my head with polarized lenses concealing my eyes and my true identity.

Squeals emanated from the children in the front row. Tiny hands reached forward like hungry seagulls. Of course, they'd have to buy the toys like everyone else.

I mentally synced with the nanobots back at my lab and ordered them to execute their programmed primary objective. This crowd, and the world, was about to witness my heroism firsthand.

Conner's hands trembled with excitement as he reached for the doll, while his mother pouted for the cameras going berserk over the new scoop.

The world darkened for a brief moment as something huge blotted out the sun. Everyone's attention was drawn skyward. A second later, chaos unfolded.

A gleaming silver pterodactyl circled overhead. A column of flames billowed out from its maw.

The nanobots within me reconfigured the cells of my teeth and fingers to create sharp fangs and giant claws. The pain was a walk in the park compared to growing wings.

I snarled in front of the microphone, the speakers amplifying my growl. "How dare you threaten Brunning City!" I expanded my wings to cheers from the crowd.

News crews jostled over the best position to catch my heroics in the act.

The ground disappeared beneath me as my wings beat powerfully, delivering me closer to the circling monster. Dirt and rubbish peppered the crowd from the downdraft. A small price to pay for their safety.

The muscles between my shoulder blades burned as my wings beat harder and faster. The pterodactyl machine neared with each surge of momentum, steel glinting in the sunlight.

A pillar of flames spewed forth, and I narrowly dodged it by banking to the left. The searing heat warmed my Kevlar body suit.

We passed side by side in midflight. Its talons slashed at my face, but the arms weren't long enough to reach.

Mine were.

My extended reinforced claws traced down the length of the machine with a metallic shriek, ripping open its insides. Sparks flew and severed wires snapped in the breeze. Now lifeless, the hunk of metal careened down to the ground at lightning speed.

With my nanobot-enhanced vision, I saw a wheelchair-bound cripple directly underneath the falling pile of scrap metal. The boy's father struggled to move him.

Instinct kicked in and I dove, wings beating hard by my sides.

Gaining.

Beside it.

The ground was meters away.

The boy's eyes were about to pop out of his head.

With the cry of someone who had accepted their fate, the father shielded the boy with his body.

I swooped down, pushing the boy and his father out of the way milliseconds before the ground was pulverized by nearly four hundred pounds of steel. Dirt showered over us.

The boy was pale and his lips quivered. "Th-thanks."

I tapped him gently on the chin. "Anytime, buddy."

The boy threw his arms out to his dad. "Dad! Did you see that?"

The boy's father nearly bowled me over as he descended on him in a mess of tears and flailing arms. "Oh, Jason. You're alive. It's a miracle."

Miracle… There was no denying the occasional pangs of guilt that jolted me in my sleep. I was forced to continuously remind myself of the grand plan. After twelve months of heroic deeds and establishing myself as a superhero and savior, the world will listen to me. Change will happen. Yes, nanobots could make that boy walk again, but unleashing that technology on the public could have devastating results. And despite the infinite good nanobots could be used for, they could also be corrupted for malevolent purposes.

I mentally activated the nanobots' secondary objective.

"Quick, someone pass me a container for the scrap metal before it disappears!" I cried.

The nanobots worked quickly, breaking down the metal pterodactyl until it completely dissolved into the ground.

I threw myself down on the ground in a desperate attempt to collect some of the evidence. Theatrics. The nanobots would relocate my work of art back to my warehouse where it would be reconfigured into my next creation, leaving no evidence to be traced back to me or my precious bots.

The press fell on me like a wave, and I was forced to pose with the boy and his father. The news crews certainly earned their paychecks. Today couldn't have worked out better for my coming plans.

The crowd tentatively returned to my presence, cautious eyes scanning the horizon for any signs of further threats.

I retreated back to the podium and addressed them one last time. "There is a monster among us, and I will not rest until this perpetrator is brought to justice! The people of Brunning City deserve to sleep peacefully at night. Under my protection, you are safe, today and always."

One reporter stepped forward, her cameraman following her like a puppy. Long, dark hair fell onto the shoulders of her beige suit. "Jessica Charmers, Nine News. Lord Chimera, do you know anything about who is behind these machines plaguing the city? Or why they disappear once defeated?" She held my gaze long and hard with her cool green eyes, demanding an answer.

"I hate to admit my shortcomings, but as of yet, I have no information on the matter. As soon as I have any word, you'll be the first to know."

It wasn't enough for her. She pursed her peach lips for a moment. "Don't you think it all seems odd? There have been no demands. What does this villain want?"

"My best guess at this point in time is that the mastermind behind these attacks is a terrorist and wants to cause widespread panic. But I have stopped every one of his creations so far, and will continue to do so until the coward shows his face, and then I'll defeat him too."

The people cheered, clapped their hands, and whistled their appreciation. But Jessica's eyebrows had knitted together in worry.

"I'm just concerned that these monsters are tests. They've all been so easy for you to defeat. What if the villain is learning your strengths and weaknesses while creating something you won't be able to defeat?" She bit her bottom lip. Hers wasn't the only worried face in the crowd. Whispers of doubt spread like a plague.

"If that is the case, so be it. I have plenty more talents hidden up my sleeve." With a final comforting smile, I launched myself into the air.

Flying over the congested streets, I alighted a few blocks from my apartment where my driverless car awaited me. Another wonderful creation I had my nanobots to thank for.

My wings, claws, and fangs retracted with all the discomfort of barbed wire sliding through my blood vessels.

The triskele tattoo appeared on the inside of my wrist once more, and I squeezed myself out of the Kevlar suit and into a comfortable pair of jeans and a t-shirt.

Leaving the key and my suit in the car, I took the elevator up to the penthouse and headed straight for the shower.

The sheer curtains flapped into my bedroom on the breeze coming through the open window. I would have loved to openly display my key in my trophy case, an entire wall of glass cabinetry opposite my bed dedicated to documenting my lifelong achievements and accolades. It would look at home beside my three framed doctorates and my New York marathon medal, but Lord Chimera couldn't be further from Andrew Jackson. It was like becoming a different person—a better person—every time I put on the mask.

My heart skipped a beat at the knock on my bedroom door. "Dad, are you home?"

"Robbie?" *What's he doing here?*

Robbie shuffled into the room barefoot, wearing sweatpants and an old band t-shirt. He rubbed his eyes like he just got out of bed, and judging by the bird's nest of hair on his head, he had. "Not much. Where've you been?"

"Nowhere."

Robbie's eyes narrowed at me. "I looked around for you earlier and couldn't find you anywhere, so I went back to bed. I thought you forgot this was my weekend with you and went to work or something."

I tousled his shaggy hair, not that it needed any more messing up. "I wouldn't forget about you. I've been in here the whole time. And you know I don't like crowds."

Robbie shrugged. "Whatever." His stomach rumbled. "I'm hungry. Got anything for lunch?"

***

Robbie sat hunched over his steak sandwich, attention barely sliding away from his phone long enough to take a bite.

"How's school going?"

Glancing up, Robbie's eyes betrayed a hint of shame.

Folding my arms over my chest, I stared him down. "What grades are you getting?"

"I got an A in computer programming." He puffed out his chest, defiance glaring me in the eye.

"Nice. But what about everything else? Math? English?" I rolled my hands in the air, waiting for him to elaborate further.

Robbie's hands pulled at the hem of his shirt. "Cs and Ds," he mumbled.

I dropped my sandwich onto my plate. "Come on, Robbie. You're so much better than that. What's going on?"

"Why do you even care?" He stormed out of the dining room, and a moment later, his bedroom door slammed shut.

Sighing heavily, I poured myself two fingers of scotch and nursed it. "Am I a bad father?" Silence answered my question. Bleak loneliness stared back at me from each wall of the room. I thought I could save the world and have a family, but keeping secrets just pushed everyone away. Being alone was one small sacrifice I had to endure to make the world a better place.

With a job less than twenty-four hours away, and a warehouse full of machinery and nanobots that needed reprogramming, I didn't have the time to make things up with Robbie right now.

Muffled music played on the other side of his bedroom door. I knocked gently then harder when he didn't respond.

"What?" he grunted.

"Turn that off and open your door."

He opened the door with a roll of his eyes. "What?"

"Something's come up at work, and I need to pop into the lab. Are you alright to stay here for a few hours?"

"Fine."

"We'll spend some time together tomorrow, I promise."

"Whatever. I don't care." He slammed the door in my face, and a moment later, the music started up again, cranked louder than before.

***

Inside my warehouse, machinery whirred to life as I thumbed through the blueprints for my next big job. The pterodactyl was a favorite of mine, but this rhino monster was going to be even better.

Last week, the CEO of King's Casino had contacted me with the task of overseeing the security of a massive money transfer. The casino was closing down for three months for renovations, and all physical money was to be transferred to a sister casino two hours away.

A perfect opportunity for a villain to try and rob them. Cue needing the protection of Lord Chimera.

A hiss of steam escaped a vent in the industrial factory line. Instead of cars, they now manufactured my next adversary. The rhino monster had a titanium and diamond reinforced horn, capable of drilling through even the toughest of metals. Its body was hollow, capable of storing three square feet of cash and casino chips. Not that I planned on stealing anything, but the machine had to look the part.

From the depths of the warehouse came an echoing clang. Blood pulsed in my ears as I walked around, searching for the source of the noise. My fear quickly subsided. A pipe had fallen on the ground. No intruder.

A chime sounded and parts emerged on a conveyor belt. My rhino took shape as robotic arms assembled the pieces into my masterpiece.

History had seen the rise of some fantastic leaders: Julius Caesar, Alexander the Great, Churchill, Napoleon, Zedong, Lincoln, Ghandi, and one day: Lord Chimera. History was our greatest teacher, and I had learned from their mistakes. Lord Chimera would rise and stay at the top forever. From Brunning City, I would move around the world until everyone accepted me as a hero. From there, I would create my united world. One leader to take Earth to its next stage of progress. I saw a bright future, a future that was being held back by governments, power, and greed.

I tested the mental connection with the nanobots, and the rhino's eyes lit up devil-red. The horn drill buzzed, the legs moved as well as I'd hoped. It looked fearsome. I put the nanobots to sleep and locked up, ready for tomorrow morning.

***

My arrival at the casino's underground parking lot was precisely on time. I was worried I would be late due to Robbie trouble. I had caught him sneaking back into his room at the crack of dawn. I didn't have time to fight with him, so I left, saving my questions for later. But I still couldn't shake the worry from my mind. He seemed hell-bent on staying on the self-destructive path he was on.

It was a brisk morning, but my nanobots were hard at work controlling my hormones and metabolizing my breakfast to keep me warm.

I greeted Samson, head of security, a middle-aged man whose bark was worse than his bite. The sleeves of his dark suit threatened to split from the jacked muscles underneath, and his face was a constant scowl.

"Chimera." Samson crushed my hand and nodded in acknowledgement of me. "Gonna take the mask off and show me who you really are?"

"*Lord* Chimera." I had the nanobots increase the density of the muscle fibers in my hand as I returned the handshake. "I think you know the answer to your question." When Samson pulled his hand away from mine, he flicked it once before resting it inside his pocket.

After a quick scan of the area, we were on the move. Everything was as discussed: three decoy trucks and three trucks carrying thirty million dollars each. Four heavily armed guards were stationed within each truck, and the drivers each had a bodyguard sitting beside them.

But that was all superfluous. They had me.

Gliding above the convoy, I kept an eye out for any hint of trouble. There was every possibility that a real criminal would attempt something.

The trucks rolled out of the undercover parking lot of the casino and snaked their way through a maze of back streets. At this time on a Sunday morning, there was very little traffic on the roads. Apart from the odd pack of arrogant cyclists who took up more of the road than they should, everything went to plan.

At the quiet intersection of Hastings and Willow Street, the convoy was forced to stop at a red light.

Now was the ideal time. I activated the rhino's nanobots with my mental link. It didn't take long before I heard the pounding of its huge hooves, growing louder and louder.

The traffic lights turned green and the trucks started rolling, but the steel frame of the rhino plowed through the first truck, sending it rolling down the empty street.

Barrels flashed as loud gunshots disturbed the peaceful silence of the morning. Zinging ricochets twanged the air after hitting the rhino.

"Chimera! Stop it!" Samson shouted.

The rhino attacked the second truck. It was one of the decoys and would act to throw suspicion off me and everyone else here.

The horn whirred to life and sparks flew as the tip drilled into the side of the vehicle.

I swooped down from above. The knuckles on my right hand became reinforced with thick calcium deposits as my fist arced down on the weakened steel behind the rhino's left ear.

Metal crumpled with the sound of a car crash, and the whirring of the horn drill faded. The lights in the rhino's eyes dimmed, and I activated the self-recycling command with a quick thought. The rhino broke down before our eyes and melted into the asphalt road as it was carried back to my warehouse through underground channels.

Another score for Lord Chimera.

Samson holstered his Glock and clapped me on the back. "Good job. I thought the big boss was an idiot for hiring you, but turns out we needed you after all."

I clapped him on the shoulder. "I'm just glad none of you *boys* got injured."

I left a scowling Samson behind me as I took to the air once more. He twirled his finger in the air, and his men bounced back into position. The convoy rolled on. The first truck remained on the scene, the driver on the phone, waving his arms about in the air as he called for a tow truck.

Most of my attention was inwardly focused. Everything was going according to my plan. The new and improved Earth was one step closer.

Once the trucks had arrived safely at the neighboring King's Casino, I looped around in the air and sped home. The sun had risen high in the sky, warming the day nicely.

I touched down at home in the early afternoon and changed out of my Kevlar suit. There was a small dent above my right shoulder blade where a bullet must have hit me. I hadn't even felt it. I had no doubt the nanobots could repair any lethal damage, but I'd rather not test out that theory.

My phone buzzed. The text was from King's Casino's CEO acknowledging a job well done. I opened up my banking app. A nice two hundred thousand dollar sum had been added to my account. Not bad for a few hours' work.

***

"Robbie?"

The house was quiet and he was nowhere to be found. He wasn't in his bedroom or any of the other four. The theatre, games room, gym, and downstairs indoor pool were all empty as well.

I picked up my phone in frustration and called him.

"Dad?"

"Where are you?" I snapped

"I'm on my way back home now." The excitement in his voice was contagious. Maybe this afternoon wouldn't be so bad after all.

"Okay, see you soon." I ended the call and poured myself a finger of scotch. The crystal decanter made a chiming sound as I replaced it on the silver tray. I couldn't remember the last time Robbie and I spent more than ten minutes together without fighting. I promised myself to try my hardest to enjoy this afternoon with him.

Taking my drink out onto the balcony, I looked down upon my city, lost in thought. Tall buildings hugged wide streets. The occasional pocket of greenery marked a park or sport's field. It was hard to keep focused on the small steps with my end goal fast approaching. But these were delicate matters that couldn't be rushed. Patience was a must.

The front door shut with a bang, and I retreated inside to see what Robbie had planned for us.

Robbie strutted through the front entranceway like he had just won a competition, and he wanted to rub it in my face. A backpack was slung over his shoulder, and he lazily threw it down on the tiled floor.

I placed my glass in the kitchen sink. "Where've you been?"

He shrugged. "Nowhere." A confident smile tugged on the corner of his mouth. "Did you hear Lord Chimera stopped a massive rhino machine from stealing millions of dollars?"

"Hm. Good on him."

"It's a pity you've never been around to see his heroics in action." An eyebrow was slightly raised, his suggestion that I was Lord Chimera bright as day.

"Yes, well, I'm sure I'll see him soon enough. He seems to have his work cut out for him with all those machines. Anyway," I waved off the nonsense, "What have you got planned for this afternoon?"

Robbie's eyes lit up. "How about a bike ride along the foreshore?"

"Sure." It was a perfect day and would hopefully stop Robbie from asking too many more questions.

***

Wind raced through my short hair as I pedaled along the bike path on the edge of the river. It wasn't quite the same feeling as flying, but it was close.

Robbie was a few lengths in front of me, his shaggy hair trailing behind him, and I wondered if I could convince him to cut it later.

I smiled and nodded to the ignorant passersby. They had no idea how their paper coffee cups, social media addictions, and branded clothes were contributing to the mess we were in. The government had them wrapped around its little finger. Keeping the people distracted while the world was opened for exploitation.

Give me one year, and that would all change.

Riding along the foreshore was peaceful. Robbie kept glancing out over the water. *This is what I was fighting for.* How many more generations before our clear blue water ran black with pollution? Would Robbie's children have fresh air to breathe? How long until greedy world leaders plunged the world into a nuclear war that would put an end to every living thing on the planet?

Our peace was shattered as an explosion of water spurted into the sky.

Screams and yells filled the air as water crashed down in a wave.

I clenched the brakes, coming to a skidding stop, watching in dumbfounded shock as one of *my* creations scrambled out of the water.

The giant metal sea serpent rolled onto its back and splashed down. The tidal wave flung young families and couples from their paddleboats and washed onto the pathway. Chaos erupted all around us, and a panicked Robbie pedaled as fast as he could away from the scene.

It's not possible.

I tried several times to sync with the nanobots in the sea serpent without luck. My mental link was broken. I had no control over them whatsoever. Fear was not an emotion I was used to, and yet it constricted my airways like an old friend.

Glancing around, I could see everyone was too busy to notice me change. With a press of my tattoo, the nanobots inside me awakened. First, they reshaped my face so no one could recognize me without my mask, then they reconfigured my respiratory system to add gills. I threw my bike aside and stripped down to my jocks. Connective tissue formed webbing between my lengthening fingers and toes.

Icy water sent my muscles into a short spasm as I dove in. Salt stung my eyes. I grew a transparent third eyelid over my corneas, just like a crocodile, and the nanobots reconfigured my corneal shape and lens focusing mechanism to help me see better in the murky water.

Blueprints raced through my mind as I powered through the water. The serpent's jaw was unstable, and tearing it apart would kill the mechanics, rendering it lifeless.

Rage fueled my strokes. Someone had been through *my* warehouse and seen *my* plans. Someone must have broken in last night. Copycats were the worst kind of villains. They lacked all imagination and creativity. And this person was turning my altruistic plan into a selfish, villainous one. *I will not stand for it.*

With a sickening cracking sound, the sea serpent crashed through one of the pylons supporting the pier that extended out into the water. Tourists and locals alike ran screaming for land, but they wouldn't all make it. The market stalls and businesses would be lost if I didn't do something soon.

The pier cracked. Wood splintered out along the jetty from the broken pylon.

I raced to the serpent and tackled it away from the pier. It flailed underwater. A powerful kick of its tail brushed me aside. The wind was knocked out of me and my throat spasmed. I struggled to get a good grip on the slippery metal.

I kept trying the mental link, but it was no use. I had no idea who was capable of comprehending my nanobots, much less reconfiguring them.

My head popped out of the water to a chant of "Lord Chimera!"

Pride swelled my chest. In times of need, people turned to me.

But it wasn't me they were cheering.

There was an imposter.

My eye twitched as a masked man swooped down from above with glorious wings. *My* wings. *My* golden mask. *My* red and blue Kevlar suit.

The serpent's mouth opened and the crowd gasped.

I commanded my nanobots to work. My gills dissolved back into normal skin and my webbing transformed into claws. Wings grew from my shoulder blades and I sped up the process despite the increasing pain.

The imposter wrenched apart the serpent's jaw like it was wrapping paper on a birthday present.

The crowd erupted into applause and my name was chanted over and over.

A wooden crack stopped the chanting. The pier dropped an inch.

The serpent dissolved, but instead of returning to my warehouse, the metal clawed its way along the pier and rebuilt the missing pylon to cheers and shouts from the masses.

The imposter Lord Chimera addressed the crowd. "Lord Chimera is a fake. He is not your hero. He is responsible for the attacks on—"

My wings completed, I burst out of the water and spear-tackled the imposter out of the sky.

"It's the villain!" the crowd cried. "Get him, Lord Chimera!"

I ground my teeth. This imposter needed to pay.

We crashed down into the water amid an explosion of bubbles, flailing claws, and thrashing wings.

The imposter gouged a deep gash across my face and blood darkened the water. I healed fast and responded with a rapid assault of my own.

The imposter's attacks weakened as my crazed claws ripped off his Kevlar suit and slashed into his chest. The imposter fought back for a few seconds before falling limp, drifting aimlessly in the water.

I pulled the pathetic mask off his face to look in the eyes of the dying villain that tried to stop me.

Shaggy hair created a halo around Robbie's head.

Few things have surprised me in my life. Fewer have made me feel bad or remorseful.

Seeing blood pour from Robbie's chest made me stop dead in my tracks.

My heart thundered as I waited for the skin to repair itself over the deep wounds across his face. His right eye had already closed up and swelled. The shock must have knocked him unconscious.

I lifted him out of the water, my wings straining against the added weight.

The crowd below hurled question after question at me, but they all melted into one big chaotic wall of noise.

Nanobots worked to strengthen my wings and lighten my bones as much as possible, but still I strained to maintain altitude.

Making a panicked beeline for home, I barely made it. We collapsed in a heap on the balcony, and I tried to stand on shaking legs. My nanobots quickly returned me back to normal, and I dragged Robbie into the room, leaving a deep crimson streak behind us on the white carpet.

"Come on, Robbie. Don't give up!" Grabbing the nearest thing I could find, I pressed an old t-shirt against his face. It quickly turned into a dripping, blood-soaked rag.

"Robbie. Stay with me. Command your nanobots to heal you." I tried and failed to sync with his bots. Part of me was amazed and proud of him for what he did. But the betrayal soured the moment.

Another blood-soaked shirt later and I knew I was losing him. His pulse weakened by the second while mine continued to beat faster and faster.

I pressed my tattoo and activated my nanobots, pooling every last one of them in my hand. I ran to the kitchen and grabbed a knife. Standing over Robbie, I cut the palm of my hand, pouring my blood over the wounds on his chest.

I set my nanobots to work, repairing Robbie and then destroying every trace of the nanobots in his system.

Robbie's eyes opened with a sigh. "Dad."

With a sob and a single tear running down my cheek, I kissed him on the forehead. "You're okay." My hands shook dreadfully.

Robbie coughed, color slowly returning to his face.

The relief that Robbie had survived started to fade as my brain registered what he had cost me. "What were you thinking?" I stood up and glared down at him on the floor. "You could have hurt yourself or anyone else there! You could have destroyed my plans!"

"No. You needed to be stopped." Robbie groaned as he stood. "This is why Mum left you, why nobody likes you. You think you're better than everyone else and that you're the only one capable of fixing things."

"Robbie, you don't understand—"

"I understand just fine!" he yelled. "You want to be rich and powerful and control everyone."

"That's not true, I—"

"Why did you do it then? Why did you make those monsters attack the city?"

"It's complicated." My fists clenched at my sides.

"Then help me understand." Robbie crossed his arms over his chest. "I followed you to your warehouse yesterday. I spent all night going through your plans, I even injected myself with a vial of nanobots."

"Why?"

His eyes shimmered as they grew wet. "Because the world doesn't need Lord Chimera. And I need my dad."

I pulled Robbie into a hug, resting his shuddering body against mine. "Sometimes people have to make sacrifices for the greater good."

He pushed away from me. "But this isn't for the greater good. This is all because you're a control freak. You don't need to make everyone do what you want. You're not a god."

I needed space. I left Robbie where he was and went to the kitchen for some water. My own son! How could he do this to me? Bringing the glass up to my lips, the absence of the tattoo on my wrist reminded me that I was now more alone than I had ever been. I felt naked without the nanobots there. I needed to get back to my warehouse and inject myself with another vial.

Robbie followed me. "You might have had good intentions, but this isn't the right way."

"Sit down." My voice was a growl. After a few deep breaths to calm myself, I continued. "You are sixteen. You shouldn't have done what you did, but it's too late now. We are going to forget this ever happened, and carry on."

He diverted his gaze. "It's too late."

"What do you mean?"

"Check the news."

A shot of adrenaline surged through me, making my muscles feel both heavy and light at the same time. Dread eased its way into my temples with a throbbing pain. "Robbie. What have you done?"

The television blinked on to a familiar face and a familiar location. Jessica Charmers from Nine News stood in front of my warehouse, which had been sealed off with crime tape. In the background, police and forensics came and went.

"No." I shook my head in disbelief. Everything. Everything was in there. All my plans, prototypes, and nanobots. Everything I needed to fix this world in the hands of others.

Jessica cleared her throat and nodded at the camera. "At this stage, authorities are unable to comment on the contents of the warehouse, but an anonymous tip leads us to believe that Lord Chimera used this location to build machines he could easily defeat to gain our trust. Who knows what his grand plans were."

The screen went black and I threw the remote on the couch, turning on my son. "You've ruined everything." The air was thin and humid. Sweat drenched my face as my heart thundered painfully in my chest.

"You wanted to create a united world. How can you do that with lies and secrets? This is how we create a united world. We trust the people we share this planet with. If you want to be a *real* hero, you'll give up on Lord Chimera and work with others to turn the world around."

"I'm nothing without Lord Chimera." Hot, prickly tears stung the edges of my eyes. The world felt like it was both closing in on me and never-ending.

"Dad, there never was a Lord Chimera, only you with a mask on. You're still the same person. Now it's time to save the world properly."

I turned my back on Robbie. "I don't know where to start."

Robbie grabbed my arm and pulled me back around. "Then give up. Just like you gave up on Mum and me. Become a failure."

Robbie was right. There was no way I could give up. I would try again, a thousand times if I had to.

Failure is never an option.

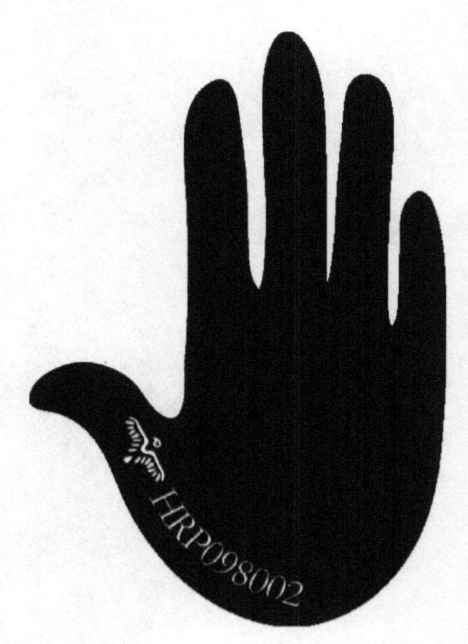

HRP098002

The Outlands

J. L. Bernard

Isaak looked at the reflective surface of the sheet metal protruding from the ground; sandstorms and high, gritty winds had polished the metal to a mirror-like surface. There was something different about him. It wasn't in his ocean-blue eyes—those had always been the same. It wasn't on his high cheekbones or coffee-colored skin. His dark-brown hair was longer than usual, hovering over his forehead and into his eyes, but that wasn't it either.

It was something else, on the inside.

A swish of chestnut, shoulder-length hair and deep emerald eyes appeared at his shoulder. The girl was a head shorter with a slender frame and distracting curves. They had been best friends for seventeen years.

"Earth to Isaak!" Ashleigh Davenport said, snapping her fingers in his face. "Are you going to crack that open or what?"

He dropped the power core nestled in his hands. Isaak frowned, looking down at the device. They were scavenging like most Wasters had to do, and Isaak's family needed the credits.

Ashleigh's grease-smeared face softened into a look of concern. "I'm sorry," she said. "I was just trying to hurry up; we shouldn't be here."

Isaak scanned the area, and she was right. She was always right, at least in his experience. Soot Raiders traveled through this wreckage, and if they found her and Isaak, no one else ever would again. They were miles from their home, Haven, and that was breaking the rules.

"I'm sorry," he said. "I'm distracted."

But he wasn't just distracted; he was hiding a horrible secret.

At first, he didn't believe it, considering that it began with a dream. In the latest one, Isaak was sitting at the kitchen table as still as a statue, but the entire house was moving as if it were alive. A strange power welled inside him that both excited and frightened him. It was strange, but somehow this power felt like it belonged. This morning, he also noticed a set of faded numbers tattooed on his right hand that hadn't been there before. They read *HRP098002*. How could he ever explain its origins to anyone? He shook his head, burying the thoughts deep. Better not to think of them now. Focus was key in the Outlands, and distractions could mean death.

Isaak began stripping the machinery. "Have you seen the latest prices for salvage, Ash? It's abominable."

She fixed her bright-green stare on him. "Abominable?" She broke down a piece of salvage without looking at it. "Seems like the Normandy Salvage Depot drops the values every day. How do they expect the Salvaging Families to live?"

Isaac scoffed; he knew his family had it worse. "How do they expect the Working Families to make it in this screwed-up world? You're paid top dollar for your parts, but us low-class wasters are slapped with a *hosting fee* to pay for our housing and food at the market in Stall Square. Dad says it's pretty much—"

"Slavery," she finished for him.

"Right," he said, a frown pinching his lips. He finished dismantling the power core and tossed the unimportant bits into a bin resting on the transport they *borrowed* from the city's hangar. Nowadays, everything was used in some way.

He turned to the piles of burnt trash, melted metal, and rusted cars spread out across the remnants of the street where they were scavenging. Dilapidated buildings that once seemed grand were gutted, empty shells of broken glass, drywall, and concrete. It was eerily silent. A smoldering breeze blew lazily through his hair, guiding his eyes upward to the tower jutting into the sky. It was like a giant, bleached bone reaching into the heavens—a monolith of death.

It was an ATMOS, or Atmospheric Transformation Maintenance and Observation Structure, and it was the catalyst that made this world possible. In 2017, a scientist by the name of James Entera brought the first ATMOS online; the ATMOS were designed to repair Earth's deteriorating atmosphere. They were nuclear-powered and accomplished their purpose by expelling robotic nanites into the air, which altered their surroundings at a molecular level. The invention performed as expected and by 2020, James Entera had installed ATMOS units all over the globe.

All the towers were linked so each hemisphere could communicate, but a system error in 2025 caused the nuclear reactors in the towers to meltdown. Yet, they continued to pump out nanites saturated with radiation. Thus began the end of the world. Now, 300 years later, survivors that lived in a place like Haven had to struggle in the endless wastes of the Outlands.

A screeching sound assaulted Isaak's ears, forcing his stomach into his throat, but it was just a street sign that had finally given in to the elements. Isaak couldn't ignore the feeling of hundreds of eyes watching him, waiting for him to screw up. Waiting to strike.

Isaak was about to return to work when he saw *it*— the only word he could use to describe the monstrosity standing about fifty feet down the street. Isaak froze as he took in the sight of the creature, but there was no mistaking it.

It was a Soot Raider.

Sweat glistened on the obsidian skin of the humanoid beast. Blood-red eyes watched with intent and foaming saliva bubbled around incisors clearly too large for its mouth. It was hairless and completely naked. The Soot Raider was unmoving, clutching a massive pipe wrench in its freakishly long fingers.

Isaak's mind moved sluggishly, the gears locked up with fear. "A-Ash. Go back to the skimmer."

"What are you going on about?" she shouted.

"Ash," he said through gritted teeth, "get to the skimmer *now*, or we're dead."

"Isaak, what—" Ashleigh gasped, dropping a piece of salvage.

Isaak swore, turning his eyes on her. Her eyes were wide as she stood awkwardly in a half-crouched stance. She barely moved a muscle.

"What do we do?" she hissed.

"I don't know."

He turned back, but the Soot Raider was gone. Alarms sounded in Isaak's mind, and his legs were moving before he knew what he was doing. A cold sweat enveloped his body and terror twisted his gut so tight he wanted to vomit. Just as he hopped onto the skimmer, a roar broke the silence of the area.

Now, three black forms blocked their path, and Ashleigh still hadn't moved.

It was almost imperceptible, but she was fidgeting with something at her waist. That's when his stomach turned somersaults; Ashleigh removed a large, adjustable wrench from the holster attached to her belt. Deliberately, she pressed a small red button near the top. Instantly, the tool began to morph as pieces of it rearranged themselves like a Rubik's Cube. Soon, she was holding a pistol.

At some point in her life, Ashleigh had designed the weapon with her father, Charles. He was a soldier and believed people should arm themselves for protection. But an accident and a wheelchair ended his fighting days. On more than one occasion, the weapon had saved her life, but Isaak couldn't see how it would save her now. Not against three of them.

"Ashleigh, don't," Isaak pleaded.

She hesitated before firing three rounds. Three bursts of electric-blue energy exploded from the sidearm's barrel before colliding with their marks. A blanket of electricity washed over the three hulking forms, but all it did was send them into a frenzy. The one carrying the wrench charged forward, and the others followed, screaming inhumanly.

Ashleigh fired at will, but the shots were wild and whizzed harmlessly past them.

Isaak swung his legs off the skimmer, but just as his foot touched the ground, he fell forward, collapsing in a heap beside the machine. He turned back to see his other leg was bound in a strap that secured the salvage they had collected. In a few moments, Ashleigh would be torn to shreds by the Soot Raiders. Her pistol clicked empty. Isaak felt the weight of debilitating fear as he realized he was going to watch his best friend die.

This was it. Fate had spoken.

"Ashleigh," he called out, reaching helplessly toward her.

She turned to him in answer, tears streaking her face. She knew what was about to happen. Time slowed. Isaac clawed at the earth, begging to be freed.

Just as the first creature gripped a handful of Ashleigh's clothes, a hazy cloud of force exploded between them, separating her from the vicious trio. The Soot Raiders crashed together in a thrashing pile. Ashleigh stumbled backward.

Isaac was speechless, but the Raiders were already scrambling to their feet, saliva dripping from their razored maws. The first one came forward again, crashing into Ashleigh and pinning her to the solid earth. A tremor of fury rose within Isaak then; he felt it emanating from his core.

"Leave her alone!" he screamed, just as a stronger force swatted the Raider away as if it were weightless. A hum of power and energy ignited within him, and tendrils of tingling warmth traveled throughout his arms and fingertips. It felt strangely familiar, as if it had been a part of him all along.

Without a second thought, Isaak reached back to the strap, and it split in half before he could touch it. Now, finally freed, Isaak let his instincts guide him.

"Ashleigh, go!" He bounded forward in three long strides and gripped her tightly, more for his benefit than for hers.

Isaak guided her to the skimmer. She didn't hesitate, yet she gave him a wary look all the same. Did she think all this was his doing? The dreams came rushing back. His skin prickled where the tattoo was etched into his skin, but this wasn't a dream anymore. He was an Outlander. He knew Ashleigh wouldn't take his secret well. A cold spot settled in his gut. They hopped on the skimmer.

"Isaak!"

He returned to the present just as the leader pounced on the front of the skimmer and started slamming the wrench into the engine compartment. Isaak reached up again, expecting the Raider to be thrown back, but he felt the power receding from his limbs in an instant.

"What are you waiting for? Let's get out of here!" Ashleigh's nails dug divots into his skin.

Isaac mashed the ignition switch. The skimmer lurched forward but then sputtered and died. The other two Raiders jerked and pulled at both sides of the transport. Isaak felt their nails tearing into his skin. Ashleigh howled in pain as one ripped through her vest and shirt. The sight of her blood was the last straw.

A roaring sound of rushing water filled his ears, and a wave of energy vibrated through his frame. All at once, Isaak felt unstoppable and afraid of what was happening to him. The energy kept building and his senses sharpened, even as the Raiders continued to maul him. Ashleigh screamed again as one of the Raiders yanked her off the skimmer, and at that moment, the floodgates opened.

The force of the power exploding through him could only be described as a rushing wind expelled from the center of a tornado. He let his voice rise as the power threw the Raiders in all directions. The wave of power blew outward, disintegrating a row of dilapidated buildings that crashed into the ATMOS.

The infinite height of it swayed back and forth as pieces of metal and glass rained down. The area of impact collapsed inward, and the ATMOS buckled under the weight from above and came crashing down. Finally, the creaking and groaning of metal subsided.

Their eyes met, and Isaak could see it; she knew exactly what he was.

"It's time to go."

Isaak didn't waste a moment and held out his hand. Ashleigh hesitated, like she was scared of him. She worked her mouth as if to say something but instead picked herself up and settled behind him.

"We need to talk," she said.

"About what, Ashleigh?"

"This…this wasn't supposed to happen?"

"What are you talking about? I don't understand."

"Not here, Isaak," she hissed. "Take us home."

She wrapped her arms around him to steady herself, but he could feel the tension running through her. With one last look at the destruction, Isaak tried to start the skimmer's engine, and after a few attempts, it roared to life. The howl of the wind followed them as he guided the skimmer toward Haven.

He might have been hearing things, but he swore Ashleigh kept repeating "What have I done?" to herself.

***

"Both of you know the ATMOS is off limits. We may be a scavenging town, but that doesn't mean you should fulfill a death wish while doing it." Ashleigh and Isaak kept their eyes glued to the floor. She sat hunched and defeated in a seat on the other side of the table in Custodian William Wisdum's small cubicle of an office. Isaak was more lost and confused than ever before.

The room reminded him of an old hospital with the stark white walls, gray floors, and bright lights. Half-completed bits of machinery that had lost the spark of inspiration cluttered the office. A few years before he was appointed to the Custodian position, William worked as an educator of sorts. Since unlimited amounts of salvage moved through the city, William used the opportunity to show citizens how to repair minor machinery and even design something new with well-constructed lessons.

He was a natural and his classes were some of the most popular to date. Ashleigh and Isaak were frequent participants and spent long hours after class talking about the next project. But all good things end and so did the classes when William assumed his new responsibilities.

"Do you two have anything to say?" William's salt-and-pepper hair left his prominent forehead exposed; his glasses rested on the bridge of his even more distinguished nose. Despite being older, his skin had an ageless look to it. William's mouth was a tight line. Isaak's attention kept returning to his intense eyes.

Isaac kept his mouth shut; he glanced at his best friend, but she was in her own world. Her jaw clenched repeatedly, and her hands were balled into tight fists. Ashleigh's cheeks were damp with tears.

"Something happened, didn't it?" William mused. "Why don't you tell me about it? Perhaps, I can help."

Ashleigh choked out a laugh. "Help? There's nothing you can do. No one can."

William focused his honey-colored eyes on her; his bifocals slightly magnified their brilliance. "That seems a little dark, Ashleigh."

"Whatever. Just drop it, please."

"No, we need to have a discussion about—"

"William," she said, her eyes blazing like green fire. "Leave. It. Alone."

He blinked slowly, his brow crinkled in thought, and turned his attention to Isaak. "What about you?"

Isaak shook his head, though his resolve was deteriorating. "I don't—"

"Isaak, stop talking!" Ashleigh hissed. Isaak stopped, feeling as if something terrible would happen if he continued.

William sighed. "Fine, don't explain. The result of your actions remains the same. Because of you two, the ATMOS has collapsed—not to mention that you've also damaged a city-owned skimmer. You won't avoid the consequences, and since you leave me no choice in the matter, I'm going to dock credits from both of your family accounts." William removed his glasses and pointed them at Ashleigh and Isaak. "Be thankful your punishments aren't more severe."

Ashleigh abruptly stood from her chair. "William, take the credits from my family's accounts instead. Please."

The corner of his eye quirked. "Okay."

Something was off. Isaak had never known William to back down from doling out a well-deserved punishment. He glanced at Ashleigh, but she wouldn't break eye contact with the Custodian.

"Can we go now?" She sighed.

"Yes," the custodian said, waving her away. "But I'd advise the both of you not to look so guilty. Entera sent a small platoon of Enforcers to determine the nature of the damage to the ATMOS."

"What do you mean?" Isaak said, unable to control the quivering in his voice.

"I'm saying that however you did it, it's got Entera looking for Outlanders."

***

"Did he say Entera? Like the 'old-world government' that's crazy-psycho about hunting *Outlanders*?" Isaak whispered the last word in Ashleigh's ear. She was deliberately ignoring him.

The two of them dodged citizens kicking up dust in the industrious hub that was Stall Square. Here, the economy of Haven, the Outland's first city, thrived on salvage trade, restoring old technology, and even baked goods. Ashleigh hadn't said a word since William dismissed them.

He grabbed the crook of her arm, and she flinched. "Ashleigh, what just happened in there?"

She jerked her arm from his grasp. The look in her eyes was like nothing he had ever seen. It was like she didn't recognize him, and it almost made him back down.

"What do you mean?" she said.

"Don't play dumb with me. You said we needed to talk."

"Isaak—"

"Just tell me what you know!" He stomped his foot and a nearby stall rattled itself to pieces. All of the vendor's wares spilled out onto the ground. A few bystanders gave him a peculiar look but returned to their business. His chest was heaving as if he had just sprinted a mile. At that moment, he wanted to burst.

"Don't do this. Not here. You need to calm down, Isaak."

Isaak felt a nervous energy pulsing through his limbs. It was fighting to get out. "Don't you get it? I'm scared, and I don't know what's going on."

Her eyes were swimming. "I know, and it's my fault. Come here." She grabbed his hand and led him to a quieter section of the square. Here there wasn't much foot traffic and one or two stalls sat unused for the time being. "Okay, just…start from the beginning."

He shook his head. "I-I've had dreams. For a while now, it's been the same dream over and over. I was moving things without touching them. I never dreamed of anything like today."

She was silent for a moment. Tears spilled down her flushed cheeks. "Why didn't you tell me sooner? I could've helped you and made sure it didn't happen again."

"Tell you," Isaak's voice strained. "I haven't told anyone. I *can't* tell anyone…you know what I am."

She swallowed. Her voice cracked. "Yes, I know."

"Wait…what do you mean by *making sure it didn't happen again*? What aren't you telling me?"

"Nothing."

Isaak's heart fluttered, and his mouth tasted like chalk. "Why are you lying to me?"

She raised her hands. "I'm not lying, Isaak."

"I don't believe you, Ashleigh," he said, feeling a tightness in his chest. He took a step back. "Whatever is happening here, you shouldn't be getting involved; bad things will happen if Entera finds out I lied about this. I have to turn myself in. I can't be this monster."

"Monster? Isaak, you can't; you know what they'll do to you!"

Someone carrying boxes on a dolly bumped into Ashleigh, nearly knocking her over. Isaak darted into the crowd, but he could hear Ashleigh calling out for him. When he was sure he had lost her, he slowed down to the exit that led to the Working Families' apartments. To his right, a metal sign on a high, wooden post caught his eye. Beside the sign was a kiosk with various Entera propaganda plastered on it.

Within the kiosk was an emergency system where anyone could report Outlander activity; Entera would be notified immediately and send a response team within the hour. His eyes kept returning to the sign. Chills crawled along his skin as he read it.

Report suspicious activity to your Custodian or nearest Enforcer. Only you can help Entera keep the New United States safe from Outlanders.

***

Isaak strummed his fingers on his parents' kitchen table in Apartment Cube 305 as he tried to find the right way to break the news. His mother sat next to him with her arm resting on the table. Worry lines pulled at her mouth and wrinkles stretched the corners of her dark blue eyes. She wore her coffee-colored hair down, and she tucked her hair behind her ears before speaking.

"Your father and I heard from William about the incident; it seems we also have to thank Ashleigh for taking your punishment. What were you thinking?"

Isaac didn't answer. He watched his father wash his greased hands and arms clean at the rusted sink set in a deteriorating countertop. His cold blue eyes were staring holes into Isaak. A shaggy, gray mane flowed around the scruff of his face; it had been a few months since his family could afford a decent haircut. On more than one occasion, Isaak had been forced to push his hair out of his eyes or tie it back somehow.

"Answer your mother," his father barked. If he could have spit fire, he probably would have. "What happened out there?"

"I don't know," Isaak said.

"Bullshit."

"Samuel," Isaak's mother said.

"Our son is old enough to understand the consequences of what he's done. Entera is searching this city right now for those responsible. William doesn't know how anyone could've caused the collapse. It's their assumption that an Outlander did it. Are they right?"

Isaak turned away from them. "I don't know."

He heard the scraping of chairs and both of his parents were in his view again. "Isaak, tell us the truth," Dad said.

Isaak shook his head furiously, trying to keep the tears at bay. "We never should have gone out there. I knew better, but…all the best salvage is out there."

"We know that, son, but that far out of the Haven is dangerous," his mother said. "It's just not worth it. Do you know what's been happening here recently?"

"Yes, people keep disappearing, and nobody can figure out why." As soon as he said it, his mind flashed back to the Soot Raiders threatening to tear them limb from limb. Hearing stories about them was one thing, but seeing a Soot Raider in person was next to impossible, or it was until today. Maybe the Soot Raiders were taking people.

"Exactly, so try to think of this from our point of view. When you go out there on your own like that, there's always a chance you might not come back," Mom said.

"Mom, I get it. Can we just drop it now?"

"No, Isaak," Dad shouted, slamming his palm onto the table, "If you don't tell us what happened, we can't help you."

"I CAN'T!" Isaak screamed as he stumbled backward over his chair. "Don't you get it? If I tell you—then I put you and Mom in danger. I won't do it!"

"You can tell us anything, Isaak," Mom said. "We promise."

"This is different. You don't want to know this; it changes everything."

"Everything's already changed," Dad answered.

Isaak needed to release the pressure building in his chest before it escaped on its own. He heard his pulse in his ears, and his hands shook uncontrollably. The kitchen table started to rattle, scattering years of dust and dirt from its surface.

Isaak clenched his fists as he tried to gain control. Once he did, he returned his chair to the upright position and sat down. "You want to know, fine; here it is. I'm an Outlander, and I think I can move things with my mind."

The house went silent. His parents exchanged a look and took each other's hands.

Mom cleared her throat. "We already know, Isaak. We have something to say as well. We're Outlanders too, and we were born this way."

Isaak felt as if the wind had been knocked out of him. "So, I'm an Outlander because of you."

His parents exchanged another glance and his father put an encouraging hand on his mother's shoulder. She finally met Isaak's gaze with a steady resolve. "You aren't our son, Isaak, but that doesn't change—"

Isaac tried to speak around the rock suddenly lodged in his throat when the front door shook several times. They froze; someone was at the door.

"This is the Enterian Enforcement Squad. We have a few questions for you!"

Isaak thought about running—there was a door that led out back—but his father was holding on so tightly he didn't think he could budge.

"Just stay calm," Dad said, licking his lips.

He moved to answer the door just as Eleanora wrapped her arms around her son's shoulders. Dad swung the door open, revealing five Enforcers suited up in black, metallic environmental suits. The fifth one, at the head of the group, wore the insignia of Entera, an eagle holding plaques made up of the branches of its organization, on his right chestplate. The four Enforcers wore helmets with blackened visors while the leader wore a helmet with a clear visor; a set of black voids stared back at them.

"Afternoon. My name is General Soloman Gray. You are welcome to call me General Sol. How are you all doing?"

"We're okay," Dad said.

"Wonderful," General Sol said with a smile in his voice. "Would you mind if we came inside?"

Isaak's father blocked the doorway for a moment that stretched for an eternity. "No," he said, stepping out of the way. "I suppose not."

"Thank you."

General Sol stepped forward with his men on his heels. Isaak hadn't noticed the energy rifles in their hands before. Pulses of blue electricity flashed through the coils around the weaponry's barrels. In the back of his mind, where the rational side was currently indisposed, Isaak could hear a piercing noise so high it seared through his eardrums like a knife. He could feel his muscles locking up and his breath going shallow. Entera was *here*—in his house. Certain death had never been so close.

General Sol held up his hands. "You all look so tense; please, this is a friendly visit. We just have a few questions for your son."

The sound droned on, increasing in volume until it was beating on Isaak's inner ear.

"May I sit?" General Sol said, indicating a chair at the table.

"Yes," Dad said, his body tense like a taut wire.

"So polite." General Sol sat in the chair. Isaak noticed a small black box with a light on the front of it clipped to his waist. It blinked like a thrumming heartbeat.

Isaak expected the general to speak then, but he sat silent, smugly looking back at them through his visor. He inclined his head.

"I feel as though I know you from somewhere. Did you used to work for us?" His eyes bored into Dad.

Dad shook his head quickly and didn't answer. Isaak was sick with fear; nausea boiled up in his throat, and a tremble quivered in his right hand. The sound sent chills washing over his body. Something was wrong.

"All right," Dad said, the impatient tone in his voice barely muzzled. "What are you doing here, General? Surely you didn't come just to harass us small town folk."

"I told you, we're here to ask questions." Annoyance seasoned his words.

"So ask them already. We have yet to cook dinner."

"Oh, am I keeping you from your meal? My apologies." General Sol turned to Isaak. "Isaak, how are you feeling? You look pale."

"I-I have a headache." Isaak pursed his lips tightly while looking at his parents. Dad's eyes widened slightly in recognition and his hand inched toward something behind his back.

"Really, is that all? Don't be shy, Isaak, you can tell me anything. I know the rumors, but Entera isn't as big and bad as we're made out to be."

Isaak shook his head. He didn't want to speak again because at any moment he was going to vomit.

"You must believe me when I say Entera is looking out for the New United States. We operate on the sole principle of protecting innocent people from Outlanders, and there can be no greater mandate."

A sudden surge of pain lanced through Isaak's stomach, and he doubled over in agony. He couldn't hold it back anymore as his body evacuated the churning contents of his belly. The relief was immediate, but the feeling was staunched by General Sol's chilling laughter.

"Ah, Isaak," he said as he tsked several times. "Did you eat something disagreeable or was it something else?"

General Sol crouched to his level, holding the blinking box in front of Isaak's face. Panic coursed through him. Isaak fell backward and crawled away on all fours just as the general stood. There was no more smile in his eyes.

"This little box is perfect for sniffing out young metahumans who can't control their abilities; you can thank the lab coats back at headquarters. Unforeseeable circumstances created the world we live in today: a barren wasteland with a few safe havens tucked away, genetically superior beings who are somehow immune to the ill effects of our irradiated planet. Entera wishes to regain control of these conditions. I'm afraid I wasn't honest with you. I actually work with the Metahuman Acquisition Program headed by the Entera Organization. I also have a legitimate question for you."

He paused, letting the words sink in. "Did you think you would escape the MAP, Outlander?"

And then the room filled with flashes of light and explosions.

A bolt of super-charged energy screeched past Isaak's head as his mother yanked him toward the back of the house. They were going to run after all.

"Don't let them escape," General Sol shouted over the gunfire.

Behind them, the kitchen disintegrated into a thousand pieces as energy rounds pelted the room. The Enforcers had taken cover near the door behind the overturned table, while General Sol stood out in the open unscathed.

Isaak staggered after his mother, but all his attention was on his father.

"Isaak, keep moving," Dad screamed as an orb similar to a miniature sun swelled in the palm of his hand.

He lobbed the burning projectile at the chest of one of the Enforcers. The impact knocked him down and shattered a section of the unlucky grunt's armor. The Enforcer screamed as his suit depressurized, exposing him to the elements. His skin began to sizzle as if it were covered in acid.

Rumors about Entera's people circled Isaak's mind. They couldn't tolerate the air of the Outlands and had to wear special suits to keep them safe. Isaak watched the Enforcer struggle for a few seconds as his skin blistered. Before Isaak could see any more, his father yanked on his arm until pain jolted through it.

They almost made it to the door before a bullet clipped Dad's shoulder. He crashed into the doorframe but still managed to shove Isaak and his mother safely out of the door.

"Go," Dad barked, stopping just outside. His shoulder was torn open to the bone, but it was like it didn't faze him.

Isaak stopped, planting his feet. "Dad, what are you doing?"

Dad's entire body was shaking as an orb the size of a basketball materialized between his hands. "You need to run, Isaak!" He grunted. "Go with your mother. I'm right behind you."

"Let me help."

Gunfire ripped through the siding of the house. Dad gritted his teeth as the orb sparked in his hands. A crashing vibration shook the house, and the door exploded outward. A second later, Dad forced the ball of energy into the house and sprinted away, tearing the collar of Isaak's shirt as he pulled him along. Then the house Isaak grew up in imploded from within, collapsing on General Sol and his men.

"I said run!"

For a few panicked moments, Isaak and his parents ran through the narrow streets of the Working Families' dilapidated apartment cubes. They stopped at the edge of the road, right where the entrance to Stall Square began, but there was no sign of General Sol or his Enforcers. A few bystanders were staring warily at them.

"Are they gone?" Isaak said as he gulped down air.

"No," his father said, squatting down. "We need to leave."

"And go where, Dad?"

"We're going to be hunted, Isaak, and they will never stop; the only solution is to take our chances in the Outlands."

"We won't make it out there! There are Soot Raiders roaming the Outlands. Ashleigh and I saw them and they nearly killed us."

"You what?" Dad shouted.

Mom took Dad's shoulder in her hands. "Sam, take a breath and let me help you with your shoulder."

He tried to shake her off. "No, I'm all right."

At first, nothing seemed to happen, but the flesh on his shoulder began to knit itself back together. Within moments, the wound was gone. Isaak didn't know how to react, and then his mother's shoulder started to bleed. It was sluggish at first, but her face paled as a gash split her shoulder wide open.

"Mom?!"

She swayed slightly, and Samuel steadied her. "I wish you wouldn't do that, Eleanora."

Her eyes were glassy, but her voice was steady as she spoke. "It's fine. You know it heals quickly."

Sure enough, just as she said it, Isaak watched the wound disappear. A gasp came from behind them. The three of them turned to see that an older man had witnessed the entire thing.

"Wait a minute," Dad pleaded, taking a step toward him.

"No," he shouted, keeping his distance. "Stay away, monster!" He turned back toward Stall Square shouting, "Outlanders! There are Outlanders in Haven!" Immediately, he made a beeline toward the emergency kiosk.

Without thinking, Isaak chased after him. A few bystanders backpedaled away from them as if they were ill with a contagious disease; a few screamed as he grabbed the older man with both hands. It was all a blur.

"Please, calm down," Isaak pleaded.

The man struck him across the cheek with his bony knuckles, and Isaak felt the skin split. A jolt of anger pulsed through him and cracks spiderwebbed through the surface of the street.

"Just stop struggling. I'm not going to hurt you!"

"Leave me alone, freak," he said, delivering another blow to Isaak's face.

The second punch loosened Isaak's grip and the man jerked himself free. He was moving again in a heartbeat, sprinting to the kiosk. Something snapped inside Isaak then, and a stampede of emotions assaulted him all at once.

"I said STOP!"

Isaak reached out to grab the man. A shockwave of invisible energy exploded from Isaak's outstretched hand. Dust and large sections of earth were pushed aside by the bulldozing force. Various stalls splintered into sawdust and unlucky patrons caught in its wake were thrown heedlessly in every direction. The emergency kiosk shattered into nothing.

At that moment, all of Stall Square fell silent. The cries of agony and fear reached Isaak's ears as he gaped in horror at the destruction wielded by his hands. Soon, the hum of whispers filled the streets. At first, they were panicked, but gradually, the patrons of Stall Square determined the culprit. They grouped together, unifying into one cohesive force.

"Isaak, stop!"

He pivoted on his heels. By instinct, he picked up a jagged board and launched it toward the voice. Next thing he knew, Ashleigh was diving to the ground. Isaak felt his stomach jump into his throat.

"Oh god, Ashleigh—I'm sorry."

She stood and warily lifted her hands in a surrendering gesture. "Isaak, please, you have to stop."

Hearing her voice, he felt a wash of relief and joy, but it quickly soured to anger. "You acted like I had used this power before. What aren't you telling me?"

Her shoulders sagged. "Isaak, I can't."

"Tell me!" he shouted as another shockwave of power shook the ground where he stood.

"I'm sorry. I never meant for any of this to happen; I was just trying to protect you."

"Protect me? From who?"

"From me!" General Sol strode into the scene with Enforcers jogging at his heels. Isaak was ready to defend himself, but in that instant, he was no longer in control of his own body. A force had clamped down on him, and it was relentless. He wasn't sure he could blink or breathe.

General Sol stood a few inches away from Isaak's face. "And no one is going to protect you from Entera."

***

Isaak squirmed in the metallic cuffs binding his wrists. He wanted to break them with his cursed abilities, but somehow the device was blocking him. It was like a sharp needle piercing his skull.

His parents had been escorted there by two of the gun-toting terrorists just a few minutes before. So, Isaak, his parents, and Ashleigh huddled together while the Enforcers rounded up patrons trying to flee the square. General Sol was speaking into a mobile console on his wrist.

Isaak turned to his mother and ground his teeth as he spoke. "Is there anything else I should know?"

She flinched and looked away. "We wanted you to have a normal life; we couldn't tell you what you are."

"What am I, then?"

"It's complicated, Isaak," Mom whispered as an Enforcer passed by.

General Sol was moving from person to person with a small handheld device. Once in a while, he would pull someone from the crowd, and the Enforcers would take them away. Some of the people threw up as they were dragged off. Some staggered. Others screamed.

Isaak shuddered. "Well, it doesn't seem like we've got much time, so talk."

"Fine," Dad said. "But you won't like what you hear." He grabbed Mom's hand. "A long time ago, I used to work for Entera."

"Are you serious? You worked for these jerks?"

"Yes, and I did exactly what General Sol is doing. I hunted Outlanders and sent them to Entera to be studied. I think, through their work, they created you; you were part of something called *The Human Rejuvenation Project*."

Isaak felt like he was going to be sick again. "What were they trying to do? Better yet, why did you do it?"

"Essentially, they were trying to redefine their genetics so they could live safely in this world—like we do. I suppose I did it for that and other reasons that aren't important anymore."

"Is that all you have to say, Dad?"

Dad rubbed his bloodshot eyes with his hand. "Isaak, listen: Entera employs the strongest Outlanders for this job; this is vital to them."

"So, General Sol—"

"Is an Outlander, just like us. I know him, Isaak. He's ruthless, unsympathetic, and incredibly powerful. We can't beat him, so it's pointless to fight him."

"So, we just give up?"

"No, we give in, and hopefully, we make it through this. Your mother and I are tired of running."

"I hope you all aren't scheming; it will only make this worse for everyone," General Sol said as he motioned for two Enforcers to split their group apart.

He turned to Dad. "I almost didn't recognize you, Samuel, but your power gave you away. How long has it been? Fifteen years since you made off with Entera's prized research and spat on everything they did for you? Do you know what you cost them?"

"Isaak is more than just *research* or data points—even if he was created in a lab. He's human just like the rest of us. As for Entera, it is a stain on the Outlands, and I realized it too late."

"You say that now, but I remember you before. You were so idealistic and loyal. You would have done anything for Entera, but *someone* changed that. Didn't they?"

He turned his attention to Mom, and Dad stepped in front of her. The general gave a short bark of laughter. "It's funny how devotion can be corrupted so easily by one beautiful face. You betrayed Entera, and they lost everything. So, without any alternative, they revived the MAP initiative, and everyone suspected of being a metahuman is detained and brought in for study. Since we found Subject 002, you, and your wife here, it begs the question: How many more of you are hiding here?"

A blood-curdling scream carried over the square from where a man and a woman were forced to one side of the plaza while a child no more than four years old was yanked away from them.

General Sol tsked. "It's so unfortunate to see families broken up. If you have yet to realize it, Samuel, the citizens of Haven have *you* to thank for their suffering."

Two distinct gunshots followed that forced bile into Isaak's throat. The parents' screaming stopped as they collapsed together in a heap. Isaak clenched his hands until the skin around his knuckles turned white.

"This could've been avoided if you hadn't stolen Subject 002. How does it feel, Samuel, to be the cause of an entire city's suffering?"

More people were divided up as the Enforcers pushed and shoved them like cattle. Some were children and some elderly. It made no difference to the general's men as they kicked those who weren't fast enough.

"Entera is the root of all suffering," Dad said, but his voice sounded far away.

A white noise had filled Isaak's ears, muffling the sounds. A tremor vibrated through his feet, and the stall on his left began to shake. He was losing control again, but this time he welcomed it. When it finally happened, he would direct his fury at the monster in front of him. As if things weren't bad enough, patrons began to run. The Enforcers didn't give chase, they merely raised their rifles and fired.

The square became a frenzy, but General Sol stayed calm and collected. The cuffs on Isaak's wrists rattled and became less constricting.

"Why are you doing this? These people don't deserve it," Isaak seethed.

"Harboring metahumans is a crime in the New United States. Your Custodian knows that, and these people know it. There is no excuse."

"But you're one of us! Surely, you don't enjoy handing us over for torture." More screaming and gunshots followed. It was turning into a massacre. "Stop it! Tell them to stop shooting people!"

"Resistance is futile. Entera doesn't tolerate insubordination."

An Enforcer forced his way into their group and lurched toward Isaak. He pushed Ashleigh out of his way, and she tripped over something, crashing into a pile of rubble. Isaak released what little control he had left, and the cuffs snapped in two. An intense focus took over, and he took a step forward. The same Enforcer trained his rifle on him.

Isaak raised his arm as the Enforcer fired. The energy bolt screamed toward him, but at the last second, it was deflected by his power. In a sweeping motion, Isaak threw the Enforcer aside like a rag doll. General Sol squared up to Isaak.

"Do it, boy," he said.

Unsure of what was guiding him, Isaak released the power and a tidal wave of energy, debris, and earth crashed into the general. Yet, he stood unburdened by the onslaught.

Laughing, he said, "Unlike you, I was born of this earth and have honed my abilities. You don't understand your gifts. Allow me to educate you!"

The stall beside Isaak jumped up from the ground and sailed toward him. Isaak turned, and the object splintered into him with the force of a locomotive. As Isaak pushed his way through the pile of boards, he could hear the sounds of fighting. His father was tossing orbs of fire at the general, but each was deflected effortlessly. Then Dad threw two larger ones simultaneously, one high and one low. The general parried the low blow, but the second made it through his defenses. It exploded like a grenade and sent pieces of the armor on his arms and torso scattering.

"Enough!" he screamed as a wave of energy flattened the area around him. "This ends here!"

Enforcers and citizens alike were knocked down by his powers. General Sol strode quickly over to Samuel, binding him still with the wave of his hand. "Samuel Lukas, ever the thorn in my side. Well, no more." A quick flick of his wrist and Dad's forearm snapped with a sickening crunch.

"No, leave him alone," Isaak begged as he tried to rise, but the power still held him down.

"When I came to this quiet little town, I never expected to find you—the one that got away." The general flicked his wrist again, and Dad's left leg broke like a toothpick. He wailed in agony, trying to sum up enough energy to attack. Mom tried to help, but the general halted her mid-step.

"Please, I'm begging you not to do this!" Isaak cried through blurry vision.

But the general was too engrossed in the moment to hear the plea. He wouldn't stop. Isaak noticed a large rock protruding from the earth, and an idea began brewing in his mind. He focused on it, and it quivered. Isaak pushed through the binding force until his arm extended toward the rock.

General Sol lifted Mom, and her hands clawed at her throat. She gasped and fought feebly against him. Desperate, Isaak pushed harder, and the rock budged a few inches and rose from the earth. Slowly, one by one, a few Enforcers collected themselves and their weapons. It was only a matter of time before Isaak lost his chance. Blinking sweat from his eyes, Isaak dove deep, coaxing every bit of his strange power to the surface. Within seconds, the force holding him down melted away, and the boulder broke through. It was the size of one of the rusted out cars Isaak had seen in the Outlands, and Isaak couldn't believe he held its weight.

"Hey, stop that!" an Enforcer commanded.

A shot whizzed past Isaak's face. Adrenaline coursed through him as he directed the boulder at the attacker. It collided with the group of Enforcers, yet Isaak still held it in the air. General Sol took his attention off Isaak's parents. His eyes went wide, and Isaak pushed the boulder at him with all his might. General Sol released his prisoners just as the rock crashed into him. He never stood a chance.

The rock split jagged down the middle, one of its halves crashing into more stalls, while the other landed on top of the general. The next few seconds felt like a millennium and Isaak could feel the exhaustion in his limbs. He expected the boulder to rise suddenly, allowing the general to resume his horror show.

As minutes passed by, the rock remained motionless. Isaak exhaled and the tension ebbed from his muscles. He sat down in the dirt, numbed by the experience. The Enforcers who remained looked lost, their weapons hanging harmlessly at their sides. The crowd started to close in around them, and the Enforcers wisely began to scatter. At some point, Ashleigh picked herself up out of the rubble. Isaak barely felt her hand on his shoulder.

"Are you okay?" she whispered.

He shook his head.

"Look, I've wanted to tell you this for a long time now, but I didn't know how to. It's my fault you didn't know about your powers. I blanked your memories. I…I'm an Outlander too."

"I don't understand, Ashleigh, how have you kept it a secret from me all this time?"

She looked down as she wrung her hands together. "You found out once, and then I made you forget."

Stunned, Isaak swallowed the lump in his throat. He didn't know what to feel.

"I know what I did was wrong, but I was trying to keep something like this from happening. My power works best when I'm touching someone, but I don't always have to. A long time ago, I learned about where you came from; I pulled the memory from your dad. When I saw you use your power for the first time, I knew someone would find out. It was too destructive to hide. I did what I thought was right."

"I don't understand." Isaak could feel himself slipping, and people were starting to notice them. He dropped to his knees, and a rumble of power bubbled to the surface.

"All right, look," she said, kneeling beside him. She pulled the hair from her left ear to the side, exposing the skin around it. "Read what that says, Isaak."

At first, he didn't see it, but his heart started racing at the sight of the tattoo. "HRP098001..." He touched the raised area on the inside of his hand. "You were part of Entera's projects too?"

"Now you understand." She laced her fingers into his. "When I was older, I realized that we were in trouble. Both of Entera's lost projects...here in Haven. When my tattoo appeared shortly after I used my powers, I thought someone was tracking me or something. Turns out, I was right. One day, maybe three years ago, you had an accident, and someone reached out to Entera. They sent a small force, but I don't think they took the threat seriously. Then a year ago, it happened again. I was always able to blank the memories of those involved. I never accounted for them reviving the MAP...or you destroying the ATMOS. I'm not going to be able to hide anything this time, Isaak. I'm sorry."

Ashleigh was on the verge of tears by that point; she was barely holding herself together. Isaak reached up and put his hand on her cheek. "It's not your fault, Ashleigh. It's Entera's fault. They created us and now they're hunting us. We didn't ask for this but—" He hesitated as a spark of an idea came to life. "The people here have seen firsthand just how Entera operates. Maybe we don't need to hide anymore."

Isaak stood and turned to a few of the people standing nearby. One of them was the old man from before. He was dusting himself off, but he snapped to attention and his eyes narrowed.

"I'm sorry about what happened before," Isaak said. "I wasn't trying to hurt you, I was just afraid of what Entera would do to us."

The man glanced to a few others standing beside him all covered in black earth and bruises. He scanned the destroyed sections of Stall Square. Bodies lay sprawled in the rubble. Groups of families huddled together, sobbing in each other's arms. Cries of pain echoed against the skeletal remains of the once immaculate trading hub. The man's stern expression softened into one of grief.

After a moment, he nodded. "I get it. You were frightened, but after today, why did you save us? I was ready to condemn you to death. Some of us might still do it anyway."

Isaak looked around, at the fleeing Enforcers, at his parents and Ashleigh, at the dead and the wounded and the grief-stricken. "I wasn't trying to save anyone. It just worked out that way. But now, I think I want to do something with this new power I have, and not just for me, but for everyone under Entera's thumb. Word of what happened here is going to spread, and this town needs to be ready for whatever Entera decides to do."

The man glanced around the Square at the people gradually filling the debris-filled streets. Isaak expected them to mob, to curse at him, Ashleigh, and his parents. But they didn't. Some began to help the injured, binding their wounds or making makeshift gurneys to carry those who couldn't walk. Others joined the swelling crowd surrounding Isaak.

Isaak took a deep breath. "After things calm down a bit, we can talk to the Custodian and figure out what we're going to do. You know as well as I do that people have been disappearing recently…and I think Entera is responsible. It's the only thing that makes sense. We just want a chance to show you that us Outlanders are not what Entera says we are. We aren't monsters. What do you think?"

He shot a quick glance at Ashleigh and his parents, who maintained their distance. His friend wore a slight smile and her shoulders didn't sag quite as low as they did before. Mom grimaced as she recovered from healing Dad's wounds, but they managed nods of approval that filled his chest with hope and confidence. He turned back to the man and held out his hand. A slight shake twitched through his palm, as he braced himself for a response.

The man looked to the people crowding around him and then stared into Isaak's eyes for what seemed like an eternity.

He gripped Isaak's hand in return. "Okay, Outlander, we're listening."

Ice Bonds

Mae Baum

At the insistent pounding on the front door, I clicked off the SyFy channel and shrugged off the warmth of my favorite fleece throw. I stubbed my toe on the edge of the coffee table as I hurried over to swing the door open. Two police officers stood on the step, a man and a woman, illuminated by the porch light. I knew them both; in a small town like ours, there are only so many officers to go around.

"Sarah," said Officer Bassett. His hat was in his hand, and his bald head shone under the light.

When I was a kid, he played poker with Dad and he'd let me rub his head for luck. The poker games had ended six years ago when Officer Basset had stood just like this and told us about Mom.

I stumbled back. *No, no, no. Dad can't be dead. This can't be happening.* Ice crept up my knuckles, and I crossed my arms, tucking my hands into my armpits to hide its cold advance.

"You father has been kidnapped," said Officer Bassett, his baritone deepened with emotion.

"K-k-kidnapped?" *Not dead. Not dead. Not like Mom.*

"He was giving a lecture at Maddox Labs," Officer Bassett continued, "when he was taken."

"'The Wonders of Virus D'," I said. Dad had been excited about that lecture. He'd been working on this project a long time, and he said it would save the world. "Why would someone take my dad?" Was it because of his work? He wouldn't have told them what it really does, not yet.

The rumble of my friend Asha's old car echoed in the quiet street as she pulled up behind the patrol car.

"We don't know, but we are doing everything we can," said Officer Huxley. She leaned forward and laid a hand on my arm.

I jerked away, tears brimming. "Yeah, sure, everything. The way you did with Mom."

"We did the best we could, Sarah." Officer Bassett squeezed his hat between his hands.

"We believe Dr. Thurmond was targeted because of his work, but you should be safe," said Officer Huxley briskly. "However, since you are only sixteen, we'd like you to stay with someone until we find your dad."

"I don't have any other family." I wiped my eyes with the sleeve of my shirt. "It's just Dad and me."

My best friends, Asha and Olivia, barreled across the lawn and up the steps. "She can stay with me," said Asha, panting. "Mom said it was okay. It's all over the news, Officer Bassett."

Officer Bassett's eyes narrowed as he pulled out his cell phone to verify.

Olivia hugged me and I was enveloped in her familiar rose perfume.

"Let's get you a bag," she said, pulling me back into the house.

Asha stood guard outside, her hands on her hips. Her thin shadow splayed across the front yard.

***

I curled up on Asha's futon couch, wrapped in an old, crocheted blanket, trying to get warm. Asha's bedroom was large and spacious, with room for her queen bed and the futon for guests. Olivia and I had stayed here so many times before.

"Having an ice power should make you immune to cold," said Olivia, dropping down next to me. She squeezed my hand in one of hers.

Pushing aside her karate uniform, Asha perched on the edge of her bed. "Of course, you're the only person we know with superpowers."

Dad had warned me not to tell anyone about my powers, even if they were faulty, but I couldn't hide them from Asha and Olivia. I was just glad my friends had gotten over their initial shock and were treating me like they always had. "I wish it actually worked when I wanted it to. Maybe then I could do something worthwhile with it."

"And get carted off to a lab for study," muttered Asha.

"Yeah," said Olivia. "That's why your dad said it had to be a secret, right?"

"I know." I growled in frustration. "You said Dad's story is on the news?"

Asha nodded and pulled out her tablet. "It's been running nonstop since it happened. But, Sarah, are you sure you want to see this?"

"Yes." My voice was frosty.

Asha came over and sat on the other side of me. With a few rapid taps, the tablet came to life and a news report began to play.

"Respected chemist, Jacob Thurmond," said the blond newscaster, "was kidnapped tonight from Maddox Lab's auditorium, just after concluding his talk. We have footage of the unknown assailant, dressed in black, taking Dr. Thurmond in front of a full auditorium."

"Maddox Lab's head of security, Dean Thorne, spoke with us about the danger Dr. Thurmond might be in. No ransom demands have been received." The newscaster went on to interview Dean Thorne about why my dad might have been kidnapped and the security measures that had been taken for Maddox Labs.

The words started to blur together. Dean's crew cut and muscled arms screamed safety, but he hadn't been able to protect my dad. Every time I saw his face, a crust of ice inched across my hands.

After the video finished, I hit the button to replay the footage. Tears leaked from my eyes, but they froze before they'd made it halfway down my cheeks.

"This isn't good for you or my tablet," said Asha, pulling it from my hands.

Asha wrapped me in a hug from one side, and Olivia enveloped the other. Squished between my two friends, I finally began to unthaw and the tears flowed freely.

***

I was on autopilot the next day, stopping at Monkey Joe's for coffee on my way into my dad's lab, where I worked part-time. I'd been helping keep his archaic filing system in order for the last couple of years.

"Cookies and cream frap with soy milk," I found myself saying instead of my usual latte. I guess I just needed a treat.

"Sarah, is that you?" asked a male voice behind me.

I swung around. "Tommy Thorne. I haven't seen you in…well, since you headed off to M.I.T."

A grin stretched across his face and he pushed his blond bangs out of his blue eyes. "Yep. Sophomore year has been a blast. Just home for break and hanging with Dean."

"You all still live on Patterson?" I asked. We used to live next door to the Thornes. When Mom died, Dad had moved us to a smaller place, saying we didn't need all the room.

The barista took Tommy's order, a soy latte, while I admired the fit of his black jeans. I mentally slapped myself.

What was I doing checking out a guy when Dad was missing?

"Yeah, the 'rents left it to us when they moved."

"Awesome," I said. "I miss the old house."

He laughed. "The neighbors still throw those crazy parties, like your mom, well, used to."

My heart squeezed, gaze dropping to the tiled floor. "Yeah, I don't know if you saw the news, but Dad's…"

He put a warm hand on my forearm. "I saw. I'm sorry, Sarah." He grimaced. "I'm sure the police will find him."

"I hope so." Tears blurred my vision. I just needed to get to the lab and do some work. The routine would soothe me. I gave a halfhearted smile. "I gotta go, Tommy. Nice to see you."

***

When I pulled up to the Maddox Labs complex, my gut twisted. Surrounded by chain-link fence and fronted by a gatehouse, the large, whitewashed buildings looked the same as they always had. They looked safe. My dad should have been safe.

Who could have taken him and why? Did it have something to do with Virus D? He was working on making it safer. I stared at my ice-covered fingers gripping the steering wheel. Too bad I'd gotten one of the early batches. If only my power worked properly, I'd be able to save Dad and actually help people. What else are superpowers good for?

I shook my head to clear it. The police were doing everything they could. Glancing up at the lab buildings again, I scowled. Shouldn't the police be swarming all over it still? They had better be doing everything they could to get Dad back.

I slammed the car door and headed toward the complex. I waved to the guard on duty and passed my key card through the machine. Even for a weekend, the place was quiet. I used the passcode to get into Dad's building.

The immaculate cages of rabbits and rats on death row greeted me, and the knot in my gut tightened. Beneath the pine-scented cleaning chemicals was something sour. Even though I'd worked here for two years, the use of animals for experiments never sat well with me, even if it was necessary.

I slipped my fingers through the thin metal bars to stroke a bunny, her fur soft and silky. "Lab rats like us ought to stick together," I whispered. Even though my dose had been an accident. Dad had warned me, again and again, to be careful around the chemical solutions. Then, like an idiot, I'd tripped and crashed into his workstation.

I grimaced and moved on toward the file cabinets. Dad and I argued about putting his work on computer like everyone else, but he insisted analog was safer. There were always files to sort and organize. Maybe if I could keep busy, I could stop thinking about the kidnapping for a minute.

There was a loud crash, and a metallic ringing echoed through the lab. Who was here? I walked through the workstations toward the sound. A file cabinet lay on its side, papers spilled across the floor. A man in black tore through the files.

I ducked behind one of the stations. Who was he? Taking a deep breath, I peered around the edge of the counter. He wore a black mask over his face and crossed swords mounted on his back. In the news footage, the man who took Dad had been dressed like this. Was this the same guy? My fingers started to feel cold, and I rubbed them against my jeans. What was he looking for?

Frost crystallized along the back of my hands. If I could just get my power to work, I could freeze his body and make him talk to me. I'd find out where my dad was and what the kidnapper wanted. A grin spread across my face, and I tensed my hands. I could do this. Concentrating on the feeling, I tried to push the ice out. A trickle of frost slid across my jeans.

My stomach dropped. Crap. No way I'd take on an armed intruder with a trickle.

I balled my fists. But I couldn't just sit here and do nothing. I had to try. My heart fluttered in my chest, but I forced myself to stand up.

"Stop right there," I said and imagined an icicle shooting from my palm. It worked! Part of me wanted to dance in glee. But it was too small and too slow.

The icicle struck his shoulder and bounced off, shattering on the linoleum floor. The man in black watched me but didn't move. A file was still open in his hands.

My heart rattled against my chest. *Why isn't he doing anything?*

Still not believing I was really doing this, I stepped forward. "Where's Dr. Thurmond?" I forced authority into my voice. "Why have you taken him?"

No response. He folded up the file and tucked it under his arm. He seemed poised for escape but hesitated.

Frost power lingered at the edge of my fingertips. My fingers twitched, but I couldn't seem to call up another icicle.

He tilted his head. His eyes were blue beneath the ski mask.

We stood separated by the file cabinet, studying one another.

"Is this about Virus D?"

The guy nodded.

I let my breath out. Information at last. "Is Dr. Thurmond okay?"

Another nod.

Tears pricked my eyes. I wiped them away with my arm. "Where is—" I started, but he had disappeared. I spun around, but I couldn't see him.

Hell no! He was not getting away that easily. I ran for the red alarm box and triggered it. The siren screamed, and the strobe lights flashed across the room. Four guards poured into the lab, running up and down the aisles.

A hand grabbed my shoulder, and I looked up into Dean Thorne's chiseled face.

"Are you okay, Sarah?"

I nodded numbly.

"Let's get you out of here." He pulled me from the room.

***

My head in my hands, I waited in Dean's office for the alert to end. The blaring alarm echoed through the building. The intruder was probably long gone. How the hell had he gotten in here to begin with? The labs had layers of security, from the guards out front to the key cards.

I squeezed my eyes shut, running the encounter over and over again through my mind, searching for anything that might help. What kind of robber dresses like a freakin' ninja? A ninja on a budget, given the black shirt and black jeans, although the swords looked real enough.

The alarms died out. I rubbed my forehead and leaned back against the upholstered chair. I glanced around the office, fancy for a security guy. A huge, mahogany desk sat in front of me and above it hung a painting of hunters chasing a fox.

The door swung open and Dean strode across the room. He leaned against the edge of his desk, staring down at me. "You okay, kid?"

I bristled. Ever since we were little, Dean had treated me like a pesky younger sister; I guess I couldn't expect it to stop now. "Yeah. More shaken than anything."

"What were you thinking, coming into the lab with everything that's going on? We're all on high alert since Dr. Thurmond's kidnapping."

I crossed my arms. "Some high alert. That ninja got by you, didn't he?"

Dean's eyebrows furrowed. "Ninja?"

"Yeah, didn't your security cameras pick up anything? He was all dressed in black, with a mask and swords."

"Just 'cause he wore black doesn't make him a ninja." Dean glowered at me and rapped his knuckles on the desk. "We saw him, but too late. He torched some files and disappeared."

"Burned files? Virus D ones?"

"To be determined." Dean rubbed his head, making his gelled hair stand up. "That damn project is more trouble than it's worth."

***

Feeling useless, I climbed back into the car. Still cold, I pulled on a sweater, wrapping its two sides tight around me. This stupid power that Virus D gave was supposed to save the world and all I got was cold.

I sighed. The head of security thought I was ridiculous for calling the intruder a ninja, but why else would he have those swords on his back? Glancing at the time on my phone, I figured Asha'd be at the dojo. There was only one in town, and she helped with the kids' classes on Saturday afternoons. I wondered if Sensei would know anything about someone who trained with swords. I doubted I'd be that lucky.

The dojo was in an old warehouse that had been converted into shops. I made my way carefully down the steep cement steps, and opened the glass door engraved "Martial Arts Center". As I entered, the pungent smell of old sweat greeted my nose. I waved to Ms. Kendra, the receptionist, and then headed down the hall to the studio. The mat was a large blue square, and two rows of seven-year-old white and yellow belts stood at attention. Sensei stood in the front with Asha next to him.

Asha caught my eye as I leaned against the cold wall where the children's parents, grandparents, and nannies waited on gray folding chairs. Class was almost over then. Clicking through my phone, I smiled at Olivia's text, "Let me knO if U need NEthing."

"U R d best," I texted back.

The class finished up and Asha came over. "How are you?" she asked, wiping a towel across her forehead and popping open her water bottle.

"Crazy," I said with an unsteady laugh. "I ran into somebody robbing the lab."

"What? What happened?" Asha dropped her long limbs into an empty folding chair, and I sat next to her.

I told her about the intruder, the files, and my conversation with Dean. "So, what do you think about the swords?"

"Well, they don't actually teach any weapons classes here. We could ask Sensei if he knows anyone in town who practices, but it's a long shot." Asha frowned.

"Yeah." I leaned my head back and stared at the unfinished ceiling. "There's no guarantee this guy's even local."

"But we've got to try, right?" Asha jumped up. "I'll ask Sensei."

I nodded, glancing at the children and parents filing in for the next class. "Send me a text if you find out anything?"

"Of course. And Olivia's still coming over tonight for pizza." She leaned over and hugged me.

"Thanks, Asha." I headed out.

The stairs always seemed even steeper on the way out. It had rained while I was inside and the cement was wet. My eyes trained on my feet, I nearly ran into a guy coming down the stairs. He reached out a hand to steady me.

"Oh, sorry," I said, glancing up at Tommy's handsome face.

"Hey, Sarah," Tommy said, his warm hand lingering on my arm. "Be careful on these slick stairs."

I blushed, feeling like an idiot. I'd been up and down these stairs a million times visiting Asha. "You visiting Sensei?"

"Yeah," he said, pushing back his bangs. "It wouldn't be right being home without stopping by. Old man was like a second dad to me."

"I can see that."

He smiled. "Well, uh, I'll see you around."

I nodded and continued up the stairs. When I reached the top, the wind cut through me and I pulled my sweater closer.

***

I listened all afternoon to the news reports, hoping they'd say something about my dad. I tried calling Officer Bassett at the station, but he had nothing to report yet.

"Don't they say something about the first twenty-four hours being most important?" I muttered as I paced across Asha's living room. Somehow, it wasn't as satisfying to pace when thick carpet cushioned my sock-clad feet, no shoes allowed.

"You should sit down. There's nothing we can do now," said Olivia, pulling a slice of greasy pizza from the box on the coffee table. She leaned back against the camel-colored couch, cradling three napkins under her food. Asha's mom would freak if we messed up her perfect furniture.

"I hate being useless." I tried to call up an icicle, but the frost just coated my fingertips. "I hate this power."

Asha came down the curved staircase, dressed in a pale blue robe and drying her long, dark hair.

I pounced. "What did Sensei say?"

"Nothing," Asha said, gesturing helplessly. "He doesn't know anyone trained in swords, at least, not locally."

"Crap." I paced back across the room.

Olivia poured Coke into three red plastic cups. She gestured to the drinks and the pizza. "Have something to eat."

"I can't eat." I sank into the couch and put my head in my hands. "My dad is out there somewhere. Who knows what they are doing to him, and the police in this town are just twiddling their thumbs waiting for evidence to fall in their laps."

"Now, that's not fair," said Asha. She'd always had a soft spot for the police since her on-again, off-again boyfriend's father was a crime scene investigator.

I glared at her. "Sure it is. They still don't know who ran my mom off the road."

Asha just stared down her nose at me, and I folded. "I'm sorry. I'm just so worried."

"I know." Asha sat down next to me. "I've wanted to punch someone all day."

"Me too." I smiled. "But it'd be a better punch if you did it."

Olivia snorted and her foot jerked, knocking one of the cups off the coffee table. It arced through the air, and we watched in horror as the liquid fell toward the off-white carpet.

Instinctively, we made a grab for the cup, even though we were too far away. Asha knocked into my left arm and Olivia bumped into my right, and a bolt of energy shot through me. Shaking, I held out a hand toward the liquid. "Freeze!"

The spiraling liquid froze solid and fell to the carpet with a thud. The empty cup bounced harmlessly after it.

Our mouths dropped open and we stared at it for a minute. Then, Asha bolted into the kitchen and came back with a broom and dustpan. She swept up the ice and disposed of it.

"My power worked," I said, staring at my hands.

"It really did." Olivia grinned as she placed the empty cup back on the table.

Asha gazed at me. "Now, who has your dad? You need to kick some butt."

I smiled. I could finally stop hiding in the shadows and really do something to help. This was going to be amazing. Looking at my full cup, I held out my hand again and shouted, "Freeze."

We all stared at it but nothing changed.

"Freeze," I said again.

The liquid remained liquid.

"What the hell?" Asha asked. "But it just worked. What's different?"

Olivia started to smile then giggled.

I spun toward her. "What's so funny?"

"I think I understand." She stood. "You need *us* to make it work well."

Rubbing my hands along my arms, I went over the sequence of events in my head. "You both touched me when I froze it."

"Yes." Olivia gestured to the carpet. "We all wanted the liquid to freeze."

"'Cause Mom would kill us," Asha said. "It's like we shared our energy with you somehow."

Olivia nodded. "I wonder if we have to be touching or just thinking the same thing."

Asha smiled slowly. "You know, I think she's right. Let's test it in the back yard."

We hurried out the back door, across the deck, and down the steps into the neatly trimmed grass, edged by manicured bushes and garden lighting. The sweet smell of hydrangea wafted over us and a bird called nearby.

Asha linked her arm through my left, and Olivia through my right. They both looked at me expectantly.

I gulped. I'd never been very good with performance pressure. I focused on the cold feeling in my hands. The frost slithered across my palms. Tensing my arms, I concentrated on pushing the ice out. Nothing.

Olivia frowned. "Maybe we have to think the same thing. What are you trying to do?"

"Shoot an icicle into the grass," I said.

"Okay," Olivia said, motioning for me to go ahead.

I felt for the energy, the bolt I'd felt before, and imagined the ice erupting from my hand. A tiny icicle shot across the grass.

"It's not working. Just like with the intruder," I said.

"Try again," said Olivia. "I know it will work."

"Sometimes it helps the kids in karate class to focus on something." Asha pulled a few rocks from an ornamental display. "We can use these as target practice."

"Okay," I said and took a deep breath and pointed to the biggest one. "That rock."

Olivia and Asha nodded, hands on my arms.

I willed the frost out toward it. Slowly, the ice formed on the surface and spread around it. When the rock was encased, I stopped.

"It worked!" Asha and Olivia shouted together.

We practiced a few more times. As long as the others focused with me, my power worked beautifully, even if they weren't touching me. If they didn't, I didn't get more than a dribble.

"Now we just need to find your dad," said Asha.

"Yeah." I kicked the iced rock. Easier said than done.

We headed back inside to finish our pizza, and Olivia clicked on the evening news. Traffic, weather, and a warehouse burned downtown. Blah, blah, blah.

"Still no ransom demands from the kidnapper of Dr. Jacob Thurmond," said the blond newscaster. "Dr. Thurmond was taken from Maddox Labs during his talk last night. Police still have no leads."

I growled at the perfectly coiffed newscaster. She looked smug, as if all of this was the culmination of her own evil plans.

Asha patted my arm comfortingly.

The newscaster continued, "Investigators tell us that Maddox Labs was again victim to a possibly related attack this morning. An assailant ransacked Dr. Thurmond's lab and burned many of the files to ash. This is a great loss…"

"He burned the files?" asked Olivia, turning to me, her eyes wide.

I shrugged. "Yeah, crazy, huh?"

Dean Thorne's face filled the screen again.

"He is so good-looking," Asha said. "His brother Tommy's not bad either. Did you see him at the dojo today?"

I nodded, thinking of Tommy's fringe of blond hair and bright blue eyes. My breath hitched. Blue eyes, just like the masked intruder. I grabbed Asha's arm. "Did Tommy ever train with swords?"

"Nobody did at the dojo," said Asha, rubbing her forehead. "But today, he said something about Kendo at college."

"What's that?" asked Olivia.

"Sword fighting."

We stared at each other.

"And the intruder I saw had blue eyes." I pointed at the TV screen. "Just like Dean and Tommy."

"Do you think it could be?" Olivia asked.

I nodded thoughtfully. "I just talked to Tommy this morning. He and Dean still live at the old house on Patterson. We should check it out. Maybe he has my dad there."

***

We pulled up in front of my old house, which was bursting with light and music, and stared at the dark, quiet Thorne residence next door.

Olivia whistled. "That's a party worthy of your mom."

My heart ached as I looked it. Mom had loved to entertain. I sighed and rubbed the back of my hand across my eyes. There wasn't time for this. We had to find Dad or at least a clue about where he might be.

"It's a big place," said Asha. "But Dean's a security guy. How could he not know if your dad was there?"

"I don't know," I said. "But we've got to check it out."

"Why don't we call the police?"

"And tell them what exactly, Olivia? It's not like we've got any real proof. Similar-looking eyes and sword fighting class? They'd laugh me out of the precinct."

As we got out, Olivia dug in the back seat and came out with an old tennis racket.

Asha snorted. "What exactly are you going to do with that?"

"Sarah's got her power and you're a black belt. I've got to have something."

We decided to go over the back wall from my old yard to the Thornes'. Dean and Tommy had grown up in that house. There wouldn't be any hidey holes that they didn't know about. We took a loop around the house and peered in the windows. Every room was dark and silent. Not that we could have heard anything over the music from next door. Asha tested every window to see if they were locked.

When I heard the click, I knew we'd gotten lucky. She opened the window and we all climbed in. "Now," I whispered. "If you were Tommy, where would you hide my dad?"

"Basement," we all said at once. All the houses on this street had pretty similar layouts. There wasn't more than a crawlspace for an attic, and Dean would have noticed Tommy using one of the bedrooms.

We tiptoed down the hallway toward the kitchen. Asha stopped and peered into each dark room, just to be sure, but no one was home.

The basement door was just off the kitchen, and we paused nervously in front of its white wood. There weren't any scratches or streaks of blood that we could see. I hadn't seen any signs of a struggle anywhere in the house. Of course, Dean would have noticed something like that, wouldn't he?

"You open it," whispered Asha, pushing Olivia forward.

"No way," squeaked Olivia.

I sighed at both of them and turned the handle. The door swung open silently. Dark stairs led down into the basement. I listened, but I didn't hear anything unusual.

We crept down the steps single file. Olivia flipped the switch at the bottom, and a lone, dangling bulb flickered to life. Asha and I turned on her and growled.

"What?" she said. "There's obviously no one here."

She was right. There were lots of piles of stuff, mostly sports equipment, and a washer and dryer. No chair with my dad tied to it. No stacks of stolen files emblazoned with the Maddox Labs logo. I kicked the washer. "This was a waste of time."

"No, wait, guys," said Asha, pushing aside a box and peering at the floor near the basement wall. "Look over here."

Olivia and I hurried over. Five little piles of ash. Neat, as if something had just disintegrated right there on the spot. I looked around. Nothing else was burned, not the boxes, not the wooden support beams, nothing. "This doesn't make any sense."

Asha smiled. "Yes, it does."

"What?" asked Olivia.

"There's a rock encased in ice in my backyard."

"So?" Olivia frowned.

"What would it look like if Sarah had fire power instead of ice?" asked Asha.

"Whoa," whispered Olivia.

Footsteps creaked on the floor above us. Olivia sped over and flicked off the light then hurried back to us.

"Tommy, where are you?" called Dean's voice above.

My breath whooshed out of me. At least it wasn't Tommy.

Asha caught my eye and jerked her head to a window high on the basement wall.

I nodded. We shifted the closed boxes to the wall, piling them on top of each other, as silently as we could. Then we scampered up them and pushed on the window. Locked.

We yanked on the latch as hard as we could, but it wouldn't budge. The lawn was right outside. We could see the house lights from the party next door dancing across it.

The basement light came on, and Dean said, "You do seem to like trouble, Sarah."

We turned to face him.

"And you've dragged your friends into this too," he said, leaning casually against the wooden support beam. "Now, what are you doing in my house?"

My breath came fast, and I couldn't help my eyes from straying to the piles of ash on the floor.

Dean laughed. "I see you found Tommy's little project. We've been working really hard to get his power under control."

I swore under my breath. Asha gripped my arm, and Olivia gasped.

He laughed. "I guess I shouldn't be admitting that."

"Probably not," I said. "Why did you take my dad?"

"Virus D, of course. Although the word virus gives it such a bad connotation, doesn't it? It's really quite the miracle drug." Dean stepped toward us.

"Why not just steal the formula from the lab?" asked Asha.

Dean winked. "She's a smart one, Sarah. A badass black belt and smart. I like that."

"So, why didn't you?" Olivia asked.

"We did get a vial, that's how Tommy got his power, but there wasn't enough for me and all your dad's damn files are encrypted." Dean pulled a gun from the waistband behind his back and aimed it at us. "And I think we may have found the ticket to making your dad do what we want. Get down now, girls."

We climbed off the boxes and stood on the floor, quivering.

I stared at the gun, a million thoughts racing through my head. He knew where my dad was. We were going to die. What the hell had we gotten into? I should have come alone; now Asha and Olivia were in this too.

Olivia touched my arm and flicked her hand. I shook my head. He was going to lead us to my dad. I knew it.

Dean trooped us up the stairs, across the kitchen, and out the side door. Music still blared from my old house, but I couldn't catch sight of anyone before he shoved us in the garage. "Hey, Tommy," he said. "Looks like we have some company."

My dad was tied to a folding chair in the middle of the room. The sleeves of his button-down shirt were rolled up, and there were burns covering his arms. His head sagged against his chest.

"Dad," I cried. My hands chilled. "Is he okay?"

"He's breathing," said Asha quietly, watching the rise and fall of his chest.

Tommy sat on a stool next to a work bench that was covered with various bottles and carafes. Something green bubbled over a Bunsen burner. He scribbled something on a paper and then looked up at us. His mouth opened as if he meant to say something but then closed again.

"Tommy's the chemist," said Dean, nudging us into a line along the wall. "I'm just the brawn."

Asha gripped one of my arms, and Olivia took the other. Asha squeezed a silent question, *Now?* I nodded and looked at Olivia. Her lip jutted out. We were ready.

I concentrated on Dean first. An ice bolt burst from my fingers. Ice coated his gun. It crept up toward his hand. He screamed when the cold hit flesh.

"Come on, girls, concentrate," I hissed. Pulling energy from them both, I froze Dean's entire body.

"Duck," yelled Asha.

I dropped to the floor.

Olivia screamed. The smell of burnt hair hit my nostrils. I grabbed Olivia, pressing my icy hand to her smoking head. Maybe the gun wasn't the most dangerous thing in the room.

Asha shouted, "Ki-ya!" as she lashed out with a kick at Tommy's head. He dodged, and she rolled away from his punch.

"Freeze him." Olivia stood shakily and picked up her racket.

"I can't. Maybe I used too much on Dean." I glanced toward him. The ice was starting to drip from the tip of his gun. "I don't think we have much time."

"Crap," said Olivia. She advanced toward Tommy with her racket held high.

Asha danced around him, trading blows and ducking a fireball that flew past her shoulder and exploded against the cement wall. She was more than a match for his martial art skills, but the firepower was an extra challenge.

I moved behind Olivia and poked her.

"What?" squeaked Olivia.

"Ice plus racket," I whispered.

She nodded.

I caught Asha's eye and motioned. She took a punch to the shoulder as she nodded.

Collecting as much energy as I could, I focused on the racket. I could hear Asha faltering as I stole her momentum, but I didn't take my eyes off it. Pushing the ice out of my fingertips, I encased the wooden racket in ice.

Asha crashed against the wall next to Mr. Thorne's old lawnmower, which was draped in a tarp. Tools slipped from their hooks and clanked as they hit the floor.

Tommy turned toward us, holding another fireball in his hands.

"Sarah," mumbled a voice. "Is that you?"

"Yes, Dad. I'm here." My dad was waking up. He was okay. Relief flowed through me.

Tommy paused, cocked his head. Glancing at my dad, he gestured toward him with the fireball. "Playtime is over."

My fingers were cold, but the ice was gone. I couldn't freeze him.

Olivia raised her ice-covered racket.

Tommy laughed harshly. "I wouldn't if I were you."

Asha coughed and struggled to rise.

"And Dean said he was the brawn," I said.

Olivia tried to laugh.

"Looks like you might have gotten a dose of Virus D too," said Tommy.

My heart was racing. "Yeah, I did."

Asha had gotten to her feet behind him. She swayed.

"We should work together, Sarah." He smiled charmingly. "We'd be a force to be reckoned with."

Asha picked up the tarp gingerly and looked at me. I glanced over at Olivia, and she nodded. This was going to work.

"A force for good?" I asked, trying to keep him talking.

He chuckled.

Asha threw the tarp over Tommy's head. I ran forward and plowed into him, knocking him off balance. Raising the iced racket, Olivia gave the best serve of her life and clocked Tommy over the head. He tumbled onto the ground, moaning. Olivia hit him again, knocking him out.

Panting, we stared down at him.

A crackling sound echoed through the garage, and we swung around. Dean's ice casing was breaking.

I ran over and yanked the gun from his hand, tossing it across the room. Asha kicked him, and he keeled over. Olivia brought the racket down on his head.

"Sarah?" asked my dad groggily.

I hurried over and hugged him. He opened his eyes and smiled.

Asha called an ambulance and the police.

***

I stood next to my dad's stretcher as the paramedics looked him over. Officer Huxley had taken our statements, and Asha and Olivia waited nearby.

Officer Bassett pushed Dean into his patrol car, and another officer was reading Tommy his rights. I was glad to see Tommy still looked too disoriented to produce a fireball. We had warned them, but the police officers didn't act as if they believed us.

"I'm glad you're okay," I said to Dad.

He squeezed my hand, then the paramedics loaded him into the ambulance. They were busy working on him, and I backed up to the fence in order to give the emergency services room to work.

"You okay?" asked Asha, as she came up beside me.

"Yeah, I think so," I said. I was still worried about my dad and his injuries, but we were back together and that was what was most important.

"We're all okay." Olivia came over and linked arms with both of us. "So, who's next?"

"What do you mean?" I asked, raising an eyebrow at her.

Asha smiled.

"Somewhere, someone needs our help." Olivia flipped her hair.

"Like a superhero?" I asked quietly.

"No, a superhero team," said Asha. "We'll have to think of a good name."

"I'll need a better weapon," said Olivia.

I looked toward the squad car where Tommy sat. "We'll have to make sure he stays in jail. Do you think they'll be able to contain him?"

"I don't know," said Asha. "But we had better be around if they can't."

"Thank you." I hugged them both to me.

Jump Discontinuity

Renee Frey

Calculations flashing across his vision, Captain James Andrews set down the stealth tilt-rotor about one hundred yards from the industrial complex. A line dotted away, making an arcing graph. Just five degrees variance and he would have crashed the aircraft. He cut the power to the engines and nodded. Three other heroes, clad in midnight blue, leapt out and ran for the complex. Andrews unfastened his safety harness and jogged after them.

More calculations swirled about his hazel eyes as they ran. It was as if someone had grafted a supercomputer into his retina. After five years, he was getting better at ignoring them when necessary. During those controlled crash landings in Iraq, however, his ability—whether magic or some freak jump in evolution—had saved his life.

Betsy Loss grinned, blue eyes twinkling as he caught up. "Nice of you to join us, Andrews."

He grunted. As the newcomer, they all teased him. From basic training to elite operatives, the military was the military. He couldn't wait for someone else to join the team—just so he could join in on the banter.

"I guess accelerated probability doesn't accelerate your running any." Betsy laughed as she lengthened her stride, empty pack bumping against her back, black, curly hair dancing with each stride.

"That's enough, Betsy." Ahead, Magellan slowed and glanced over his shoulder. "He's here, and he landed us safely with no lights. Makes the rest of this easy."

Betsy rolled her eyes. Melion, the last member of the team, snorted. She was probably choking back her own snarky comments. Despite himself, Andrews smiled.

As they neared the building, they slowed and hid just outside the pool of light surrounding the complex. The building itself was nondescript. Plain blocks cemented together, built for fortification, not beauty. With floodlights only illuminating fifty feet or so around the building, the team's approach was too easy. Andrews started actively reviewing the mathematical equations popping up across objects. He honed in on the building, scanning until he found the weak point of the structure. He pointed. At the base, where a drain pipe had eroded the foundation, was a collapsible pressure point. Melion crouched low and slunk into the illuminated area. Her red hair burnished in the light. The crew held their breaths. No alarm sounded.

Melion darted to the side of the building, fast despite her Amazonian stature, touched the wall, and closed her eyes. After a pause, she smiled and opened them. Her talent, recognizing and analyzing inanimate objects, confirmed Andrews' prediction. She reached into a pouch and placed a small cube on the wall, pressed a button, then ran back toward the group, out of the revealing floodlights.

BOOM!

The charge created a small opening in the wall. No alarm yet, but it was only a matter of time before someone came to investigate the explosion. Betsy and Melion started toward it.

"Bring the bird back—we'll be coming out hot," Magellan barked.

Andrews nodded and jogged back toward the plane. The others would recover the stolen information and plant charges to detonate the warehouse as they left. Andrews scowled. Undoubtedly, there would be people in the building. The explosion would likely kill them. He hated that. But Major, leader of the Nationalists, had insisted on destroying the complex, claiming it was crucial to the mission. At least Andrews wouldn't have to plant or detonate the charges. Being a pilot had its advantages, both here and in Operations Desert Storm and Enduring Freedom.

He ignored his accelerated probability as he raced across the dark, silent field. His talent had started while he was a pilot in the Air Force, a chance occurrence in moments of danger. Now, it happened all the time. He couldn't turn it off. Mathematical representations of the probability of things happening, graphs indicating the results, now overlaid everything he looked at. Even running in the dark, a line would pop up, or a graph. Some days, it was downright nauseating. But it had saved his life in Iraq and Afghanistan, and now he could do even more for his country—as a Nationalist.

Restart and pre-flight check of the tilt-rotor took mere minutes. He skipped a few steps, but what pilot didn't? The wings hummed as the tilting mechanism locked the nacelles in the vertical position. An alarm wailed in the distance. Time to move.

Andrews focused his ability. With his talent, he could fly dark, with no lights or navigational equipment. As long as he interpreted the math correctly, he could select the best route. He navigated as close to the ground as he could, until a darting line indicated he better pull up. The chopping of the rotors filled the air. Hovering next to the building, he released a rope ladder for the others to climb into the cargo bay. It snapped and swirled in the rotor's vortex.

Right on time. His three teammates clustered around the rope. Magellan finally caught the moving target and held it steady. Melion scaled the rope, muscles heaving with the strain of her added cargo. She climbed the rope as one born to it. Magellan, almost invisible with his dark skin in the night, was right behind her, struggling to keep up with her blistering pace.

Betsy waited below, right hand extended, left hand to her temples. She was always last, using her neurocognitive deficit powers to hide their presence from others. A guard leapt out from the hole in the building. Betsy held out a hand, palm glowing. The guard stopped then turned and began walking away. A double tap on the cockpit door told Andrews the pair made it safely to the hold. Andrews was about to radio Betsy when she broke away and clutched at the rope. He began their ascent, trusting in Magellan and Melion to pull in the rope—and Betsy.

The bright light of the explosions burst behind him. Andrews pushed the throttle and got them the hell out of there.

A moment later, Magellan joined him in the cockpit.

"Did you get it all?" Andrews asked.

Magellan smiled. "Yes. The Russians won't be starting riots anytime soon. It will take them months to find another data mine, and without the technology to hide what they were doing—"

"Good." Andrews' tension evaporated. The hard part was over. What had started as false news websites had grown into a full-blown communications crisis. The Russians were hijacking entire networks and communications platforms and sending distorted messages to incite the general population. Riots and other pockets of violence had started and grown, making a small hacking operation into a prime security concern.

Major had decided that full-scale destruction was their only option. The technology relied on massive amounts of archived information, as well as a new processor that allowed for lightning-fast creation and compilation of data into a new "news item." Stealing what they could and destroying the source had been the only option open to the

Nationalists. *It was the only option.* Andrews kept telling himself that. Even after serving in two wars, he found it hard to just hate "the Enemy" and slaughter them. *Remember, this is for the greater good. Focus on that, instead of the children whose father won't be coming home in the morning.* He still felt guilty.

Magellan pressed a couple of buttons. "Black Eagle to Base. Magellan speaking. Authorization November Alpha Tango. Over."

Andrews' headphones crackled before the response came through. "Roger that, Magellan. Report."

"Target destroyed. Intel recovered safely. No casualties on our side."

"Great job." That robust voice could only belong to Major. "Status of team?"

Magellan glanced over at Andrews and grinned. "They never saw us coming, sir. New guy here can fly blind, no problem."

"Good, good. I'll expect a full report later. I'll brief you on the next mission then."

Magellan chuckled. "We'll be ready."

Andrews turned on the autopilot and stretched. He still couldn't believe he was part of an elite government task force, using a special ability to save the world. Major had noticed how Andrews always succeeded in his missions—always. Andrews lived and saved others in situations where other pilots had perished. Afraid that what he saw might be some sort of mental disorder, the Captain had kept quiet about his abilities. Now, he knew them for what they were—and could use them.

"We are the perfect team." Magellan smirked.

"Hm?" Andrews wasn't expecting conversation—he and Magellan usually just decompressed in the cockpit after a mission.

Magellan shrugged his burly shoulders. "I just think our skills are a perfect complement."

Betsy poked her head into the cockpit. "Aw, Magellan! I heard you talking to Major, but I didn't expect to hear a love story!" She turned to yell back into the cargo hold. "Hey, Melion, get a load of this. We got a pair of doves flying this Osprey!"

Melion's response made even Magellan wince.

Betsy waved a hand. "She's just tired. So, what's so great about you two?"

Magellan's lips thinned. "I was saying that our talents complement each other. Not just the two of us, but the whole team."

Betsy smiled. "You're right! With your global positioning, Andrews' accelerated probability, Melion's psychometry, and my neurocognitive deficit, we can find anything, get in anywhere, and understand any weapon or person used against us."

Andrews thought it over. "But no one is invincible."

Betsy snorted. "Whatever, Andrews." She left the cockpit as abruptly as she had entered.

Magellan shrugged. "Well, that's about what I was going to say." He rolled his eyes.

Andrews laughed. Betsy's bubbly personality would take some getting used to. "Yeah, I'm sure that's *exactly* how you would have said it." He stifled a yawn.

Magellan glanced at his watch. "You should get a quick nap. After using your powers so much, you need it. I'll wake you for the air refueling."

Andrews closed his eyes. It felt like mere moments later when Magellan woke him. He wished he could have slept more, but someone had to monitor the flight.

"Of course you make me do the air refueling." Andrews rubbed the sleep out of his eyes.

Magellan shrugged. "You're the better pilot. We have each other's backs. Didn't we just discuss this?"

Andrews shook his head as he took the stick. Magellan was right. And Andrews should be used to the partnership and camaraderie of working with a close-knit team from his military background. *I guess the more things change, the more they stay the same.*

By the time Andrews finished refueling, Magellan was asleep, his snores echoing in the cockpit. Andrews stretched and refocused. Only six hours to go.

Five hours later, a transmission came through.

"Major to Black Eagle. Do you copy? Over."

Andrews started slightly. It was unusual for Major to contact them after their final report. He toggled the radio.

"Black Eagle to Major, this is Captain Andrews. Over."

"Andrews. I need you to start transmitting the recovered data. It's extremely time-sensitive. Normally, I would wait until you arrived, but—"

"Sure, no problem. Any place in particular you want me to start?"

"There should be a black-and-red flash drive. Have one of the girls use the remote connection to upload it onto the mainframe."

"Roger that, Major."

"Thanks, Andrews—I owe you."

Andrews shook Magellan awake. "Need you to take the stick. Major has a project for Betsy and Melion."

Magellan rubbed his eyes and grunted, leaning forward to study the navigational equipment. Andrews undid his harness and slipped out of the cockpit. Betsy and Melion were both passed out in their bunks. Andrews sighed. Betsy was probably exhausted from mentally distracting the security guards to cover their getaway. Andrews considered waking them but decided against it. He could log in and begin the upload just as easily.

He crossed to the cargo hold and searched through the recovered items. Melion couldn't identify and tag items quickly because of her powers. No matter how much she tried to control them, sometimes they slipped out, so it would take longer on some items and tire her out quickly. They normally deferred the job of tagging evidence and intel to the intelligence specialists on base instead.

After a moment, he located the flash drive. He re-secured the cargo and returned to the main hold.

The Black Eagle was outfitted with state-of-the-art equipment, including onboard computer terminals that accessed the virtual network. Andrews logged in and inserted the flash drive. He copied the files and, after navigating to the appropriate directory, began uploading them. He rolled his shoulders. Estimated time to completion: thirty minutes. *Must be lots of files.* One title streaming across the screen caught his eye: False Flag Mission Iranian Implication. He hesitated then opened the flash drive directory again. Searching for the file name, he located it. Andrews' finger hovered over the mouse button. He wasn't a spy. But he was an operative. And if there was a false flag mission planned— maybe it was time-critical, and he should try to stop it.

He clicked and began reading the document.

False Flag Mission: Iranian Implication

Objective: To declare war on Iran

Method: Plan an assassination on major world leaders, implicating Iran in their deaths. Russian Intelligence will cooperate with the United States National Security Council to execute and carry out the mission.

Contacts: Kenneth Banners, director NSC, Vladimir Bortners, director FSB, Major, director Eagle Missions

Andrews stopped short. Major? *Major* was in on a secret false flag mission? Did that mean…

He went to continue reading when the "upload complete" dialogue box interrupted. He clicked "OK." The screen blanked. He tried to open the flash drive again but was prompted to enter a password. Andrews scowled. Of course, once uploaded, the data was automatically encrypted. He tried his credentials, but a huge blinking "Access Denied" flashed across the screen. Andrews pursed his lips.

He didn't know enough to do anything. Just enough to be worried. He turned and studied the two sleeping women. They were a team. Magellan was right. But could he trust them with this?

Andrews lost track of how long he stood there, musing. They had been destroying a false info hacking center. There was every possibility that the information on the flash drive was false, a gaslight. He removed the flash drive and studied it. Nothing to indicate the owner or the purpose. And how would Major know about this specific item?

"Andrews! Landing time!" Magellan's deep voice boomed from the cockpit. Andrews jumped then pocketed the drive. Maybe he could find someone who could hack the encryption. He returned to the cockpit and strapped himself in.

"Beginning landing sequence," he murmured.

"What? Can't hear you." Magellan was busy punching buttons.

"Beginning landing sequence." Andrews pulled the microphone to his lips as he spoke. He also began toggling knobs.

"Black Eagle to Home Base, requesting permission to land."

They landed without a hitch. Major stood on the edge of the runway, trench coat flapping in the breeze. Tall and imposing, with a scar bisecting one eye, he was waiting for them. Andrews' heart raced.

Andrews tried to speak casually. "I'll taxi her to the hangar." Would Major realize he had the flash drive? Hopefully he could buy a few extra minutes and try to copy it.

Magellan grunted and unfastened himself. "Suit yourself. I can't wait to get out of this uniform." The floor vibrated with his pounding steps.

Once all three had exited, Andrews taxied the plane toward the hangar. Major glanced over, his good eye focused on the cockpit. Andrews swallowed the lump in his throat then waved and smiled. Major nodded then looked back to the team. Everything seemed normal, right down to the sun shining on the black tarmac and reflecting off the white paint. Andrews pulled into the hangar and began final shut down when his radio blipped. He went to toggle it then stopped. The channel was private, not one usually used by the Nationalists. He hesitated then placed his earphones on.

"This is Captain Andrews."

"Captain Andrews. I must meet with you. Privately. It is a matter of national security. Be at Washington Monument this evening at 1800."

"Who is this? Why should I—" The transmission died. Andrews clenched a fist. He had no idea who had sent the message. What should he do? First the weird file on the flash drive, now this. Was it an enemy operative, trying to lure him into a trap or implicate him in a crime? The Nationalist's operating procedure for any secret transmission like this was crystal clear: report the message to Major, and let him decide how to proceed.

But if Major had flipped, and was working against the United States…

Andrews pulled the thumb drive out of his arm pocket. Nothing special about it, save the red-and-black coloring. He should return it. He had never dealt with such issues when serving in the Air Force. The rules were made and followed. There were no gray areas. But what should he do when he couldn't trust the man in charge? His powers only worked in real situations, with actual things happening—not in the what-ifs of espionage.

A mechanic's head popped into view. "Andrews? You coming? Major wants to see Team Black—something about a mission on Friday."

Andrews tucked the flash drive back in his pocket. "Coming—just one second." He rolled his shoulders and tried to relax. He could figure this out. He unfastened his safety harness and exited the aircraft. The hangar was tall and airy. Andrews drew in and released a deep breath. He would figure this out. His footsteps echoed as he left the hangar, pausing only to give a salute to the security patrol at the exit.

A blast of cold air wafted over him as he entered the office. Typical gray tile floors and awful fluorescent lights surrounded him, just like his old offices in the Air Force. A quick glance at the white board told him where to go. "Nationalists: Briefing Room Six." Andrews started down the hall. Usually, the pervasive silence was a welcome respite. Today, it unnerved him. He kept circling back to his situation.

Andrews stopped and opened the door. A television, tuned to the World News Network, played in the background. "The United States President and the Canadian Prime Minister will take their yearly retreat together this weekend…"

Magellan grabbed a remote and turned the TV off. "You missed the coverage—the mission is being reported."

Andrews stopped. "You mean they already reported the raid?"

Melion rolled her eyes. "People have been posting about it on my Facebook for several hours now. I hate the media blackout while we are in transit." She crossed her arms, full lips pursed.

Betsy nodded, her blue eyes serious for once. "I hate this round-the-clock news coverage. Half the time, I feel that the news reports our mission before we lift off. And what is reported is so slanted…"

Magellan shrugged. "It's being called a rebel attack. Russia is blaming the Ukrainians and trying to justify military action."

"But this was supposed to prevent action against the other Eastern Bloc countries." Andrews scratched his chin, hoping he hid his nervousness.

"Look, I don't write the news." Magellan crossed his arms and leaned back in his chair.

I should ask them about it. We are supposed to be a team. Maybe they have had something like this happen before. Andrews swallowed the lump in his throat then began, "Well, Major asked for some files to get uploaded as we returned. I did that, but—"

Betsy and Melion sprung to their feet. Magellan stood, slower than the women, but didn't waste any time. Andrews turned around. Major stood directly behind him in the doorway. With close-cropped hair and a permanent scowl, there was no questioning where Major's military career had begun—with the Marines. Andrews lifted his right hand, touching the third finger to his eyebrow in a salute. Major returned the gesture.

"Have a seat, team."

The women and Magellan returned to their seats. Andrews walked around the long table and found the last unoccupied chair. He sat and struggled not to fidget. He turned off his emotions. Stoicism would save him—Major wouldn't suspect anything, especially since Andrews never really showed emotion anyways.

"Thanks to the data sent during your return flight, we learned that several key military targets are gathering in a compound in the Maldives this Friday."

Andrews' breath caught. Friday was the day for that false flag mission. If only he had read faster.

"The Maldives?" Betsy frowned. "What could they possibly want there?"

"Everyone takes vacations." Magellan shrugged. "Why would evil warlords be any different?"

"Or terrorists," Major added. "So your mission is simple. Navigate to the compound. Destroy it. Cut the head off of the terrorist snake, as it were."

"Seems simple enough," commented Melion. "What time?"

"Report at 0600. Dismissed." Major turned and left.

Both women stood and headed toward the door. Andrews' heart thumped harder. He wished he could look at something, anything, and activate his ability, give him a hint. Should he go along with it? Report his findings?

"I—I don't know if I can go." There. He said it.

Melion whirled around. "Why not?"

Betsy planted her hands on her hips, frowning.

Magellan didn't move, but his gaze bored into Andrews.

Andrews took a deep breath. "I wanted to tell you, but I didn't have the chance. I saw something when I was uploading those files—"

"Then why didn't you tell Major?" Melion slapped both hands down on the table. "You know the rules."

Andrews steeled himself. Melion, all fiery temper, was right—at least as far as she knew. She respected strength—he would need to be strong in his assertion if she were to understand. "I know the rules," he said curtly. "I would appreciate it if you would hear me out." If he could trust anyone, it would be his team.

Her green eyes narrowed. After a heartbeat, she nodded. "Fine."

Andrews glanced around at the others. "And both of you?"

Magellan gave his usual shrug.

Betsy shook her head. "No."

"No?" Every muscle in Andrews' body tensed.

"Andrews, you are new. A rookie to the Nationalists. You haven't seen what happens. No matter what you saw, what you think happened, you have to take it to Major."

"And what if it implicates him?" Andrews stood. "Why should I blindly trust him?"

He looked at each of them. Betsy stood square, all five feet of her resolute. Magellan avoided his eyes. And Melion crossed her arms, met his gaze, then looked away.

No one can answer this. Guess I'm on my own.

"I just need time to think about this." Andrews shoved past Betsy and left the room.

***

It was almost 1800 hours. Andrews surveyed the area around the National Mall. People meandered up and down the pristine sidewalks surrounding the central lawn. This late, most of the museums were empty. He scanned all around the park. Nothing. His powers didn't suggest anything out of the ordinary. He sighed and made his way toward Washington Monument. The last few visitors were leaving as the sun set. Soon, the area would be practically abandoned. Andrews stopped next to the monument and waited. Every nerve tingled. He was taking a huge risk—but he had to know the truth.

His watch beeped. Andrews pressed a button on the side to turn it off. It was time. A stranger, pale-skinned and blond, clad in a nondescript black suit, walked up.

"Captain Andrews?" A perfectly chiseled face framed with graying sideburns smiled at him. The stranger's stormy eyes emanated an icy chill. The man's thick Russian accent made understanding him difficult.

The captain studied the newcomer. He decided he didn't trust the man's smile or outstretched hand. "Depends—who's asking?"

The stranger laughed. "Mikhail. Russian Intelligence. I received a ping on our flash drive. So you have the intel."

Andrews' lips tightened. Apparently, Mikhail had put some sort of a bug in the flash drive that would notify him if the file was opened. Something that also recorded who was logged in when the file was accessed. Impressive.

"I don't know what you're talking about." Andrews gazed at the man impassively, wishing that he had Magellan's or Melion's height instead of barely reaching five foot ten.

"Comrade, I know you read file. You know that tomorrow they plan to assassinate your president and the Canadian prime minister. To blame it on Iran. A joint operation between our countries. Clean house, as you say." Mikhail lit a cigarette. "You read file, no?"

"And if I did?" Andrews kept his face relaxed. Inside, however, his stomach roiled. *I wish I had read faster. What if this is all a setup? A move from Russia for counterintel?* He clenched his fists then, with effort, relaxed them. *But what if it's real?*

Mikhail puffed out a breath of smoke. "Then you know why mission must be stopped. I confirm for you. If not, I must act to stop."

Andrews considered. "How do you know that I won't take this straight to my superiors? That I'm not a plant looking for rogue spies?"

Mikhail laughed. "Major came up with idea. He hates the President. Wants new one. He also hates terrorists, wants any excuse to invade Middle East. If you were going to tell him, you would have already done so." He dropped the cigarette and put it out with a toe. "Tomorrow, you stop mission, da?"

As soon as Andrews heard Major's name, his chest contracted. There was no way he could take Betsy's advice now. *How do I find out the truth?*

"That would make me a traitor to my country—halting a mission on the word of a Russian spy."

"This Russian is trying to help. I betray my country to help you." His eyes narrowed. "Don't take that so light."

"How do I prove what you're saying? I can't do anything on conjecture." *Here's hoping I get something.*

"No proof. You must use your power."

"My power? But—"

Mikhail drew a fist back and punched him across the jaw. Mathematical equations screamed across his eyes, too quickly for Andrews to react. He rolled backward with the punch and flipped up into a fighting stance, fists at the ready. Mikhail jumped away. He soared, spanning over thirty yards. Andrews' jaw dropped. That was impossible. Going against every logical thought in Andrews' brain, Mikhail lunged again, cresting through the air right toward the captain.

Andrews dodged. "How are you doing that?"

"You think America only place with talented intelligence? Make this look good. For your sake." Mikhail darted again.

"What are you talking about?" Andrews tucked and twisted, narrowly avoiding the onslaught.

"Preserve your innocence. Fight me. Make it believable, *Comrade*." Mikhail socked Andrews in the gut. Luckily, the Captain was prepared for this and struck back. Mikhail danced backward, just out of range.

Andrews grimaced. He had hoped to keep the meeting a secret. He faked an approach then ran the other way—the way his calculations told him Mikhail would jump. Andrews sprinted for all he was worth. He couldn't run fast enough. Mikhail landed several yards from Andrews. Andrews halted, studying the Russian through narrowed eyes. Mikhail walked toward him. Thousands of calculations diminished to three.

"You can't even land punch." Mikhail's shout echoed off the surrounding buildings.

Andrews smiled. He knew exactly what he needed to do. "No. You are too good for me."

Mikhail sneered. "Great American powers not so great in the real world, are they?"

The whop whop of a chopper drew both their eyes. Andrews sighed. Balanced News. Any hope of secrecy was gone.

Looking back at Mikhail, Andrews shrugged. "My ability can't compensate for you leaping football fields in a single bound. So, I guess I get slugged to make it look good?"

"No."

"No?"

"You get eliminated!" With that resonating statement, Mikhail rushed forward.

Andrews was ready. He ducked and swept his leg forward in a spinning kick, tripping Mikhail as the Russian's legs bent to leap up. A cracking sound told Andrews that he had shattered the man's shin.

"I told you truth. Will bring proof—soon," Mikhail gasped.

Andrews snorted. He had to get back to headquarters—and fast. With the news helicopters covering what happened, his only hope was getting the mission underway before the news broke.

Andrews' mind raced along with his feet. Maybe he should just come clean to Major. Explain what he saw, share the details of the meeting, and follow orders. Be a good soldier.

But what if it's true? Could I really just step aside and allow this?

No. His heart thudded faster, and not just because he was running. He couldn't take the information to Major. Protocol be damned. If Major was involved, it would be suicide. Even if Betsy was right, and it was a setup. Andrews' hands were tied. He was complicit now just by meeting with Mikhail. If the whole thing was an attempt to remove Andrews, discredit him and end his career, he had fallen right into the trap. At best, he would be court-martialed and dishonorably discharged.

A cold sweat broke over his brow. Of course, the Constitution allowed for the death penalty for one specific crime: treason.

I might not make it out of this alive. His hands trembled. Carrie, his wife, and his four kids were at home. He wouldn't even have the chance to speak with them before facing the impending consequences.

There was no winning situation. No matter what he did, Andrews would fail in being a patriot. Would fail to uphold the oaths he took as an Air Force Academy cadet years ago.

Panting, Andrews drew close to Home Base as the dark of night changed to a foggy dawn. An extra contingent of security guards crowded the gate. Apparently, he hadn't been able to outrun the news. Scanning the perimeter, he smiled as he located a weak point. Glancing back at the guard shack, Andrews confirmed that the coast was clear then made his move.

He wiped his slick palms on his pants. He had to decide—and fast. He raced toward the airfield, where his team should be waiting for him. Where they would leave on their mission. Where he would either be a traitor, or a hero.

The other three Nationalists were waiting on the tarmac.

"Andrews. Glad you could make it. Here are the coordinates." Magellan handed a sheet of paper over.

"Verified with your global positioning?" Andrews tried to smile. He felt as if he would vomit.

Magellan laughed. "Of course!"

"Once we're there, you should be able to identify the best place for the charges." Melion smiled at him.

Andrews nodded rather than answer. If they got in the air, he could tell them, privately, on the plane.

They began boarding the Osprey. Betsy hung back. "You okay? Doesn't normally take you this long. You love flying."

Andrews shook his head. "I—I'm having a hard time focusing. Nervous, I guess."

"Did you talk to Major, like I told you?"

"Eh, I mentioned it. He told me not to worry." The lie fell glibly off of his tongue. Andrews hated himself for it.

Betsy nodded. Melion poked her head out. "Who's that?"

Andrews whirled around. Mikhail.

"Proof. Here." The Russian was there, holding a dossier folder.

"How do I know it's real?" Andrews glared at Mikhail. He needed answers now. The secret of how the Russian healed so quickly from a major broken bone could wait.

"Andrews? Who is this? What is going on?" Melion jumped down from the loading dock. "What are you doing here?"

Mikhail ignored Melion. Looking square at Andrews, he shrugged. "You will have to make decision. Decide who to trust. Your leader, who will say anything to get result, who cares only for self—or enemy spy here at great personal cost to prevent disaster."

Andrews snatched the dossier and began flipping through it.

Communications from Major, copied, confirming the worst. The file activated his ability. Major planned to betray them all.

"I knew it." The deep voice of Major was unmistakable.

Andrews froze.

"Consorting with the enemy, Andrews? I thought better of you."

Andrews whirled around. "What do you mean?"

Betsy and Magellan also jumped down onto the tarmac.

Major snorted. "Betsy told me all about your personal crisis."

Andrews glanced over at Betsy, who raised her chin despite the shadow of shame blanketing her eyes.

"I also know about the meeting last night," Major continued. "Cut the crap, Andrews. Make a decision. Either do your job, and leave to plant those detonating charges, or else prepare for a court-martial."

"How do you explain this?" Andrews thrust the file toward Major.

Major smiled and reached behind his back.

"No—" yelped Mikhail.

Major drew a handgun and fired. BAM! Mikhail was down, bleeding out.

Major studied Andrews' face. "My power is perfect aim. I don't even have to look at the target or see it. That is why I am the leader. I see perfectly. You can trust me—and you should have trusted me from the beginning."

"But the False Flag—"

"I have the facts, Andrews. Not some flash drive you recovered from a *false news warehouse*."

"But according to this dossier, that wasn't a counterintelligence mission. It was a government cover-up. They were disseminating that information to sway voters—"

"Shut up." Major backhanded Andrews. "I have the facts. Period. So what if they are not the facts you see with your eyes. What I say is the truth. Always."

Andrews backed away, shaking his head. "I want to believe that you are a patriot at heart—that you want what is best for the country."

Major smiled. "I do, Andrews. And what is best for the country is for you to do as ordered: blow up the compound in the Maldives."

"No." Andrews read the calculations and ducked. Another blast told him he had just escaped having his brains blown out.

"Major!" That was Betsy.

"What are you doing?" Melion appeared in Andrews' peripheral vision.

Major glanced around then hefted his gun. "Who are you going to believe? Me or that traitor scum over there?"

Andrews took advantage of the distraction and dropped and rolled under the aircraft.

"Here's what is 'going on.'" Major swiveled to face the others. "Captain Andrews here doubts our mission. He is questioning my honesty and integrity. Bad. Very bad. Dishonest." He pivoted back toward Andrews, his face dead. "I think we should take care of this problem now. Before he does anything—unfixable."

Andrews rolled into the nearby hangar and made a run for it. Another shot sounded. Andrews looked back. He couldn't see anything. He ran.

"Andrews! Get back here!" Heavy footsteps rang out. Major was in pursuit.

Andrews tried a door. Locked.

Keep running.

Tried the next door. It opened. He darted inside then ran down the hall. There was no way he could stand against someone with perfect aim. Not without the proper setup. He looked all around. No place to hide. He kept barreling down the hall.

The door he came in slammed. Major was in the building. He was running out of time. Andrews ducked into a conference room and hid behind a desk. Best probability, but still only fifty percent. A TV blared, covering any noises Andrews made. *Certified News Network to the rescue.*

"Andrews! Come out and answer for your crimes!"

Major was in the room. Andrews swallowed. He thought fleetingly of the wife and kids he would never see again—and steeled himself. He stood slowly and stared down Major. He refused to die like a coward.

The other three Nationalists burst into the room behind Major.

"What do you mean?" Magellan grabbed Major. "Major, everyone on this team has doubts. It happens when working counterintel. You told me this yourself, when I started. Explain why Andrews should not be retrained, given the benefit of the doubt."

Major sneered. "He consorted with a spy—a Russian spy!"

"So?" Melion crossed her arms and planted her feet, standing between Andrews and Major. "We've all had to go undercover. Andrews saw something that raised concerns for him. He investigated. You usually applaud initiative. What's changed?"

Major started backing away. Andrews snarled then leapt forward. The equations flew. Andrews dodged to the side, avoiding another shot. He whirled and closed—rendering Major's gun ineffective. A punch disarmed the traitor; a tackle disabled him.

The dossier flew across the floor, papers scattering.

Betsy picked one up and scanned it. Her lips thinned. "Andrews is right. You're a liar."

Melion dashed over and knelt into Major's back. "I don't like liars," she sneered.

Magellan recovered Major's gun. He targeted the traitor's head. "I suggest you hold very still, sir."

The strains of "Hail to the Chief" blared from the television. As one, all eyes riveted on the television.

"And the President arrives for his retreat with the Canadian Prime Minister in the Maldives. We are hopeful this new method of diplomacy—mixing pleasure with business and allowing true human connections—will allow for a greater relationship between these two great nations."

The building from the mission filled the screen. In front of it, both leaders shook hands and walked in.

The Tiger of Geminia

Mckayla Eaton

Dampness hangs in the air, the kind I can feel in my bones. That's what happens when you get old—your body starts predicting the weather better than the satellites and thermometers.

My reflection walks along beside me in the outer glass wall of the Geminia Central Hospital. It surprises me how much my shoulders are hunched and how prominent my limp has become—an injury from my youth. My mirrored image (a man who seems too old to be myself) bothers me more today than it has previously. Maybe the Corp was right; am I too old for this?

I slip through the revolving doors of the hospital. Inside, the stark white lobby has no glass to torment me with my reflection. It's quiet. Nurses and doctors whisper in doorways and people sit silently on seats covered in soft fabric. The televisions on the walls are muted, dimmed, and showing reruns of cartoons to occupy the children.

I walk to the pretty secretary who's seated at an ivory topped-desk, her eyes fixed on the screen in front of her and nails clicking softly on the keys.

"I'm here to see a Lilly Ambers," I say, sliding my card across the desk.

She picks it up a moment later, flashing me a professional smile. "Of course, Mr. Taitt. Let me look her up." She clicks on the keys again.

"She's in maternity ward eight. Take the elevator to the fourth floor and go down the hall to your left until you find doors marked M8. She is in room one twenty-five."

I thank her and take back my card, slipping it into my pocket.

In the elevator, I breathe in deeply, chest swelling, before pressing the button. The four is illuminated with a red light and the elevator hums gently as it carries me to my destination. I recall a much more terrifying elevator ride I took once, when I had first met Lilly. She was my first assignment—I was twenty-five. By all accounts too young, but too full of reckless confidence to notice.

***

The elevator had been an old, rattling machine trapped within a brick shaft inside one of the oldest buildings in the city. St. Amber's was a home and private school for girls. The death trap of an elevator had been in the section of the school that housed orphans. I'd been sent there by the Corp to interview a young girl who showed signs of possessing an extraordinary skill.

I had arrived at the top floor with my stomach in my throat, white knuckling the thin iron bars of the elevator, trying to keep down my lunch. I had long been plagued by a fear of heights, and hurtling vertically inside a ramshackle box was nightmare material.

It was not helped any by the short, stout nun that awaited me.

"Good morning, Mr. Taitt," she said, beaming at me. She was the kind of woman who could suffocate a person with glee alone. "I'm Sister Marge, and we are so blessed that you could come."

She turned and started down the narrow brick hallway. I pushed aside the sliding grate and stepped from the elevator with shaking legs. I was sure my cheeks were green.

"Lilly is a special little girl," Sister Marge said. "She's twelve now but she's been here since she was a babe. We never knew the parents—poor thing. She would have been adopted right away, but she was so little and sickly that we decided to keep her with us until she was stronger. She did get better, but unfortunately the sickly complexion stayed with her and this deters potential parents. Just awful."

She stopped before a door with a dainty white wooden cross nailed to it and spoke quietly. "One day, all the girls were at their prayers, and I walked by Lilly's room to find her, well, floating. Now, as you must imagine, I thought the child was blessed by the Lord and had reached some sort of divine state in her prayers. I left quickly and said nothing to her because such things are the business of God and his children, but then she started doing it with alarming frequency and not only in prayer. She did it at meals and at choir practice. One day, I found her just floating down the hallway."

The nun shook her head. "It's unnatural, Mr. Taitt. The priest wanted to exorcise the child, but I thought perhaps we would call you first."

"Thank you for calling the Corp, Sister. It was wise of you, and if we can assist in any way, we will." I tried to imitate the authoritative tone the more senior guys at the Corp used when dealing with people outside the organization. To my ears, the stiff language felt fake, like I was a little boy trying to wear my father's suit, so I was relieved when Sister Marge simply nodded, then rapped her plump knuckles against the door.

"Lilly, darling. There is someone here to see you."

"Come in," a young voice called from inside.

Sister Marge opened the door, revealing a very pale young girl. Her long, black hair was pleated into twin braids, which hung below her as she levitated above her bed. She was lying in the air, horizontal, just as comfortably as if her head rested on the pillow. She wore the white blouse, navy vest, and gray skirt that all St. Amber's girls wore. A white rosary dangled from her skirt pocket.

She sprung up to sit cross-legged as we came in. "Hello."

"Lilly, this is Mr. Taitt."

"Hello, little girl." I pulled the stack of prim white business cards I'd had printed that morning from my pocket. In my haste, I spilled them on the floorboards. The girl giggled and, embarrassed, I hurried to collect them before offering one to her.

"I work for the Corp and assist in training the heroically inclined. I'm here to assess your reported extra-ordinary abilities."

"Am I heroically inclined?" she asked. She reached for the card but only managed to fumble toward it as she floated higher.

"Well, from what I'm seeing, it appears the reports of your abilities are true and Judeo-Christian values tend to be a benefit—so long as non-violence and 'thou shall not kill' tendencies aren't instilled too deeply."

Sister Marge's mouth fell open, her little eyes becoming round and wide.

I ignored her as I watched the girl floating slowly toward the ceiling. I'd seen a lot of weird things while training at the Corp and levitating wasn't a particularly unique ability, as far as powers went, but I was sure I could turn her into a great hero nonetheless.

She held her hands above her just before hitting her head on the roof and pushed herself back toward the bed. She landed on the mattress and quickly reached forward between her knees, grabbing the bed frame to keep seated. She took my card.

"The Corp," she said. "They make superheroes, right?"

"We find potential superheroes and help improve on their innate abilities," I explained.

"So, you don't make them in a lab?" she asked, turning the card over in her fingers.

"No. That's simple superstition."

She laughed. "Superstition about superheroes."

"Can you control your floating, Miss Lilly?"

"It's just Lilly," she said. She put the card on the bed, looking bashful as she grabbed the bed frame with her other hand to keep herself from floating away. "Not really."

"What happens if you float outside? Will you float higher indefinitely?"

"No. I can't do it when I'm scared, so if I get too high I get afraid."

"Then you float back down?"

"I fall."

"I see. That is problematic."

"Can you make it stop?"

"I can help you to control it. But, Lilly, I'm not a therapist. I train heroes. If it's a cure you want, then I can give you some recommendations for a doctor."

She stared at the floor in thought. "What if I don't want either?"

"I'm afraid we can't allow that. Orphans such as yourself typically make good heroes, but statistically, they make better villains. We can't allow you to keep your ability without proper instruction."

She looked to Sister Marge who, thankfully, said nothing. She was leaving the decision solely to Lilly. Years later, I had often wondered if it was this choice, this taste of freedom, which had led Lilly to her decision.

"I'll go with you."

***

Lilly came to live with me in my apartment in Eastern Ridge, a wealthy neighborhood near the center of the city. It was a large penthouse apartment paid for by the Corp. I would have preferred something less grandiose, but the Corp already had an image in mind for the superhero they hoped Lilly would become. Geminia was a particularly troubled city with a crime rate beyond that of cities twice its size. Even the "good" neighborhoods like Eastern Ridge were plagued by criminals, and few dared to walk the streets alone at night. The city needed help, and the Corp thought it would be best to have something flashy, a superhero with a strong community presence who could be a model for the citizens.

Lilly had other intentions, but her real resistance would not manifest until much later.

I had her begin meditating, but it seemed to be too similar to her prayers and did little in helping her control her levitating. I had to switch tactics—nothing was as easy or as straightforward as the Corp had made it seem in training. Superpowers were pretty predictable, easy to manage, but people were not so simple.

"This is stupid," Lilly said when I made her stand on a board resting two feet above the carpet in our living room. I'd propped it up by putting a cinder block under each end.

"The biggest problem with your power is that it doesn't work when you're afraid. It would be more beneficial if it did precisely the opposite."

She walked slowly across the narrow beam, one foot in front of the other. I held out my hands as if to catch her if she fell.

"So, I'm practicing my balance? I don't see how that's going to help."

Had I complained so much when I was her age? Yes, I probably had.

As she came up beside me, I suddenly gave her a hearty shove.

She gasped and fell sideways off the board, landing with a thump on the carpet.

"Hey, what was that for?" she asked, brushing her hair out of her face.

"I'm going to push you off, and you're going to try and levitate to keep yourself from falling."

"But I won't be afraid if I know you're going to push me."

I helped her get back on the board. "You're going to try and stay on. It's like a game."

She smiled and turned to face me.

I tried pushing her off again, avoiding her hands as she flailed in an attempt to keep me away. It didn't take me long to push her off again. She rose, rubbing the hip she'd landed on, and returned to the board.

"Bend your knees this time," I instructed her. "Try and avoid me by moving sideways away from me."

"That's not fair, you're stronger than me."

"Lots of people are stronger than you, little girl; you can't let that stop you."

This time, she stayed on much longer. Once or twice, she managed to avoid a harsh landing by levitating, but it seemed more of a fluke than an act of will. We practiced this exercise often and, slowly, she improved.

Along with this, I had her studying law and philosophy. I had to instill in her a strong ethical code. The Corp believed diversity was good and that not all heroes should have the same ethics. We allowed them, to a degree, to decide what was good and bad and what boundaries existed between the two. We couldn't allow them to be systematic about it and think that every case could be found in a textbook. They had to develop the ability to judge situations quickly and on a case-by-case basis.

Luckily, Lilly took to her lessons quickly, with a kind of ferocious dedication that reminded me of myself when I was still training. At first, she was obsessed with knowing my opinion on everything, but I tried my best not to impart my own biases on her. She realized this and soon found ways of catching me off guard, questioning me while we watched television together or were out getting groceries rather than when we were studying so that I was not so careful with my words. I felt these slip-ups to be my own failings, despite the intended manipulation on her part. I wanted to be perfect, like my own mentors. I think I may have been trying too hard back then to be a man older, and wiser, than I was—the man Lilly saw me as.

"I'm not naive, Mr. Taitt," Lilly told me once. "I want to know what you think because you've studied these things longer than me, but I know if I'm to be a real superhero that I'll have to find my own conclusions."

After that, I stopped withholding my views, and we often debated long into the night about what was or was not just.

I was her primary adviser (what the Corp called a handler) but not her sole mentor. Agent B, whom Lilly referred to as Aunt B when she wasn't present, came weekly to train her in martial arts.

Gunner, an ex-detective, created elaborate puzzles for her to solve which often took her all over the city.

Mrs. Mod from the Corp's Health Department was the only one Lilly, and I, disliked. She came monthly, bringing her needles, and charts, and cold hands, preforming tests even I was not privy too. She made Lilly strip behind a sheet set up in the living room, despite my suggestion of using her bedroom. I always found myself wanting to leave the apartment for the sake of her privacy while at the same time paranoid about leaving her alone with the unsettling woman. I took to making an elaborate tea with various ingredients which kept me busy in the kitchen until she was finished.

One night after a visit from Agent B, Lilly bid me goodnight quite earlier than normal. Chalking it up to a particularly tiring exercise, I initially thought nothing of it. But Lilly had always been a creature of habit, and this was unlike her. My curiosity grew too much for me and I went to her room. When she didn't respond to my knocking, I went in. Her room was empty, but then I noticed her window open and my heart leapt.

I ran to it and saw her hovering just outside, eyes closed as she concentrated. I said nothing, not wanting to startle her. She was levitating twelve stories above the street.

Eventually, she opened her eyes and looked right at me. She wavered and fell, shrieking as she hurtled toward the ground.

"Lilly!" I shouted, leaning recklessly out the window. My stomach lurched.

Lilly floated back up, looking embarrassed. "It's okay, Mr. Taitt, I've got it."

I put a hand to my chest, gasping for air as I reached out to help her back inside.

With her feet safely on the ground, I shut the window and then pulled her to me in a hug.

She laughed. "I'm fine, Mr. Taitt. I can control it now. Soon, I'll be a superhero."

***

It was years later that Lilly got her first taste of crime. I had taken her to jails to see the types of people she'd be putting away. We started walking the streets at night in dark coats. At first, only I was armed. Then, after a lot of practice at a firing range, I bought her a pair of handguns. In later years, she took to carrying four. And after she'd nearly met her match with a villain capable of manipulating bullets with his mind, she'd added blades to her arsenal.

It only took a year before she insisted on going out alone. Despite the weapons, she always tried her best to stop crimes without death. In two years, she'd nearly scrubbed the streets clean of the scum that had once clogged it. It took two more years after that for me to stop worrying so much when she went out. I was thirty-two then, and the Corp was pushing me to take on another assignment. I was hesitant; I'd been with Lilly for seven years and, because she was an orphan, I was her only family. But at the same time, I was excited to have a new hero to work with, new problems to solve. I told myself I waited just a little longer for Lilly's sake, but looking back, it was me who couldn't let go.

The day of Lilly's nineteenth birthday, she'd come home early. Around three in the morning, I heard the sound of her feet sprinting across the roof just before she threw herself off the building and plunged through the balcony door, which I kept open for her.

She landed in a squat and threw off her black hood. Against the wishes of the Corp, who'd wanted a bright colorful costume, she wore only black. Over a tank top, she wore a thin sweater with two cat-like black ears sticking up from the top. She wore a mask (also against the wishes of the Corp, who'd wanted a known face and public identity) that was nothing more than an orange strip of fabric with black stripes and two holes for her hazel eyes. I never knew if it was the mask or her fierceness that had made the papers dub her the Tiger of Geminia.

She'd removed her mask, and I could see the worry in her face.

"What's wrong?" I asked, setting aside the book I'd been reading to keep myself awake.

"Bank robbery," she said, slumping down on to the couch beside me, resting her feet on the coffee table. "I heard it on the radio. Robbery in progress. But when I got there, all the perps were tied up."

I frowned. "Someone else had stopped the robbery?"

"That's what it looks like."

The incident was peculiar, but with no evidence of who had done it, there was little to do about it and it was soon forgotten. Until two weeks later, when it was repeated. This time, it was a break and enter. The third time, it was a hostage situation at a school.

The fourth time, Lilly came back, returning again through the balcony doors, with the long stem of a flower grasped in her fingers. It was a lily, a tiger lily.

It became the calling card of the person who seemed to want to help her catch criminals. One day, months later, it arrived with a note.

"He wants to meet me," Lilly informed me.

"I don't think that's a good idea."

"Why not?" She seemed crestfallen.

"Lilly, you have no idea who this person is. What if he means you harm?"

"He's fighting crime, Taitt; he's no villain."

"There's little difference between a hero and a villain."

She rolled her eyes. "I'll be careful."

There was nothing I could do to dissuade her—so I followed her.

Hopping from rooftop to rooftop, she was impossible to track in the city, but I listened to the police radio and was lucky enough to be close by when a call came in for domestic abuse in a condo on the twentieth floor of a building in the West Side. I reluctantly got in the elevator and was surprised to see there were only nineteen floors. I sighed, pressing the button for the roof.

It was empty when I got there. The ledges were lined with garden boxes filled with exotic plants. There was an arbor strung with lights that looked like tiny lanterns. I quickly ducked beside the rooftop entrance, hidden in shadow.

A moment later, a dark figure flipped over the side of the roof—he'd climbed straight up the side like a human gecko. He wore a mask like Lilly's, but it was straight black, blue eyes peeking out from the eyeholes. His blond hair was nearly yellow in the light of the lamps. He wore a white shirt under a black vest and black pants but had on a short cape, which he pulled around himself quickly before sitting on a garden box out of the light. He was nearly invisible.

Lilly jumped down a moment later from the top of the roof entrance. I held my breath, waiting for her to look back with an accusing glare, but she walked forward under the arbor. She hadn't seen me.

She had seen the man though, turning toward him right away, which impressed me and evidently disappointed him.

"You missed my entrance," he said with a coy smile on his lips.

"I'm sure it was dramatic," Lilly said, staying a safe distance away from him. "Do you have a name, stranger?"

"Do you?"

"I believe you know it."

He shrugged and stood from the garden box, pulling out a beautiful tiger lily. He wore black fingerless gloves and his fingertips were badly callused. He offered her the flower.

"Why are you stopping crimes?" Lilly asked, not moving to take it.

"I'm a hero; it's what I do."

"This is my city."

"You don't appreciate the help?"

"I do; however, I think it would be more beneficial if we worked together rather than racing to crime scenes."

"I hoped we might be able to arrange something like that," he said and stepped closer to the light, still holding the flower.

He seemed younger than I had assumed he'd be, perhaps a few years younger than Lilly.

I saw a smile creep onto her face, and she stepped forward, taking the flower.

"I think I would like that."

***

In the past, when superheroes were left to their own devices, they would often team up and create large groups. The thought was that with a wide variety of powers, there was no crime they couldn't stop. This worked for a while, but the honeymoon was always brief.

Too many personalities, too many ethical codes, made for frequent disagreements and schisms which often left cities marred by the disgruntled superheroes who abandoned them.

When the Corp was still in its infancy, they'd tried creating such a group, grooming them to hold very similar ethics and complementary powers. Great lengths were taken to make sure no heroic toes were stepped on. Still, it failed. Going forward, thoughts of superhero teams were abandoned and even discouraged.

So, when news of the Tiger and a new mysterious hero hit the headlines, it didn't take long for the Corp to contact me.

Dear Mr. Taitt, the letter said, *the latest reports from Geminia cause us anxiety. As you are aware, the working together of superheroes has been proved disadvantageous. We strongly suggest that you deter your charge from further behavior of this sort.*

We look forward to your cooperation.

I sighed and set the letter on my desk, picking up instead a document showing the statistical crime rate of Geminia. It was at an all-time low and had shot past our neighboring cities. Geminia had no need for a superhero, let alone two.

I dug out the stack of city crime files from my desk drawer. The Corp always kept their records as up-to-date as possible, and we got a new shipment on a quarterly basis. I'd just finished separating the cities with the most alarming crime rates when Lilly came home.

She used the door to our apartment this time, and I set the files aside as I heard her key in the door and laughter in the hall. She stepped in, carrying a large pink stuffed frog, and Marcus walked in after her. I had a hard time not thinking of him as a puppy—all big eyes and blond hair and following Lilly everywhere she went.

"Hey, Taitt," he said to me. "You look like you know how to have a good time." He nodded toward the papers on my desk.

"I'm working," I replied.

"Yeah, I know that…" He coughed and looked at Lilly.

"I'll see you tomorrow," she said, giving him the dismissal he was so obviously begging for.

He took her hand in his and kissed the back of it. He always did that, like he thought he was a knight or something.

Lilly flashed him a smile before shutting the door behind him and kicking off her boots, which were spotless— she didn't like her feet touching the ground and always stayed at least half an inch above it.

With crime so low, Lilly had taken to spending her nights experiencing the city in ways she'd never got to as a youth. I was reminded then that she was only capable of such excursions because of her rebellious decision to keep her identity a secret. I had always been quietly happy with that choice, but now her rebellious nature worried me—and not only because I found her boyfriend to be a bit of a goof.

Her smile faded quickly as she looked to me again. She crawled into the armchair by my desk, hugging her carnival winnings to her chest in a pose that made me forget she was nearly twenty.

"Did he win that for you?"

"*He* has a name," she said.

Marcus. I'd known his name and had met him on a number of occasions, but not saying his name, ignoring his relation to her, made my life a little less complicated. It wasn't that I didn't like him—he reminded me a bit of myself when I was his age. Of course, that's probably what worried me.

"Lilly, listen. I…" I trailed off as she snatched the Corp's letter from my desk. Her eyes flickered over the words.

"They want to separate us?" she said, putting aside the frog.

"Superhero teams often end in tragedy. You know this, Lilly. We studied such cases in the textbooks. I can refer you to the sections—"

She stood, balling up the letter and throwing it to the ground. "I am not a child, and I am not a textbook. I am nineteen years old and I will make my own decisions."

I laughed despite myself, and she accused me with her eyes. "You have always made your own decisions, Lilly. I am but a humble adviser." I made my tone more serious. "But the Corp is not, and though it is in their best interest to keep their distance from heroes and their handlers, they will step in if they feel things have gone far enough amiss."

I could tell this distressed her, and she began pacing around the living room. Eventually, she buried her face in her hands.

"What am I supposed to do?" she said into her palms.

I went to her, putting an arm around her shoulders. "Lilly, it might not be so bad to let him go. It would be for the good of your city."

"Our city," she said, wiping her eyes. "This is his home too."

I nodded. My words to her were the most rational answer I had to offer. It was undoubtedly the best choice to tell Marcus he had to go find some other city to take care of. He was a homegrown hero. No handler. Not under the direct supervision of the Corp.

I knew what was best, but I went to sleep early that night anyway. I left my desk a mess with the city stats I'd been examining, which was out of character for me. I told myself that I had been tired and stressed, but in my heart, I knew I left those things out in the hopes that Lilly would look at them.

She did. She no doubt saw that Geminia was in outstanding shape and that there were many other cities that could use the help of a superhero—or two. I could have chosen a particularly bad off city and left its statistics alone on my desk, but I left them all out so that the next morning when I found her room empty and her things gone and had to call the Corp to report her AWOL, I told them with complete honesty I had not the slightest inclination where she had gone.

The Corp was rightfully upset but knew Lilly had always been something of a troubled assignment, and after grumbling about it for a few months, they gave me another charge.

***

Over the years, I had many heroes in training in my care. One could crush solid stone between his palms and another had powers of regeneration. There was a boy with an unhealthy fascination with fire I convinced the Corp to take a chance on and a young woman who was my only loss: a villain. Even now, she still writes from time to time, always signing off: *With love, from your mistake.*

And in my own small act of rebellion, I respond.

For a long while, I hoped to wake one morning to a story in the papers about the Tiger fighting crime with her partner in some other city, but such news never came. Nor any letters.

It wasn't until nine years later that I heard from her. It was a late-night phone call.

"Hello?" I said sleepily.

"Taitt, it's me." There was a pause. "Lilly."

I could hear her take a shaky breath. "Are you alright, little girl?"

She laughed, but it was hollow. "I'm trying to be strong, Taitt." She sighed. "Meet me at Geminia Central Hospital tomorrow morning."

"I can meet you now. Are you hurt?"

"No. I just need to think and get some rest." She hung up.

I stayed awake the rest of the night, sitting at my desk, waiting for morning.

***

I stumble out of the silver-walled elevator and release the breath I'd held from the ground floor. The walls of the hospital are sterile and smell of disinfectant and "scent-free" fabric softer.

I push through the doors marked M8. The maternity ward.

I watch the numbers on the doors as I pass and quickly find hers. It's across from a nurses' station currently manned by a short woman who reminds me of the nun at Lilly's orphanage, though with much less enthusiasm. I nod to her, pointing to the door. She nods back and I go in.

There's Lilly lying on the cot, propped up with a mountain of pillows. She's cut her dark hair short, black ringlets restrained with a headband of black fabric. She's lost some of her sickly complexion and her cheeks contain a pink hue I've never seen before.

In her arms is a small, pink baby. It yawns and rests lazily on her chest.

Lilly looks up at me and smiles. "Mr. Taitt. I'm sorry I haven't kept in touch. I didn't think the Corp would like that very much."

"You wouldn't be the first of my charges I've kept in touch with to the displeasure of the Corp. But I am glad you've reached out to me now. I am honored to get to see your dear child." I hesitated. "May I hold her?"

Lilly nods and I remove my damp coat, abandoning it on a chair, and take the infant from her arms.

"His name is Justine," she says.

As I hold the little boy, I notice how much he resembles Marcus. The man's absence troubles me, but Lilly doesn't give me the opportunity to ask about it.

"He's dead. We were working out of Marie Port together, but he's been working alone for months because I've been pregnant. There was a call about a burning building. He never came home and they dug his body out of the rubble a few days later."

"I'm sorry—"

"It was the Corp, Taitt."

I believe her. "The Corp will know you've come back, Lilly."

She nods and I can see tears welling up in her eyes. "I don't know what to do, Taitt. I didn't have anywhere else to go."

I hand her son back to her and get out my phone. "I'm going to make a phone call. I may know somewhere you can stay. You won't like it, but it's only temporary."

I go out in the hallway to make the call—knowing full well that it may mean I never see Lilly again.

***

I spend the next few months in an anxious stupor. The Corp harasses me almost daily with phone calls, emails, angry notes slipped under the door when I refuse to answer. I tell them, honestly, that I don't know where she is.

Yes, I saw her at the hospital.

Yes, she blamed the Corp for Marcus's death.

Yes, she was mad about it—furious, actually.

No, I have no idea if her baby has superpowers.

On this last point, they are particularly curious. Eventually, they realize I know nothing, and they relent.

I receive notification of my impending retirement—the third one I've received—and for a third time, I get it revoked, pleading my case to the Corp, and am permitted a few more years of service.

I decide I can't prove the Corp murdered Marcus and also that I'm ninety-nine percent certain they did. But I figure I can do more good training heroes than I can getting revenge.

Eventually, a letter comes.

Dearest Taitt,

I'm well and up to no good. I received the package you sent, safe and sound, and although its chatter is nearly as unbearable as your own, I have done my best to make sure it's comfortable. I'll have you know we are not the best of roommates, but at least we have our dislike of the Corp in common—and you, of course.

With love, your mistake.

p.s. The brat can already levitate.

Enclosed with the letter was a pressed tiger lily.

I slip the flower between the pages of a thick textbook and burn the letter.

As I watch it go up in smoke, I wonder if I should be counting Lilly as another failure. The Corp certainly did.

I smile as the flames consume the paper and decide that next time I get that notification of retirement, I'll accept it and use my freedom to train just one more superhero: a tiger cub.

Childhood's Last Nemesis

Kristy Perkins

Shelley Marchant wondered what life was like for people who didn't have archnemeses. She came to the conclusion that being Glow Kid always seemed like a better idea when she wasn't facing down an egotistical germophile who had just escaped from prison.

Again.

The Plague Queen laughed maniacally as she raised a hand that glowed with squalid power. The lurid green light made the cramped alley look like a gateway to the underworld, complete with a twisted metal ladder and the detritus of forlorn human life.

"Duck!" Davy leaped in front of Shelley, his bright blue costume a blur.

Shelley bit back a retort and ducked behind a dumpster. The blast of green energy shot overhead, ricocheting off the brick walls to end up harmless in a garbage can. Even the Plague Queen's power couldn't make that cesspool of an alley any worse. The residue from the blast made everything glow as the acid decomposed.

"Remind me why two sidekicks are handling this?" Davy wheezed, his tweenage haircut covering his eyes. "Even if you are a graduating senior."

"Because," Shelley huffed, raising a can lid to block the second blast. It knocked her back a few feet. "She's a nuisance, and everyone else is busy." Maybe a little more than a nuisance, but that last part was true. Somehow, fighting germy pseudo-royalty always fell to Shelley, even though she was a teenager, and there had to be someone better equipped to deal with it. But Plague Queen was obsessive and Shelley had enhanced healing that gave her a slight advantage. Still, college wouldn't be any easier.

Davy squeaked as he rolled out of the way of the next shot and crashed into a trash can. Shelley groaned. The kid had no awareness of his surroundings. At least Plague Queen didn't seem interested in pressing the advantage.

There was a lull between blasts, so Shelley jumped to the nearby ladder. Plague Queen was ready, and sprayed goo in a targeted stream. Shelley dropped back to the ground. As soon as the green goop made contact with the wall, she scrambled up the ladder and pulled herself onto the fire escape. She nearly stabbed her own foot on a jagged metal pole, and even though she would have healed in seconds, it would have hurt.

The Plague Queen snarled, her eyes glowing green. "Why don't you just die already, Glow Kid!" She raised her sword high.

Davy made a noise of disgust in the background. He hated being ignored. Shelley didn't care.

"Do you even know how to use that thing?" Shelley smirked and gestured at the sword.

The woman in the alley rolled her eyes, but she did shift her handhold to something a bit more stable. "I will annihilate you, of course. I've given you more than enough time to petition for mercy, and…"

They were up to the monologuing stage of the fight already? Shelley pulled back into the shadows and sat back on her heels. Finally, a moment to breathe. She tugged a bottle of water out of her utility belt and took a sip. The cut on her arm was itching its way to healing, and the burbling acid in the street was finally fading. Meanwhile, the royal pain in the alley below was pacing back and forth, in full speech-mode.

"…my clear superiority in battle. For a teenager you put up an exemplary fight, but even you must comprehend…"

The Plague Queen was an eloquent grandstander. Shelley had passed high school English with straight As thanks to the years of wordy monologues. She tightened her ponytail and re-clipped her bangs out of her face. The shadows on the roof made it hard to see Shelley in her black uniform. Even the green stripe down the side was cast into darkness.

"…even the indomitable Lightning Lady will bow before my magnificent…"

The woman did have a certain image she liked to portray. Her unkempt brown hair was held in place by a glowing green crown that threatened to mesmerize if Shelley wasn't careful. Which Shelley always was. The black bustier was a new touch. Not a flattering look with all those spiky edges. Over the last decade of fighting, "Her Majesty" had gone through a number of looks. Only a few of the changes were prompted by practicality, and the most recent alterations were definitely the influence of prison buddies.

"…should dwindle and perish in the face of my prodigious…"

Shelley adjusted her mask and checked her utility belt. She'd been too distracted to stock up on marbles after the lunchtime battle, so she was going to have to wing this. She eyed her tagalong. Davy was still down, flopped to the concrete, not even a hint of fire apparent. Worrisome, but Shelley would just have to trust he would get back up again, like she always had herself.

"…down here and challenge me, you craven imbecile!"

Oops. That was annoyance. The villainess hated it when Shelley missed the end of her prepared speeches. It didn't matter if no one else was even there to hear it, so long as Shelley acknowledged it. "Sure thing, Royal Diarrhea," she shouted, and stabbed her left hand down on the spike.

Shooting pains went up her arm but her hand itself was numb. No time to be subtle. Bright red blood oozed out of the wound, coating the spike. She pulled it out with her right hand and threw. The spike landed a few feet away from Plague Queen and rolled a half-hearted three inches closer.

"Missed me!" Plague Queen taunted.

Shelley smirked in spite of the throbbing in her hand. Her nemesis always fell for that one. They'd been fighting for years, on and off, and somehow she never remembered that Shelley's powers worked just as well from a distance as up close.

The blood on the spike sizzled, and the chemical reaction came to its explosive conclusion. Shelley snickered as Plague Queen was knocked down. Davy leaped up in time to catch the woman with nullifying handcuffs before she could blink. So predictable, even the junior probationary sidekick of a sidekick could defeat her.

Shelley was going to miss her predictability.

She sighed and then leaped down to ground level. Hit the ground hard, though. Ignoring the damage to her knees in favor of her image, she sauntered over like it hadn't done anything to her at all. Her healing would handle it soon enough anyway. "Hey, Maya. How's it going?"

The Plague Queen, aka Maya Remis, scowled up at Shelley from under smudged mascara. "It's still insulting you don't bother with my formally chosen name. At least I have the dignity to use your codename."

"I bet they haven't even cleaned out your cell from the escape," Shelley said cheerfully. "That'll make things easier when you move back in."

Maya snorted. "Yes, because I didn't have anything better to do with my evening than go back to that rat hole.

Besides, I'm fresh out of prison. It's traditional to cause a little chaos."

"First, it's already past ten, and we both know the only chaos you had planned was to steal someone's Netflix and catch up on whatever TV shows you missed when you were in solitary. And—" Shelley did some quick and only peripherally related calculations in her head. "Crap."

Davy's head snapped up. "Did more people escape from prison?"

"No." Shelley tugged at her mask. "I just officially missed Sondra's graduation party."

"Graduation party?" Maya perked up.

Shelley closed her eyes. That was careless. Maya knew her first name and age, but definitely had no idea who her friends and family were. Details got people killed, damn it.

Fortunately, Maya was distracted by one of her pet peeves. "Of course you're only just barely graduating high school. I still can't believe those cretins allowed you to start your hero career when you were eight. I didn't start work as a criminal until I was old enough to pretend I could vote!"

Six years ago, Maya had figured out how old Shelley was, and they'd already been nemeses on and off for three years. She'd actually stopped a fight mid-blow and lectured the assembled heroes on child endangerment. Kind of hypocritical considering the source of a fair amount of that danger, and that Maya herself had been a teenager when they started fighting.

Maya cackled. Shelley lunged, heart in her throat, but it was too late. Maya was gone in a toxic haze. Shelley snarled at the empty air. Davy looked glumly at the ruined remains of the suppression cuffs. He hadn't secured them properly. The slip gave Shelley serious potential for ulcers if she thought about it, but she pushed it down. Davy would learn.

He'd have to, if she decided to give up superheroing.

"Look, Flame," she said, putting a careful emphasis on his codename after her earlier slip, "if you want to take over my route when I'm gone, you need to know this stuff backward and forward, like knowing when a suspect can generate bacteria that eats through metal. You didn't know how to handle Princess Bacteria back there, and that's not the worst thing, but Lightning Lady can't always handle it. This is why major superheroes like her have sidekicks like us. You need to be able to step up and handle the details."

Shelley wanted to keep going, give the kid a lecture he wouldn't forget, but it was late. She huffed a breath and stared up at the night sky. No stars. "Go on. Time to go home. We're not getting her tonight, and you have a swim meet."

Davy nodded, mumbled some kind of response, then slunk off into the night. He was exhausted, and Mrs. Valdez was no pushover coach. Shelley sighed and rubbed at her face, which just smeared blood all over before she caught herself. She flexed her hand. Her healing factor never caught up as fast as she would like. Ten minutes later, the wound had at least closed, but taking down the mugger on Eighth Street was painful.

It was midnight before she finished her route, but that was normal. Her parents didn't even look up from the TV when she stumbled in the front door, coat covering her costume and mask stowed in a pocket. For the sake of peace, it was best for Shelley to pretend she'd had a civilian evening. That didn't mean they weren't aware of exactly what she'd been doing.

"Hey, sweetie. How was the party?" Mom asked. Shelley happened to know she was using the same calm tone she used when interrogating supervillains. If it wasn't for the faint blue corona around Mom's hands, it might have worked. The pale light gave away the power use to those who knew to look.

Shelley rolled her shoulders, irritated but determined to act casual. "Fine. It wasn't really my kind of thing, so I came home when it started getting crazy."

Dad gave her a look. He always knew when she was lying, thanks to his super-senses. It was kind of wasted on Shelley, though, because she didn't lie about anything interesting. She would tell them she was having coffee with friends when she was really at the library all afternoon, or she would say she was on a date when she was really covering for another sidekick. Her parents were obsessed with her having *the typical teenage experience*, which was their way of saying she needed friends who couldn't destroy office buildings.

Ironic, considering it was their DNA and their friends who'd gotten Shelley into this business.

Dad didn't call her on the lie this time, though. Shelley grinned. She grabbed a sandwich from the fridge and slunk upstairs to her room. After a quick scrub to get the blood off, it was time for the post-patrol phone check. Possibly her least favorite thing ever, with all the people she'd been ignoring demanding immediate attention all at once. One message in particular had her staring at her phone, biting into her sandwich morosely.

That party was supposed to prove that she could handle a civilian life and schedule. More than that, it was a last hurrah before everything changed, one way or another. And Shelley had missed it.

Even though it was just a voicemail, she pasted a sickly-sweet smile on her face as the phone rang. "Hey, Sondra, it's Shelley. So sorry I missed your party. I caught this nasty bug and didn't want to infect anyone. If you're up for it, I can take you for coffee tomorrow. Well, technically it'll be Jack taking you because I can't afford so much as a muffin right now, but I promise I will make it up to you! Please text me and let me know you don't hate me. Bye!" Her face was sore by the end of the message, and belatedly, she realized she probably should have made the effort to actually sound sick. Shelley really needed sleep.

Next was a quick text exchange with Jack, who sent a lot of grumbling emojis about how his girlfriend was so careless with his money. She snapped back that he could afford it and he owed her for the mess with Plague Queen, since his father was the supposed super-genius who had built the prison she kept escaping from. That made it kind of his fault.

And then she rattled off a check-in to an hour-old text from Rachel Meech, aka Lightning Lady, aka Shelley's mentor, who was justifiably concerned over the fact that Shelley wasn't answering her phone after the recent supervillain jailbreak. The woman hated leaving Shelley on her own for any kind of mission, even a simple patrol, but Rachel was just too busy. Shelley made sure to emphasize no one got hurt, so the woman wouldn't get any more overprotective, and included a promise to write a full report in the morning. Shelley yawned. It was too late for all the usual post-patrol stuff.

With that finished, she had officially freed up the rest of her evening to meditate. Her mother called it brooding.

Her parents were thrilled she was going away to college. They never really wanted Shelley to follow in their footsteps, but there was only so much you could do with a kid who developed powers at age six. Letting her become a sidekick was their way of controlling how close she got to the world of superheroing. Leaving for college would put all that on hold and possibly derail it forever.

Most of the other people she knew thought college was a bad idea, whether they knew about her nightly career or not. They told her she'd miss everyone, or she'd hate meeting new people. Then they'd remind her that she hadn't even chosen a degree, or that her grades weren't that good. And then they would mutter something about other people not having the options she did, which brought Shelley's ire up just thinking about it.

But if she didn't go to college, that left only one option.

Being a sidekick was getting old, but she wasn't sure she wanted to commit to being a full-fledged hero. She'd need to seriously up her training, develop a day job, and push her powers to the breaking point. She snorted. Because that sounded so appealing. But not doing at least something with her abilities was equally unimaginable.

Rachel had an opinion, of course, which would have been the case even if she wasn't Shelley's mentor. She always had an opinion about this kind of thing. She was the kind of manically cheerful person who assumed everyone would be so much happier if they just lived their lives exactly like her. In this case, her opinion was that Shelley was an essential part of the city's superhero movement, and leaving would upset the delicate ecosystem that was the balance between heroes and villains.

A duck quacked, and quacked, and quacked. Right. New ringtone.

Shelley blearily checked her phone, holding it over her head as she stuffed the last of the sandwich in her mouth. There was an alert stating "the villainess known as Plague Queen has been spotted downtown." There was more after that, but the words blurred together. It was safe to assume something was under attack, probably a coffee shop. Reporters were ridiculous, but even they wouldn't bother if she was just sitting at a table nonchalantly.

Shelley stared at the ceiling. She needed to stay in, look at some of those college leaflets. It was after the due date for most of them, but Mom would definitely use her powers if it meant getting Shelley into something normal. But that only worked if she decided she actually wanted to go.

What she needed was sleep. Shelley yawned broadly. She ought to leave well enough alone and get some sleep, but there were some jobs you just didn't leave half done. She was on her feet and strapping on her utility belt before the yawn had properly finished. Someone needed to stop Maya.

Davy, baby-faced freshman that he was, got left behind because Shelley didn't presently have the brainpower needed to come up with an excuse for his parents. She called Jack instead, the loyal boyfriend and was rewarded with… nothing. He didn't answer. She flicked his picture and headed downstairs.

She almost made it out the door, but her mom stepped out from the kitchen just as Shelley put a hand on the doorknob. The raised eyebrow was quite clear in indicating a request for information.

Shelley shrugged. "I got invited to an after-party. It's not a big deal, just some people from school. There shouldn't be beer or anything, but if there is, I promise I'll say no." She grinned.

Mom sighed. "Just be careful. These…parties, can get rough."

"I know." Shelley gave her a quick hug. "I'll be good. Love you!"

She darted out the door before it became too tempting for her mom to stop her.

***

Plague Queen was not the kind of villain to spend months planning the perfect heist or spend more than five minutes making a plan. As such, she got caught a lot. She also narrowly evaded capture a lot and piggybacked on other escape plans a lot. It made Shelley's schedule a nightmare, but at least she didn't have to spend hours outthinking her opponent's every move. Instagram was a girl's best friend when it came to tracking villain sightings. It was less dangerous for Shelley to go after the woman on her own than it would be if it was any other villain because if it was a trap, it was hastily laid. The most likely scenarios were an attempt at grandstanding or just mayhem with the aim to draw things into a duel.

Shelley found her enemy exactly where she expected: the balcony of a building that just happened to be across from a coffee shop. Just trendy enough to be a great place to spread a virus across the city, and high up. Maya loved high places for battles. They had better vantage points to share her wonderful speeches to the masses when she was so inclined.

Shelley climbed onto the roof, jumped down, and landed next to Maya. The woman twitched, but didn't stop staring out into space.

"Please tell me you're not waiting for the TV crews to show up." Shelley sighed loudly. She flipped the rock she'd grabbed from the roof in her hand.

"I can always just pursue you to wherever you go to college and harass you there. Until you capitulate, of course." Maya snarled and threw out a hand. The wall behind Shelley seethed with florescent germs.

Three feet away and still a miss. Honestly, it was embarrassing to witness. Shelley smirked and leaned against the railing. "Joke's on you, because I don't even know where I'm going to college."

Maya froze mid-flourish. "Please, tell me you at least applied." She shook her head, looking like a disapproving parent. Then she spun in a circle and hurled a ring of vomitous orange fluid in all directions.

Shelley leaped, twisted, landed, and threw. The rock coated in her blood erupted into flames. Maya dodged, and the fight was on.

And on, and on, and on. Maya thrust with her shiny new blades, and Shelley didn't have anything to throw so she twisted back. She kicked at Maya's wrist. Maya slipped aside, and they fell into a pattern of strike and evade. Exhausting, but something she could do by sheer muscle memory which left plenty of time to think. Why hadn't she restocked on marbles when she was at home? There were a whole handful, right in her desk drawer.

And why was it so hard to fight Maya tonight? Normally, Shelley put her down after the first exchange of banter. Now it was the second time in one night they'd fought, and it was taking ten minutes.

Shelley misjudged a leap. Her foot slipped and she went down, banging her head hard enough to make her ears ring while Maya laughed. The world was fuzzy, but not concussion fuzzy. She pushed to her feet.

Plague Queen punched her, and Shelley tumbled over the balcony railing. She grabbed blindly, and was saved by the ubiquitous window washer's platform that was always there when needed. Sort of.

The rusty screws in the winches let go with a shriek, and Shelley kept right on falling. It took long enough she calculated the likelihood of ending up with broken bones. A high estimate, even with her healing and knowing how to land.

All the estimates in the world didn't stop her wanting to scream from the heart-stopping, time-freezing drop.

She slammed into the top of a blessedly plastic dumpster, and skidded off onto the hard ground. When she hit the cement, there was nothing but the jagged, blinding pain of a broken collarbone. And the observation of a faint clump of stars barely visible through the city haze.

Because it wasn't enough to just feel the pain, she groaned. "Owww."

Maya reached the ground a few minutes later, without plummeting and thus without the pain involved in Shelley's approach. Those skirts of hers probably made it hard to navigate stairs. She leaned over Shelley, blocking the view of the stars. "While part of me wants this battle to continue for all time, it's much easier for me to take over this city if you die right here."

"Do you ever wonder why we're doing this?" Shelley said dazedly. Her bones throbbed as they began to knit back together.

"No." Maya visibly shook off the question. "I'm doing this so I can finally get rid of you and be done with this ridiculous battle."

That was a lie, but Shelley was in too much pain to figure out why. "I know people who will kill you if you kill me."

Maya laughed. "I'm not going to kill you. Murder draws too much attention, unless it's done at the right moment." She raised her arm high, poisoned blade gleaming in the fuzzy yellow streetlights. She had never used swords before her last stint in prison.

Something rocketed overhead, silver and gleaming, to land on the opposite side of the street. The hero known as Steel Comet stood tall and proud, the arm of his exosuit raised and ready to fire. Shelley could almost see a hint of a genuine Jack smirk in his stance. Maya made a noise of frustration and darted away, billowing black cloak hiding her in the shadows.

Shelley rolled onto her stomach and tried to push to her feet. Jack was there in two seconds to help her aching muscles do their job. They'd done this before, even before they'd started dating. She knew to let go of pride and let him help her, and he knew better than to offer sympathy for any injuries. She was healing, and fussing wouldn't make it go any faster.

Jack still hovered. "We should get ice cream. I get the hero discount at a shop not too far from here because I saved the owner's daughter. We can make a date of it." He retracted one of the suit gloves and held her hand properly. The sensation of his thumb rubbing the back of her hand was pleasant enough to jar her out of pain-related introspection.

"Is my mask still on?" she asked blearily.

He winced. "Yeah, but I'd get in trouble if I dragged you in looking like that. I'll get it, you wait here." He leaned her against the wall and darted out into the night.

Shelley almost yelled for him to come back, but after the fight, ice cream sounded appealing, so she let herself relax against the wall. Besides, he got so cute when he tried to be a good boyfriend. He worried he wasn't good enough for her, so he made weird little gestures like ice cream when she was beat half to hell.

Jack was generically attractive. Not handsome enough to stand out, but enough that he took a decent picture. It was hard to tell his ethnicity, even though Shelley knew he was three-quarters Hispanic. Honestly, his generic appearance made him a more appealing boyfriend. He was smart and rich, and if he was also super hot Shelley wouldn't stand a chance. He insisted otherwise when it came up, but she knew her limitations, and Jack's. She wouldn't be his type if he had the full trifecta of shallow high school appeal. As it was, only six of the girls in their class had tried to steal him away.

Her breathing stuttered. For all her musing about where her life was going, Shelley hadn't considered how Jack might fit in. How long could their relationship last? What would happen once the pressures of adult life overtook their teenage pocket of bliss?

"Chocolate?" Jack grinned at her, waving the blessed ice cream in front of her exhausted eyes.

She accepted the cone gratefully and gulped it down. Hot flashes tore through her as her collarbone mended, and the hairline fracture in her foot felt like bees crawling. The ice cream helped.

"You're thinking about the future, right?" Jack asked after Shelley settled back against the wall.

"How can you tell?" She tugged at her mask.

"Because you're always thinking about the future lately. Like your mom says, you brood. It's not always the healthiest approach."

Not him too. Shelley snorted. Everyone was telling her to make up her mind, but they never gave her the time to actually do it. "I don't have time for a lecture about how I spend my free time. I have a villain to stop."

She pushed off the wall and marched into the night, ignoring the twinges that reminded her she wasn't completely healed yet. At least the itching had stopped.

Jack's metal suit rasped as he trotted after her. "What? What did I say?"

"Nothing. You said nothing." She kept walking, stiff and stilted. "It's just that—" She hissed a breath through her teeth. "I don't know what I want to do next, and it's all confusing and no one is helpful and I don't even know who I am now!"

"You're the Glow Kid," Jack said, catching up to her increasingly rapid pace. He grabbed her arm and forced her to slow down. "You're the best sidekick in the whole city, and not just because you work with Lightning Lady. Because you're awesome, babe." He kissed her cheek, the edge of his faceplate scratching her ear.

"And you are a cheeseball."

"Yup."

Shelley reached out and squeezed his uncovered hand. "I always hated that codename. Has nothing to do with my powers or me. Just an extension of Lightning Lady, like I'm not anything without her."

Jack turned his hand until he held Shelley's more firmly. "So do what you planned way back at the beginning of senior year, before you got weird about this. Go to college, take a few years' break from saving the world, and come back and be a brand new hero. You barely use your powers as Glow Kid, so people might not even make the connection."

She stopped walking. "But is it actually me planning it, or is it just what I think everyone wants?"

Jack laughed and slung an arm around her shoulders. "Shell-bell, no one makes you do anything. They might think they're controlling you, but you're really just doing what you want. The second guessing is all you."

He leaned in for a real kiss. She obliged him, settling into the familiar feel of his arms, even if he was in the suit and the elbow joint pinched her. Besides, his kissing skills made up for any pinches.

"Now, go save the city from that hack." He grinned at her.

Shelley rolled her eyes, but she matched his smile. "You're coming with me, super-suit."

***

"Pay attention to me!" Maya shrieked as the news copter darted away. Her voice was shrill enough to be heard easily in the street below. By the alerts on Shelley's phone, that was the third helicopter to note Maya's location and then fly away to find more interesting villains. Shelley looked up and sighed. Again with the rooftops and the climbing. At least finding Maya was easy. Now it was time for a showdown.

Jack flew ahead and found a perch behind a water tank on the building next door, under strict orders to observe unless action was absolutely necessary. There were, after all, rules to this kind of thing. This was Shelley's nemesis, so it had to be her fight.

Shelley stolidly climbed her third fire escape of the evening to get to Maya's chosen arena. The villainess must have exhausted her prepared speeches because the instant

Shelley's head popped over the edge of the building, she shot off a blast of poisonous green gel.

Shelley ducked as more gel blasted overhead. She flipped up over the parapet and dashed to the industrial air conditioner. It was getting to be a late night. Her phone said it was past four in the morning, and Shelley was starting to feel the tiny flutter in her chest that meant she was exhausted. At the rate she was forced to heal, she was already going to sleep until four in the afternoon. And of course, she still hadn't stocked up on marbles, so this wasn't going to be easy anyway.

She tugged at the edge of her mask. "Please, just surrender, so I can go home already!" She chanced a look around the edge of the air conditioner.

Maya blasted orange goo at her. It didn't look or smell quite like the usual toxins, but Shelley still wasn't going to lick it and test it out. She ducked back behind cover. Maya just kept blasting sloppy orange whatever-it-was in Shelley's general direction. She didn't even hit the air conditioner. The liquid slopped everywhere, gurgling and glugging, and it made Shelley twitchy. She vaulted over the blockade and onto the lone dry patch on the roof.

Plague Queen smirked and raised her fists. Lightning shot out from her gauntlets, and the orange stuff was vaporized, filling the air with a noxious gas. Smelled like burning rubber. A numb sensation flooded Shelley's system, starting from her skin and working inward.

Shelley cursed. Complete paralysis in two seconds.

Maya picked up a brick and threw it. It hit Shelley's ribs hard enough to bruise, and it made her inflexible muscles wobble. She fell and landed on her wrist hard enough the bone snapping was audible. The scream was muffled by the paralysis.

Jack yelled and shot a plasma blast over Maya's head. She wheeled around, cape swirling, and shot off a wrist rocket. Since when did she have access to that kind of tech? It was distinctly irritating.

The rocket smashed squarely into Jack's chest armor.

Jack fell from his perch and hit the rooftop with a crash. No. No, no, no, no. Shelley's heartbeat pounded in her ears, but it didn't change the fact that she couldn't even move a pinky yet. Maya circled her hand and a wave of poisonous gas spread across the whole rooftop. Shelley choked and gasped. She willed her burning lungs to keep working, for just a little longer. The adrenaline and the poison were enough to get her healing factor into high gear, and pinprick pain spread across her body as the paralysis faded by force.

The poison cloud dissipated, but not because Maya was done. Because she was laughing. Shelley rolled over and used shaky muscles to push herself upright. This wasn't right. She wasn't going to let her final battle end like this.

She couldn't help sneaking a glance at the unmoving silver armor. Jack wasn't getting up, but that didn't mean anything. His dad kept messing with the safety protocols in the suit, which meant sometimes it completely immobilized him because playing dead was supposedly safer. Either that or he really was dead, or injured, and it didn't matter because in any of the options there was nothing Shelley could do for him. She pulled in a shaky breath and forced herself to even out before she hyperventilated. Cradling her injured arm, Shelley maneuvered until she was between Plague Queen and Jack. Her healing would protect her from attacks that would kill him. Probably.

"I'm not letting you win," she said, throat hoarse from the gas.

Maya just stood there, smirking, her cape swirling around her dramatically, thanks to the air conditioner backwash.

"Why are you doing all this?" Shelley raised an impatient finger, trying not to clench her jaw shut. "And I'm not talking about general motivations or whatever stupid plan you've come up with to once again bring the city to its knees." She blinked. "Actually, I am talking about that. It's a good starting point. What is your plan?"

Maya shrugged. "A simple one. Generate a nasty virus, use various dispersal techniques to spread it across the city, then sell the cure to the highest bidder. The usual." She raised a vial of blue liquid. "I've already got the antidote formula ready."

"Right." Shelley tugged at her mask, needing the reminder it hadn't fallen off. "You could have delivered the virus any time this evening. You could have picked some crowded restaurant or a mall somewhere, but instead you waited for me to find you on an out-of-the-way rooftop. Why? What do you want from me, since you clearly don't care about your grand plan actually working?"

Maya blinked, and then she smiled. Shelley would swear the woman's teeth oozed. "I wondered if you would notice. I did have every intention of simply escaping, but then I found out what you were really doing tonight."

It was Shelley's turn to blink.

Maya scoffed. "I spent years fighting you, molding you as the perfect adversary, making sure that I would be your first great enemy on your path to becoming a superhero. And you were just going to end this, without even telling me. I could have come up with something impressive, catastrophic even, but instead you were content to leave on such a dull note." Her eyes glittered. "I wasn't. So I did this."

"Sorry I didn't tell you," Shelley snapped. "I've had a lot on my mind, and finding the appropriate ending to our fight wasn't really a priority." She waved her hands in the air helplessly.

Plague Queen threw a shuriken. Since when did she use throwing stars? Stupid prison buddies. Shelley fell to the ground, yanking the blade out of her arm with a tiny squeal of pain. Not fun.

Maya stalked closer. "You're leaving. I wanted to say goodbye, and to make something very clear. There is no way out of this life. Not for you, not for me, not for all those hapless little people who cower below. Just you and me, and a lot of pain, for all eternity." Maya smiled. Her crown glinted in the moonlight. "I'll wound you, perhaps even kill you, and you'll heal again and again, and we'll fight this fight for all eternity. Maybe someday you'll finally get someone to make one of those little bombs that will put me down for good."

Huh.

She didn't know.

All this time, and Maya hadn't figured out Shelley's power. Healing was just a side effect that kept her alive while her blood did its work. After all the information Shelley had accidentally let slip, she couldn't help the smug smile.

Shelley kept quiet and watched blood seep slowly out of her wounds and drip to the ground. It changed to a cool forest green and inched closer and closer to Maya's feet. The instant her blood was out of her body, Shelley could change it, remaking the proteins and DNA and even the very molecules until it was the chemical she needed it to be.

Boom.

Not a big boom. Just enough to destroy Maya's concentration. The woman fell back, stumbling and tripping over her cape hem. Shelley shifted into a ready stance, her mind finally clear.

She threw her weight behind the first punch. Maya countered, but her nostrils flared. Shelley followed up, keeping Maya on the defensive, focused on the fight at hand rather than creating a virus. Maya flailed. Only a few of her punches made it past Shelley's guard. The woman was already panting for breath, and all Shelley had to do was wait for the right moment. Maya kept backing away.

Shelley lashed out. The cuffs caught Maya's wrists and locked into place. Two seconds later they were active, glowing a faint blue. It didn't matter how nasty a virus was if you didn't have access to the powers that let you cook it up. Maya still charged.

Shelley hit the button on her wrist console just as Maya crashed into her. The momentum carried the woman over Shelley's head. She watched as the magnets in the bindings dragged Plague Queen right across the rooftop and stuck her to the nice large metal air conditioner.

Maya squawked in outrage. Shelley took a moment to breathe, to let her pounding heart settle down and her taut nerves relax. She was sore and still a little paralyzed, but the fight was clearly over. Maya couldn't get her legs under her enough to support her, so she was forced on her knees. Besides, you didn't twist your spine like a candy cane unless you didn't have a choice. Those spikes in the bustier did not look comfortable. Shelley got to her feet and sauntered over.

"Here's what's going to happen, Plague Queen."

Maya straightened up awkwardly at the use of her preferred moniker.

Shelley stabbed a finger at her. "You're going to go back to prison, and you're either going to stay there for about a decade or else you're going to get used to kids like Flame being the ones to put you down, and I'm not interrupting my college education to stop you every time you have a hissy fit."

"A decade!" Maya's jaw tightened. "You're an ignorant child, but you're not that stupid. I'm not leaving you alone just to get a hero career started."

"Good for you. It's not for a career. I'll be in college." Shelley took a step back. Maya's viruses didn't really affect her, but sometimes she was a carrier if she wasn't careful.

Maya's eyes went vague and her lips moved. Her mouth dropped open. "Oh, god, you're getting a medical degree. I'm going to be miserable."

Shelley smirked. "Yep. I'm hoping you'll get so bored you'll give up crime. Failing that, just know that I am going to come back someday, and when I do you'll regret it." She tilted her head to one side, and her smile got bigger. Maya's look couldn't be more horrified. "You didn't think I was going to be a sidekick forever, did you? When I come back, I'm a full-fledged superhero. And I will beat you, once and for all. So I would start looking for a new career in the interim, unless you want to find your way into obscurity as my most pathetic bad guy. My childhood villain, with your place alongside the monsters under the bed."

As Maya spluttered and fumed, trapped in her bonds, Shelley fell back into her favorite pastime, which was contemplation, not the brooding her parents accused her of.

Maya wasn't going away. She was too entrenched, too set in her ways. She didn't see choices. Shelley did, and a swell of pity informed her decision. She would leave, come back, and there would be Plague Queen, waiting. Maybe she would up her strategy game, learn how to use her new weapons better, and become more of a threat. Maybe she would stagnate even more, and Shelley would be forced to end her permanently. Either way, Maya wasn't going to move on.

Shelley hid the sad thought with arms crossed over her chest and a wry smirk.

Sirens were audible in the distance, and Jack was stumbling to his feet. He gave her a quick salute and blasted off, heading to their usual post-fight meeting spot. Shelley's heart throbbed in her chest and tears of relief gathered at the corners of her eyes.

But enough of that. Shelley tapped a button on her wristband and left a release key on the rooftop for the police to find, well out of Maya's reach. Time for her favorite part.

She stepped up onto the parapet. "By the way, when I get back, I'm not going by Glow Kid anymore. It's Hemorrhage. I'll see you when I've got my doctorate." Shelley smirked and did a backflip over the edge.

It was a bit higher than she remembered. Shelley hit the ground harder than necessary, and couldn't even swear or Maya might hear. She slipped into the shadows of the nearest alleyway before the sirens were close enough to make her ears ring. They could clean it up on their own, and she was too tired to answer questions. She'd done enough explaining that night.

Once she was in the alley, she took a few minutes to massage her legs. The landing was murder on her knees, but it was such a cool exit. The move had potential as a signature move, when she took up her superhero mantle one day. She had plans to make, pros and cons to consider now she knew what she was doing.

Shelley Marchant waved an unseen goodbye to her archnemesis, and then she got on with her life.

I Choose

Renée Harvey

I stare at the smashed cookie jar in front of me, a pink and red and green kitty shattered with broken cookies all over the kitchen floor. All I wanted was one sweet, chewy, chocolate chip cookie, and it's not that hard to climb onto the counter to get it. I put the lid back and everything.

And then bumped it on my way back down.

Mommy said "no cookies". She won't be happy. Maybe I can hide the pieces?

I stretch my hands out, instinctively reaching for the part of me that lets me make things disappear, and some of the broken pieces start to go away.

The kitchen door squeaks behind me. I hear Mommy gasp. It's too late. Trembling, I close my eyes, forgetting about my hiding ability, and expecting the worst.

"Child," Mommy says, her voice strangely calm. "What happened?"

Clenching my hands by my sides, I don't say anything. I can't.

"You wanted a cookie, didn't you?"

Tears leak out of my eyes, and I feel Mommy turn me around and pull me close. She's not mad. This is the worst thing I've ever done, and she's not yelling.

I cry. My shoulders shake. Big fat tears roll down my cheeks and into her shoulder, but Mommy holds me tight.

When I begin to hiccup, she wipes my wet face. "You know what you did was wrong," she says, her blue eyes very serious.

I nod. I'll never touch another cookie jar again.

"I mean about using your talent to hide the mess."

I stare at the pieces around us with shaky breaths.

She sighs and picks me up, then carries me to the sofa. My favorite superhero book is laying on the cushion. Snuggling me close, she holds the book while I turn the pages.

"My child," she says softly, drying a stray tear.

"Mm?"

"You see these guys?"

"That's Patriot and Thunder."

"That's right." She smiles. "And you see these guys?"

I wrinkle my nose. "That's Red Face and Orb."

She chuckles. "They all have pretty cool superpowers, huh?"

Patriot is super strong, and Thunder makes storms. Red Face has lots of cool tools, and Orb has an army. They're all really smart. I grin, glancing to her before turning the page.

She points to a picture in the middle. "You see how while Patriot and Thunder use their talents to save the day, Red Face and Orb have to be stopped?"

I nod, and she catches my eye. Her blue eyes are gentler now, but still serious.

"Just like you, they learned as children to make good choices, but do you see how they each chose differently?" She rubs my cheek, and I turn to the next page. It's Patriot declaring victory over Red Face.

"One day," Mommy says. "You're going to have to decide whether you'll be a hero or a villain, too."

***

The school lunch bell rings, and I stuff my notebook and Metal Man pen in my backpack before joining my friends, Chris and Taylor, in the crazy long line trailing out of our middle school's cafeteria.

"It's beef olé today," Chris tells me with a grin. A bunch of classmates walk by, and I see the stuffed taco bowl on the tray by the canned peaches and thin blonde brownie. The smell of cheddar cheese and greasy meat lingers.

Taylor pretends to gag. "More like barf olé."

I wrinkle my nose, grateful Taylor hasn't actually replaced the taco filling with vomit this time. "That's gross, Taylor."

"Will you ever just bring your own food so we don't have to listen to you threaten ours?" Chris asks, scooting up the line. Taylor laughs.

Inching forward, we collect our milk and filled trays, and settle at our picnic table in the middle of the room with our classmates chattering around us, their conversations a dull roar and easy to tune out.

"You took the geography test this morning, right?" Chris asks.

Taylor nods with a fork already buried in the lettuce/cheese/beef mess. "Super easy, if you've been paying attention in class. I know I aced it, and the bonus questions at the end were a breeze."

The test involves filling in a blank map of Europe with all the country names, and I'm taking it last class of the day. Instinctively, I mentally run through the countries' list: *Iceland, Norway, Sweden, Denmark, UK, Ireland—wait, Finland's in there, too...*

Chris picks at the peaches. "What were those bonus questions? Multiple choice again, right?"

Taylor swallows a bite of taco. "Mm-hm. Culture questions, just like last time."

Spearing a peach, Chris asks, "Which countries were they about?"

A sudden curiosity fills me, so strong I feel like I can't survive the next few hours before I take the test myself. Taylor will tell us. Taylor's a good friend. Taylor would never make us—

Wait.

I mentally push against the curiosity with a frown toward Chris. Hadn't the lesson about cheating been learned last time? I open my milk carton. "Come on, Chris. You've been to class same as us."

The influence fades away as Chris scowls. "Yeah, but you know how important my grades are to my parents. If I get another ninety-five, they'll make me quit the drama club."

Taylor scoffs. "And my parents pay me a dollar for every grade over ninety on my report card."

"Are they really still trying to compare you to your rich uncle?" I ask, then down half the milk carton.

Chris stiffens, freezing with a peach stuck on the end of the fork.

"What'd he do now?" Taylor asks.

Chris's voice drops almost too low to hear in this room. "He paid off his vacation home in Spain on top of bailing out my dad's plumbing business again."

And without the good grades, Chris will never get into an Ivy League school to compete with Rich Uncle Owen's natural ability to collect money. What would it hurt to just give Chris the answers to the culture questions? Is it my place to stop Taylor from telling? If Taylor were to write them down, I could hide the paper.

These thoughts are mine; I don't feel Chris's influence now. I chew my lip.

"But, Mommy, how will I know what choice is right?"

"You'll know by what happens at the end, my child. Does the choice bring harm to yourself and others, or does it make you and those around you happy?"

Taylor's already reaching for a notebook and fountain pen. "Let me write them down in case Mrs. Eagle-Ears is listening."

I feel the tickling curiosity creep over me again and have to stop myself from leaning over the table to see the answers.

"Taylor, stop." I face Chris. "You know all the countries and where they go, right?"

Slowly, Chris nods.

"Then you'll do just fine on the test. Those culture questions are bonus, anyway."

Chris's gaze narrows. My throat constricts as my face heats up from the betrayed feelings washing over me.

"Come on," Taylor argues. "It's just the one test."

If Taylor gives in to this test, Chris will insist on every other one for the rest of the year. I pull my geography book out of my bag; it has the study guide tucked into the pages. "We can go over it together."

Chris drops the fork back to the tray and gets up.

"Where are you…" My words trail off as Chris's glare deepens. Betrayal has become fierce, hot anger. Chris is going away, that's where.

I watch Chris stride across the cafeteria and return the tray, the hard plastic slapping against the metal counter audible even where we are in the crowded room, and then my friend disappears out the door. Is this going to make us happy?

Taylor's very quiet, and I go back to picking at my food, unable to focus on my book, and not really hungry anymore.

"You're right," Taylor murmurs, giving me a repentant grin before diving back into the beef olé.

***

"Carmen's throwing a senior grad party Friday night," Taylor says, jumping in front of me. "Did you hear? Are you going?"

I wince, glancing to the clock above the principal's office as I walk by. Two minutes to get to History and that final presentation on the rise of the superhero in conjunction with World War II. "I haven't decided. Last party I had time for was your birthday last the summer."

Taylor grips my shoulder. "Then you have to come. I've heard Carmen's parties are awesome."

"I don't know." Mom has plans for Saturday before the ceremony at one, and I still have to remember what's not written on my notecards for this history project.

"Hey," Taylor says, stopping outside the math room. "I'll pick you up at nine."

I nod as I continue down the hall, and slip into my desk right before the bell rings. I've heard of Carmen's parties. All the cool kids go, but that's never been me. What if Taylor ends up hanging out with other people? What if I do something embarrassing?

I wonder if I can hide myself; I've never tried that before.

The teacher calls for the first victim presenter, and I ruefully grumble with the rest of the class. Carmen's party can come later.

Before I know it, it's Friday, and Taylor's honking outside my house. "You ready?"

"Ready or not," I reply, and as we pull up to Carmen's estate, the setting sun gleams off the full-length windows.

Inside, the living room bigger than my kitchen, family room, and garage combined, the bass thumps with contemporary music, and my class dances on the imported rug with soda cans and pretzels in hand. I eye the food table decorated with a "Congratulations, Class!" tablecloth and laden with snacks. I'll start there with Taylor and see what happens.

As it turns out, the music is awesome, the party is fun, and time passes like a dream.

"Look what we've got!" A couple of jocks push their way through the crowded room to the table with more soda boxes. That would taste awesome, as the last disappeared about half an hour ago. Several people around me cheer in reply, and I work my way back to the table, adding my own whoop as I reach for the boxes being ripped open. The *click-hiss* of cans popping fills the room, momentarily overwhelming the bass, and a thick smell permeates the air.

I freeze as I eye the closest box. That's not soda. It's beer. I look around, and, except for Mark, who got held back in second grade, my classmates are eighteen at the most. We could get in trouble for this. Big time. It only takes a second for me to make the boxes disappear, my mental command for them to fade so strong that I don't have to do more than stare at them. Several of my classmates grasp empty air where the cans used to be.

"Hey, where'd they go?"

"Aw, no fair!"

My heart starts beating fast as several sets of eyes turn to me.

"Give them back," one of the jocks demands, flexing his muscles.

I shake my head, but my brain refuses to obey, and the cans reappear on the table. Cheers sound around me, but I'm shaking. I back away, closing my eyes, and willing myself to be invisible just as the cans had been.

Taylor's laughing with a group of classmates by one of the support columns, and I manage to only step on three toes and bump one soda cup on my way over. The owners complain, but I ignore them for the moment.

"Hey, can we leave?" I ask, wanting Taylor to see me, but only managing to make myself visible enough that I feel like I'm still hiding under a hoodie.

Taylor takes a moment to focus on me. "What's the matter? I can hardly see you."

I open my mouth to explain, but Sasha wanders over with some beer cans in hand. I can't focus clearly enough to make them disappear.

"Who wants some?" Sasha asks, waving one of the cans. "Flynn's on the way to get more."

Along with the others, Taylor reaches for Sasha's offerings, but I'm just solid enough to push the hand away. Both of us know better. "I have an early morning tomorrow, and you probably do, too. Can we go now, please?"

"Come on," Taylor complains. "Let's just stay for a few more minutes. It won't hurt anything." The group gives me know-it-all smirks, and I want to fade again. Don't they remember how last year three of the kids went out drinking the night before graduation and got in a huge wreck? One of them was still in the hospital for the ceremony, and the other two were loopy, bandaged messes.

I make myself fully visible, my face burning up so bad. "No. We need to go now. Please." I hope I don't have to say anything else. Luckily, Taylor follows me to the car. We climb in, and I secure my seatbelt as the engine rumbles to life.

As we drive up the crazy long driveway, I stare into the darkness, wondering if I need to do something else about this. I can't rat out the entire class right before graduation, can I? Not without admitting I'd been there myself. Mom would freak if she knew.

Still, shouldn't I tell someone?

"Mommy, what do heroes do?"

"They help people, my child. They love their family and neighbors, and they are friends to strangers."

I finger Orb's picture. Orb has friends and a family, but he's mean to them. "What does a villain do?"

Mommy looks very sad. "Villains are selfish. They do things that end up hurting others because they care more about themselves than the people around them."

I trace Green Machine's profile etched into my phone cover. "Should we stop by the police station on the way home?"

Taylor gives a sharp laugh. "About that party? Are you kidding? They'll be fine." The gravel in front of my house crunches under the tires as we come to a stop. "See you tomorrow at the ceremony."

"See you."

The next day, I find a bleary-eyed Taylor fumbling with the red graduation gown as we're lining up.

"Didn't you go home after you dropped me off?" I mutter, helping to get the zipper unstuck from the fabric.

Taylor pulls the zipper up with a cocky grin. "Nope. Went back to Carmen's. You should've come. It was a blast!"

The band starts playing "Pomp and Circumstance" before I can think of a reply, and I follow the rest of my class through the ceremony in the gym.

The principal hands out the last of the diplomas then turns back to the audience with a piece of paper in hand. "Also graduating today, but unable to be with us, are Sasha Breezly, Travis Sommers, Flynn Newdell, and Eva Kritzopoli. They were admitted to Memorial Hospital last night with crash-related injuries."

Sasha and Flynn...they were at the party last night. A glance to Taylor reveals a suddenly solemn expression on my friend's face, and that's not the only one in the stilled room. I swallow and look to the four empty chairs amid my classmates.

I should've said something. I should've done something more.

***

A college Saturday means the weekly morning grocery trip before attacking a mountain of homework in the afternoon. Gotta love this life. Glancing in my handbasket, I see I've got enough ham and cheese to survive the zombie apocalypse, so I'll grab a jar of peanut butter and a couple loaves of bread before heading back to the dorms. Morgan said I need to study for my next Communications test before our date tonight. My turn to cover the movie tickets, and Morgan's for the popcorn. It's tempting to sneak in a couple sodas, but Morgan's right; the theater employees have to get their paychecks somehow.

From the bread aisle, I hear a child's whimper, and turn the corner to find a red-faced, pig-tailed little girl with tears streaming down her cheeks as she stands beside the jams and jellies. The rest of the aisle is vacant, and I don't remember passing anyone on the way over. There's no one else around her. She's lost.

"It's ok," I say, kneeling down a pace away so I don't scare her. "Are you trying to find your parents?"

She gives me a wet, wary look before turning away, and my heart pounds as I worry about her running off and becoming impossible to find, or worse, becoming one of those kids on the "lost" posters hanging by the restrooms. This store isn't that big. Her parents can't be that far away. "Come on, I'll help you find them." I beckon for her to follow me back out of the aisle to where she'll be more visible. "Do you see them?" I ask her, and she hesitantly follows me, keeping her little fists clenched tight by her sides.

"Molly!" a woman shouts from the freezer section at the other end of the store and abandons a shopping cart by a couple attendants as she runs toward us. The little girl sobs harder as the woman sweeps her up, holds her tight, and whispers soothing words.

I back up, glad the little girl found her mother, and seeing nothing else for me to do. I need bread and—

The mother's stern features stop me. She's glaring a scathing, vicious look probably reserved for the creepers and addicts that put the "lost" wall in existence. I swallow hard and walk away.

"Mommy, my superpower's not that big. I can't change the world like Patriot."

***

Morgan grins my way with a challenge in those bright brown eyes as we leave the furniture store, and I hear keys jangle.

"No, my turn!" I shout, and we race across the parking lot like a couple kids at a playground. I tug my keys out of my pocket as I run, fumbling the three for the right one, and push Morgan's hand out of the way to get my key in the sedan's lock first.

"No fair!" Morgan complains as we hear the door unlock.

I grin back. "I win."

With rolled eyes and false exasperation, Morgan slides into the passenger seat. We just bought our first sofa together and are headed back to our sparse-for-now apartment to meet the furniture guys when they show up. The sun is bright and the roads are clear. I flip the turn signal on the way out of the parking lot, wait for the cars to pass, and turn onto the three-lane road as Morgan cranks up the music. "Immortals" is on, and we belt out the chorus together, laughing when I miss the repeat. Green light ahead, stale, but I can make it, and my foot presses a little harder on the gas pedal as we reach the intersection.

There's a metallic squeal.

With a jerk, I'm thrown into my door. My hands fly off the steering wheel, flailing as the airbag bursts open.

The sky spins.

Metal crunches.

Tires screech.

And then it's all over.

My stomach rises to my throat, and I swallow it back down.

There is a dead calm, save for a hiss, mostly drowned out by my shallow heartbeat pounding in my ears.

I blink. The world is tilted, and the sunlight's too bright.

My seatbelt. I think I can unbuckle it.

My door. I think I can open it.

My hands fumble for the lever, quaking and tingly. The door swings open.

I fall to the asphalt. It's sharp on my palms and knees. I hear my own breathing. The sunlight gleaming off my new wedding band stings.

Morgan. Is Morgan okay?

And the other car. Where did they come from?

My legs are like jelly; I can't stand—my arms are barely holding me up as I kneel here on the street.

Nope; falling.

My elbows give way, and my chin smacks the pavement. My head suddenly feels like someone's reaching into my skull and squeezing my brain.

I have to reach Morgan. The car didn't hit my side.

Crawling, one painful inch at a time, I make my way around the front and blink against the sunlight. Our passenger side is all smashed in. A medium green truck is crunched into Morgan's door. There's glass everywhere. There's a woman shouting from inside the truck.

"Didn't you see the red light?" she screams, poking her head out the window. "My child is sitting back here!"

A red? I don't remember a red. It was green. I'm sure of it.

But what if she's right? What if I just caused this whole wreck, destroyed two vehicles, and did who knows what to Morgan and this lady's family? I can't have done all that. I want to fade, to disappear, and maybe the lady will forget what I look like.

There are sirens in the background. The police, the fire department, the ambulance.

Morgan.

Morgan has medical allergies. I have to tell the paramedics.

Still, what if all this was my fault? Is there some way I can make this go away?

Mommy brushes my cheek. "My child, your ability to turn things invisible is just a tool. You have a power that's even better, and with it, you can save the world."

"A better power, Mommy?"

Mommy nods with a little smile.

"What is it?"

"The power to choose."

Tires crunch on the pavement around me. Authoritative voices start shouting orders to pull the cars apart, to watch out for injuries, to block off the road. My fault or not, I can't hide anything about this. What's done is done, and Morgan needs help.

"Are you okay?" a paramedic asks as he stoops down beside me. "What happened?"

I point to the car. "Morgan needs help, and there's a child in the truck—"

"The others are helping them," the paramedic says. "Let's get you to the ambulance. Can you walk?"

I can with help. The paramedic sits me on the ground and presses an ice pack to my head.

"Get some morphine for this one," another paramedic commands as his companion wheels a gurney up to the ambulance. The vehicles have been pulled away from each other, and Morgan's door is hanging open. The woman from the truck is still screaming, but now it's at the paramedic reaching into the back of her vehicle.

I look back to the gurney. Morgan's lying there, slightly elevated, but with a bandaged arm, bruised face, and neck in a brace. The paramedic is filling a syringe with something clear.

"Is that morphine?" I ask as loud as I can, a hand outstretched to make it disappear if I have to. My voice sounds hoarse, and it feels like I'm talking around a frog just to form the words. The paramedic turns to talk to someone else, vial and syringe still in hand. She sets the vial on the gurney and lifts Morgan's arm.

"No!" In an instant, I hide the vial, separating the molecules so far apart, she has nothing physical to hold on to. She whirls around; her gaze settles on me, hand still outstretched.

"Did you do that?" she protests. "Where's the medicine?"

"It's morphine," I croak. "Morgan's allergic to morphine."

Understanding crosses her face, and her gaze falls to where Morgan's allergy bracelet rests below the bandages. I put the medicine back in her hand. Morgan will be fine. The paramedics know what to do now. I glance back to the wreck scene, and a sinking feeling settles in my stomach. Guilty or not, I'd like to hide. With the cost of the vehicles and the medical bills that insurance won't cover, this is going to take a long time to pay for.

I look between Patriot and Red Face.

I look between Thunder and Orb.

I look back to Mommy's wise blue eyes.

"Mommy, I'm going to be a hero."

Mommy smiles and hugs me tight. "Yes, my child. You are."

A police officer kneels beside me. "The woman who owns the truck says you ran a red light. Care to elaborate?"

"I remember the light being green," I answer, holding the ice pack tight to my head.

The officer cringes. "Are you sure?"

The doubts swirl within my aching head, but I'm not going to hide. I may not be like Thunder or Patriot— powerful enough to defeat armies!—but I will still do what's right.

"It was a stale green. I know it was."

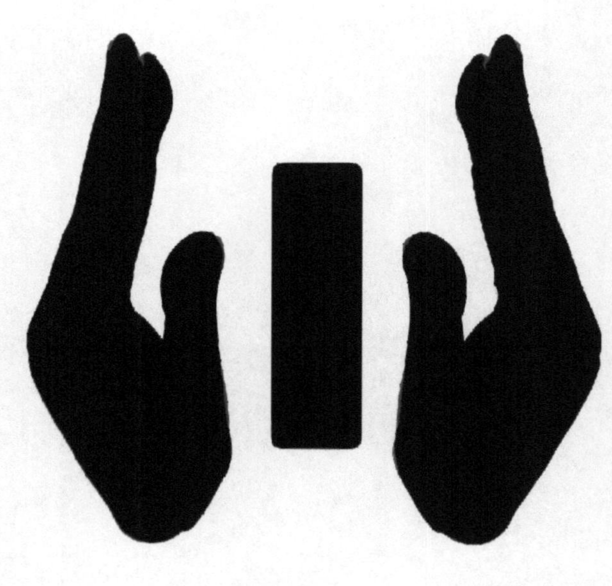

In a Breath

Heather Hayden

Voices hummed nearby, their words muffled by the thick layer of water between Rosemary and the surface. She let her body sink lower into the pond's dark depths. Blackwell Pond was normally a secluded area, perfect for swimming at any time of day—or night, as it happened to be.

The gills on Rosemary's neck fluttered as she drew in another breath of cold water and pressed it through them. It wouldn't be the first time a pair of lovers had stumbled upon the little clearing. She could almost picture the scene—a young couple, perhaps already drunk on alcohol and love and moonlight, wandering through the woods. It was dark tonight, only stars and a crescent moon for light, just enough to make the fairybells' white petals glow.

Irritation made Rosemary's skin itch. Or maybe that was her skin itself—she was getting close to another shedding season, when the tiny scales that coated her neck, arms, and chest started peeling off in sheets to reveal new, tender scales beneath. She gritted her teeth, refusing to scratch. Too much motion might stir the waters, and she wanted to give the impression of the pond being dead and empty. Lovers rarely ventured into the water, preferring to lie in the soft bed of flowers and moss and wish upon the stars.

She'd imagined bringing Will here, before...

Rosemary sucked in a deeper breath this time. Her lungs hurt, as they always did when she used her gills for a long time. She didn't need fresh air, but she longed for it. *Please just go away*, she thought at the people on the shore. *Find some other clearing. This one's* mine.

The voices grew louder despite the wall of water between her and the speakers. Sometimes, she wished she didn't have the ability to hear things underwater. The tone was too sharp to be friendly—were they having a lovers' spat? Rosemary dug her fingers into the soft muck at the bottom of the pond, distracting herself from thoughts of Will... *No, don't think about him.*

No need to think about anything. There was the water, and there was her. Pond and girl. *Focus on the water. Let it wash everything away. Forget about it all—*

SPLASH.

Something struck the surface of the pond and plunged downward, almost too quickly for Rosemary to dodge. She swam away, letting the waves assist her movement. No need for anyone to notice her presence. *Maybe they'll go away when they realize how cold the water is. Or maybe I should go up there, give them a fright.* She grinned at the thought, imagining how startled they'd be. Water-breathers like her weren't uncommon in the area, but most people wouldn't expect one to be swimming around a secluded pond on a cool spring night.

More shouts penetrated her thoughts. She was closer to the surface now, making it easier to identify the voices. Both male—and counting the person in the water, that made three people at least in the clearing. A party of some sort? Rosemary held back a groan. *I might be stuck here for a while.*

Words filtered through the water, warped but recognizable. "What if someone finds the body?"

Rosemary's heart skipped a beat. *Body?*

"Who's going to find it all the way out here? Let's go."

A chill crept through Rosemary's body. Her attention shifted to the person who had—she thought—jumped into the water. There was movement from that direction still, but not the friendly disturbance of swimming. More a violent thrashing, as though someone was fighting for their life.

Rosemary took a breath of water. Then another. The struggling was getting slower, and the shouting had stopped. But there was no way to know for sure they'd left. She had a mental image of her parents discovering her body next to this one. *This is none of my business. I'm only sixteen. I shouldn't…*

Some superheroes started when they were sixteen, part of her whispered. *Or younger.*

Her legs moved almost of their own accord, sharp scissoring that took her across the pond to where the person was weakly struggling. Her hands swept over the body, which jerked away from her touch. Clothing. Skin. An arm. She followed it to tightly bound rope. No way to cut it; her knife was in her jacket, tucked under a bush. A rush of bubbles made her yank her head back. Whoever it was had just released their breath. They'd drown soon if she didn't act.

Grasping the person under their arms, Rosemary pushed off from the floor of the pond, kicking hard. Years of swimming had strengthened her muscles, and she had plenty of oxygen to feed them from her gills. Even the water aided her, pushing her forward rather than dragging her back. Her dive training instructor had been impressed with her abilities, even if they did exclude her from non-super competitions.

What if the men aren't gone yet? Anyone who dumped a bound, living human being into a pond wasn't going to hesitate to kill a high school girl.

They were leaving. She shook her head and broke the surface. Her lungs longed to suck air in greedily, but she kept her breaths shallow as she towed her burden to shore. The person had gone limp—whether from understanding she was trying to help, or worse, she wasn't sure. Rosemary's eyes roved across the clearing, seeking any sign of movement, but it was still. An owl hooted somewhere in the distance.

They were gone. *Whoever they were.*

Still, Rosemary was cautious as she walked across the small lip of sand, dragging the person onto solid ground. Only once they were both out of the water did she look down to assess the situation.

The victim was a young man, maybe college age, maybe a little older. His skin was pale, a stark contrast to the dark hair plastered over his eyes and cheeks. The clothing he wore was soaked, possibly ruined, given that it appeared to be a casual suit of some kind.

Rosemary took all of this in as she knelt beside him and checked for a pulse and any sign of breath. No pulse and no stirring of air near his mouth or nose.

"You're lucky I took CPR training last month," Rosemary muttered to him as she checked that his airway was clear. "Please don't die." *I might be your only chance.* As she started chest compressions, all her mother's warnings not to go swimming at night, not to forget her phone, hung heavy over her head. If he died because she couldn't call for help— no. *Focus, Rosemary. Compressions. Rescue breaths. Compressions. You can do this.*

Halfway through her second set of compressions, she felt him shudder. A racking cough shook his body, and he rolled over, hacking. Rosemary winced, scanning the clearing again, half-expecting gun-waving assassins to come running out of the trees.

The man's coughing lessened and became a wheezing breath. He started to struggle again.

"Hold on." Rosemary patted his shoulder. "I'll cut the ropes."

She fetched her jacket and pocketknife then started slashing at the bindings. The wet rope caught on the blade, and she hadn't sharpened the knife in some time. As she sawed away, the thought occurred to her that freeing him might not be a good idea. *You have no idea why he was being drowned in the first place. What if he's as bad as the people who put him there?*

Her movements slowed.

"Th-thank you," the man wheezed. "You saved my life."

A bad guy wouldn't say thank you, right? Rosemary finished cutting the rope around his wrists then moved to the binding around his ankles.

The man sat up as she sliced through the second rope. He was shivering now, and she draped her jacket around his shoulders.

"Can you walk?" She rubbed her neck. "It's a ways back to my house, but I can call an ambulance from there, or drive you to the hospital—"

He shook his head. "No! No hospital. I'll be fine." With some wobbling, he got to his feet, waving her back when she tried to assist. "You should go. I'll be fine."

"I don't think so. You could still have water in your lungs. You need to go to the hospital—"

"I'll. Be. Fine." Something dark flashed across his face, an expression that made Rosemary take a step back, then another. "It would be best if you forget you ever saw me." He tossed her the jacket—she caught it by reflex, clasping it to her chest. It was already warm from his body heat, and damp. Her fingers tightened around her knife. It wasn't much defense, but it was something.

With one last sharp look, he turned and walked away, moving with a brisk pace that did not fit a man who had almost drowned only minutes before. Rosemary swallowed. *He must be a super, too. How long would it have taken him to drown? And who were those people? Why did they…* She shuddered from a cold that wasn't entirely due to her wet bathing suit. *Don't think about it. Forget it.*

She turned to the pond. Its surface had already stilled, a pool of darkness in the silver-edged grass. Sand was churned on the shore where she had dragged him. Something glinted in the moonlight.

Frowning, Rosemary walked over and scooped up the small, cylindrical object. The metal casing was cold, almost chilly against her skin, and about the size of a lipstick case. A quick inspection revealed no opening, no seam, nothing that could explain its purpose. *What is it doing here? Did he drop it?*

The man had already vanished into the trees. Rosemary hesitated then tucked the cylinder into her jacket pocket. If he hadn't missed it, he might not return for it, and she hated seeing litter near the pond.

A cracking twig made her jump. She looked around, but nothing moved in the darkness. Shuddering, Rosemary shoved her damp, sandy feet into her sneakers and ran home.

She'd left the front door unlocked. After slipping in, she clicked the lock and deadbolt then sneaked upstairs to her room. There, she changed into dry clothes and went to bed. But it was a long time before she slept, and her dreams were filled with nightmares of dark water and gunshots.

The gunshots continued as she woke up, and Rosemary huddled in her blankets, half-asleep, until she realized the sounds were coming from the television. Of course, it was Saturday. Her dad was home and watching old Westerns. Which meant it was afternoon already. Half the day gone.

Yawning, she stumbled downstairs and grabbed a bagel from the breadbox. Her dad wouldn't stir from the couch until the movie was over.

"Rosemary!" Dad appeared in the kitchen door as if summoned by her thoughts, though that thankfully wasn't the case. Neither of her parents had powers. Still, so much for avoiding him.

"Afternoon," she mumbled around a bite of bagel. Her appetite started to shrivel away. *Is he going to ask me about their divorce again?*

The corners of his mouth turned down, and his blue eyes—the same shade as hers—held worry. "You slept in today. Were you out swimming again last night?"

Her parents had never expressly forbidden her from doing so, but they weren't fond of it, especially Dad. "...yes?"

"I don't want you going out again, not for the next few weeks." The finality in his tone was hard as rock.

"What?" Rosemary almost dropped her bagel. "Why?"

"There's a fugitive super who was last seen in the area. GG officers are searching for him now, but he's eluded capture so far. I don't want you going out alone, not even to the bus stop. If they haven't caught him by Monday, I'll drive you to school."

Global Government officers here? In Blackwell? Rosemary's eyes widened. "Why is he a fugitive?"

Dad shook his head, frown lines deepening. "All they're saying is that he's a super and extremely dangerous. They haven't even released what his powers are—maybe they don't know."

That wasn't too surprising, given how many supers existed unknown, either because they didn't use their powers or didn't know they had them. Rosemary had loved her gift since discovering it as a kid, but it wasn't particularly powerful. Some supers had much stronger powers, though, and plenty of them used those gifts for selfish reasons. However, they usually targeted the cities. Why would one have come to Blackwell, hours from the nearest metropolis?

Rosemary gulped and took a bite of bagel, trying not to let her hands shake. *What if the fugitive was one of the men at the pond last night? Should I tell Dad what happened?* He might ban her from visiting the pond ever again if she did. *No, they'll catch the fugitive. I'll just have to stay away from the pond for a while. After last night, that won't be hard.*

"Rosemary," Dad prompted. "I want you to promise not to go back to the pond for now."

She swallowed then nodded. "I promise."

"Thank you." He turned and headed for the door, then stopped and looked over his shoulder. "Have you given it any thought?" His expression grew hopeful then fell when she shook her head. "You need to come to a decision soon. Your mother's leaving next month."

"I know." Rosemary looked down at her bagel. "I haven't decided yet."

Her parents had decided that "to make things easier", they would offer her the choice of who to stay with after their divorce. She could split her time or spend it all with one parent. They had agreed not to pressure her on the specifics. But that didn't mean they were going to stop asking her to make a decision.

Dad sighed and rubbed his left temple. "Well, please let us know as soon as you do."

"I will," she said in a small voice, not meeting his gaze.

Another sigh followed him back to the living room. A moment later, the TV's sound turned up again.

Rosemary poured a glass of orange juice, her thoughts swirling as violently as the liquid. *Should I stay here, where everything is familiar, or go somewhere else where I can start a new life? One without...*

She slammed the fridge door shut, cutting off that thought, and went upstairs to get dressed and start her homework.

Before she got started on her essay, though, she did a quick search for information regarding the fugitive. The local news site had an announcement splashed across its main page.

DANGEROUS FUGITIVE SUPER LOOSE IN BLACKWELL AREA. ALL CITIZENS SHOULD USE EXTREME CAUTION AND AVOID TRAVELING ALONE.

There was a picture of the man as well. Rosemary's hands jerked to cover her mouth as she bit back a cry of shock.

It was the same man she had saved from drowning the night before.

Her fingers shaking, Rosemary clicked on the article to read more.

> *A dangerous super, known only by his alias "Biovibe," was last seen in the Blackwell area. Any information that might lead to his capture must be reported to the local police or the Global Government operatives directing the search for this fugitive. Anyone who lends him aid or hinders the investigation will be charged with treason against the Global Government and prosecuted to the fullest extent of the law.*

Rosemary clicked around the site but couldn't find anything more. *That's it?* Her eyebrows drew together, and she began browsing other news sites, looking for more information.

There was nothing. Which was odd, because all the other fugitive supers she could locate information on had either their true identities revealed, or at least some detail regarding their powers. Biovibe had nothing.

Maybe he has some rare power the GG is concerned about? Or maybe they really don't know what his ability is. Or who he is. Rosemary shuddered. *Some superhero I turned out to be. If the GG found out, would they really charge me with treason?* Brushing away that unsettling thought, she got up and went to her backpack to fetch some books she'd picked up for research. Her jacket had landed on top of it last night when she'd returned home.

As she drew her backpack from under the jacket, something thumped on the floor.

Rosemary dropped her backpack and dug a hand into her jacket pocket. She drew out the metal cylinder. It sat in her palm like an unmelting ice cube. *Could this be why the GG is after him? What about those men who tried to drown him? Do they want it, too? What could it be?*

Someone knocked on her bedroom door. Rosemary flinched and shoved the cylinder back into her jacket pocket. "Yes?"

"I'm going out," Dad called through the door. "Dinner will be at six. Your mom will be home around five." His voice was perfectly neutral as he spoke, as it always was when he mentioned her mother these days.

"Okay."

After draping her jacket over her chair, Rosemary unzipped her backpack and started pulling books from it. It would take her at least a few hours to skim through them and write a five-page essay. In the meantime, her thoughts kept returning to Biovibe. *Who is he? And why is he on the run?*

***

Uploading her finished essay only took a few seconds. Rosemary stood and stretched. She could smell something savory baking downstairs, but there was still half an hour or so until dinner. After piling the research books into her backpack, Rosemary sat down again and checked all the news sites. Still no updates on Biovibe.

She pulled the cylinder from her jacket and turned it over in her hands. *Maybe I can find information about this.*

Unsure how to start, Rosemary searched for small metal cylinders. That brought up millions of results, but nothing in the images seemed to match it more than superficially. It was well-polished and seemed to be solid.

The metal was heavy, but not overly so, and remained cool no matter how long she held it.

Trying to locate the metal it was made of also proved impossible. After carefully weighing it on the kitchen scale, measuring its length and diameter, and then calculating its density, all Rosemary could be sure of was that it wasn't pure metal. At least not pure enough to closely match any density on any chart of metals she could find. With the density offering no help, Rosemary had to rely on the cylinder's color—bright silver—and plenty of metals and alloys matched that description.

By the time her computer's clock ticked over to 6PM, she was ready to give up. Leaving the cylinder on her desk, she trudged downstairs to dinner.

It was chicken and salad tonight, boring by Rosemary's standards, but neither of her parents spent much time cooking lately. They preferred simple meals or ordering in, anything that meant dinner would be over sooner. The atmosphere was quiet but tense around the kitchen table, and Rosemary's shoulders hunched.

Why can't you just get along? She glanced from Mom to Dad. Both were looking at their plates.

As though sensing her gaze, Mom looked up. "Have you finished your homework, Rosemary?"

"Almost." It was Rosemary's turn to look down at her plate. She could see the unspoken question in her mother's eyes and still had no idea how to answer it. *Maybe I should just split my time between them. But then I'd have to keep switching schools. Or be homeschooled…which isn't a bad idea…*

"Don't leave it all to the last minute," Dad warned.

"I won't." Rosemary poked at her chicken with her fork, holding back a sigh. *He's not just talking about homework.*

"I picked up your favorite cookies for dessert," Mom added. "You can take a few for lunch tomorrow."

Rosemary nodded and took another bite of bland chicken. Her parents' forks clinked on their plates.

Mom sipped her water. "I'm surprised you didn't invite Carrie over this weekend."

Rosemary's fork slipped in her hand, clanking against her plate. "Didn't feel like it." Heat flushed across her face.

Dad set down his fork. "If you do invite her over, make sure she gets a ride from someone. They still haven't caught that fugitive."

"Yes, Dad," she mumbled. *I won't be inviting her over, so it doesn't matter.*

Silence fell again and remained unbroken for the rest of the meal. After dinner, Rosemary retreated upstairs, no longer wanting to face her parents.

There was still nothing new about Biovibe on any of the news sites. Rosemary spun the cylinder on her desk. It rolled smoothly, making a rumbling sound against the worn wood grain. Worry pooled in her stomach, souring what little dinner she had eaten.

"What should I do?" she whispered.

She wanted a swim, badly. She needed to submerge herself in water, let it wash away everything, all her worries and cares and fears.

Too bad she couldn't go swimming tonight. Not after what happened last time. She could still hear the words echoing through the water. *What if someone finds the body?*

Bile scoured Rosemary's throat as she swallowed it down.

The cylinder on her desk continued to spin. She slapped it with her palm, halting it in its tracks. Did this have something to do with everything happening in Blackwell? If so, why? What was so special about a little piece of metal?

***

Tapping on her window drew Rosemary out of a dream where she was running through a forest of giant metallic cylinders that hummed with a terrifying energy. She rolled over, yawning, and snuggled back into the blankets, but the tapping continued.

Did Mrs. Plummer's canary get loose again? Groaning, Rosemary pulled her pillow over her head, but the repetitive sound was at just the right frequency to drill through the stuffing into her ears.

"Stupid bird," she grumbled, shuffling over to the window in the dark. She pulled the curtain aside, expecting to find the bird perched on her windowsill.

Instead, Biovibe's pale face hovered there, lit by the crescent moon's light. His hand was raised by his ear, perhaps to knock again.

Rosemary sucked a scream down with a heavy breath. Her hand jerked to automatically cover her window again. *Calm down, you're still dreaming. Go back to sleep.*

The tapping started again, this time more insistent.

Against her better judgment, she peeked through the curtains. Biovibe's expression was a strained one, complete with a grimace that carved deep lines in his face. He gestured for her to open the window.

She shook her head violently.

His eyes narrowed and he beckoned her closer, mouthing words she couldn't quite hear.

Clutching the curtain, she leaned over until her breath misted on the glass.

"Cylinder?" Biovibe asked, his voice muffled by the thick layer of glass.

It is his, then. Rosemary gave a slow nod, unsure if she should tell him the truth.

A look of relief sliced across his face, erasing the lines of exhaustion for a moment. "Not safe now. Pond. Midnight. Tomorrow."

"No," she said aloud, moving back.

His expression became a pleading one. "Please." She read the word on his lips.

Frowning, Rosemary went to fetch the cylinder from her desk. She could give it to him and be done with it. But when she returned, he was gone. Only a faint mist remained on the window, glowing in the headlights of a passing car. She brushed it away with the sleeve of her pajama top, but part of it lingered—on the other side of the glass.

Her hand pressed against the window, feeling its chill. *It wasn't a dream.* She looked down at the metal cylinder cupped in her hand. *I need to tell someone about this.*

But who? Her parents would ground her forever if they found out what happened at the pond, and if she told the police, it would only be a matter of time before Mom and Dad heard about it.

A few weeks ago, she would have told Carrie. She and Carrie had shared everything together. That was the problem. Rosemary leaned her forehead on the window, hoping the cold might push away her growing headache, push away the memory rising to the surface like a bubble of deadly gas.

Rosemary's favorite place to sit and eat lunch was an old tree stump behind the sports storage shed. It was secluded enough for some peace and quiet but not enough to encourage smokers or drinkers to hang around. She'd spent half of her lunch break looking for Will, but he wasn't answering his phone. Her stomach's rumbling had finally drawn her away.

As she approached the shed, she heard the sound of giggling. It sounded like Carrie, but Carrie never ate outside—she thrived on the hum and bustle of the cafeteria. Confused, Rosemary walked around the corner.

Carrie and Will saw her at the same time, and their twin looks of guilt plunged like daggers into her chest.

Hot tears dripped down Rosemary's cheeks and she brushed them away angrily. Carrie had tried to talk to her, had "explained" that Will was uncomfortable around Rosemary because she was a super.

Rosemary had ignored her former best friend, had ignored everyone for the past few weeks. And now she found she had no one she could call, no one she could talk to. She and Carrie hadn't needed anyone else before…

Sniffling, Rosemary shuffled back to her bed, where she curled up under her comforter, still clutching the cylinder. *What am I going to do?*

The right thing would be to take it to the police. Carrie would probably agree with that—Carrie's father served on the force. She even joked sometimes about Rosemary becoming a superhero, with Carrie as her wisecracking, taser-wielding sidekick. Not that Rosemary's abilities were that powerful or useful for fighting supervillains. But Rosemary had still daydreamed about it, imagined scenarios—often ridiculous—where she swooped in to save the day, Carrie at her side.

Rosemary's hand tightened around the cylinder. Her head ached from crying and exhaustion. *I don't need her. I'll figure it out tomorrow. Myself.*

***

The morning sun was dim and gray—rain was settling in for the day. Rosemary would have stayed under her blankets longer, but their warmth made her scales itch and something hard was pressing into her hip.

Groaning, she rolled over and dug out the offending object. Right. The cylinder. Maybe she'd just toss it. Then she could be done with all of this subterfuge.

What if Biovibe breaks in looking for it? Or comes after me? She hesitated, looking down at it.

The doorbell rang, making her jump. It rang again. *Mom and Dad must not be up yet.* When the bell rang a third time, Rosemary threw on jeans and a t-shirt and trotted down the stairs. She tucked the cylinder into her pocket on the way.

"Hello?" Dad's voice echoed clearly down the hall, and Rosemary halted at the base of the staircase. He must have run from the guest room, where he was sleeping. For some reason, he sounded surprised and a little concerned. "May I help you?"

"We're investigating the fugitive super," a masculine voice said. His tone was smooth and professional…and strangely familiar. "May we ask you a few questions?"

Rosemary's brows drew together as she crept down the hall to get a better look. A mirror was hung between the pictures of her grandparents—Mom loved to check her hair before leaving for work. It was in the perfect position for Rosemary to see the front door.

Two uniformed men stood before the door. Both had tasers on their holsters, along with guns of some sort—ballistic or energy, she wasn't sure. Their badges weren't the copper-rimmed insignia of the local police force, or even the silver ones of the county force. Gold meant Global Government.

Rosemary sucked in a breath. *They must be looking for Biovibe. What if they found out I helped him?*

Neither was particularly memorable—same shade of brown hair, identical sunglasses, and about the same height. One had a slightly darker afternoon shadow around the jaw. Rosemary dubbed them Shaven and Unshaven as she continued to eavesdrop.

Shaven spoke again. "A security camera outside the Blackwell gas station caught footage of a man matching Biovibe's height and build walking along this road late last night. We're checking in with the residents in this area to see if anyone saw anything suspicious."

The tenseness in her shoulders relaxed a bit. *They aren't here for me.*

"Did you notice anything unusual?" The more the man spoke, the more familiar his voice seemed, but Rosemary couldn't place where she had heard it before.

Dad shook his head. "I haven't seen anything."

Unshaven's head lifted, and Rosemary had the uneasy sense that he was looking at her through the mirror. She drew back until she couldn't see them any longer, but it was too late.

"Maybe your daughter saw something." He raised his voice. "Come on out, there's no need to lurk in the hall."

"Rosemary!" Dad called sharply. "Come here."

She shuffled down the hall, her steps slow and unsure. Her heart pounded in her chest. Something was wrong, but she wasn't sure what.

Dad scowled at her, probably angry she'd been eavesdropping. "Have you seen the fugitive?"

Rosemary shook her head, not trusting her voice.

He turned to the officers. "There you go. I'm sorry we can't help you."

"Thank you for your time," Shaven said stiffly. "Have a good day." The way he said the farewell made it sound more like a threat. He turned to the other officer. "Let's go."

A shudder ran down Rosemary's back and she took a step away, even as Dad closed the door, blocking her sight of the two men. *I know where I heard that voice before. He was one of the men at the pond. The ones who tried to drown Biovibe. Why would GG officers do something like that?* Her hand slipped into her pocket, touching the cool metal cylinder. *Is this what everything's all about?*

"Rosemary?"

She looked to him. "Yes, Dad?"

He frowned. "Please don't answer the door for a few days. There's something about those two I don't trust." Dad glanced at the door and sighed. "I hope this whole situation is sorted out soon."

Unsure how to reply, Rosemary simply nodded and headed to the kitchen for breakfast.

***

The cylinder stayed in Rosemary's pocket throughout breakfast, since her parents were in the kitchen. She volunteered to do the dishes, hoping to have a chance to get rid of the cylinder, but Mom offered to dry and refused to take no as answer.

"I found some cheap flights to Milton," Mom said as she dried a stack of plates. They clinked, punctuating her words. "This would be a good time to order tickets."

Rosemary squeezed the sponge and started scrubbing at a frying pan with more vigor. "I haven't made a decision yet."

"All right." Mom's voice was quiet, with a hint of sadness reflected in her expression. "School's almost over, though, and my new job is starting in a month. You can't keep dragging it out like this, Rosemary."

"*You* decided to get divorced." Rosemary dropped the frying pan on the counter a little harder than necessary.

"I know it's been hard for you, it's been hard for us as well—"

"Then stop pressuring me!" Rosemary flung the last dish—a metal spatula—into the frying pan and tossed the sponge onto its drying pad. "I'm going to do some homework."

"Rosemary…"

She ran upstairs, ignoring Mom's call. The cylinder pressed against her hip, a reminder that she still hadn't thrown it out.

Sitting at her desk, Rosemary spun the cylinder on the wood as she tried to focus on homework. Too many questions were boiling in her mind, though, heated by fear and worry and frustration. *Should I meet Biovibe tonight? Should I go with Mom or stay here with Dad? What should I do with the cylinder?*

***

As evening approached, Rosemary had no idea what she was going to do come midnight. Without a better option, she went to take a bath. The warm water would be soothing on her scales, anyway, since they'd been itching all day.

She soaked in the bath, alternating between breathing through her gills and her lungs. The water wasn't as oxygen-rich as she would have liked, but it was a relief to drift underwater for a bit and let everything fade away.

After a long soak, Rosemary returned to her bedroom, wrapped in a comfy blue bathrobe. The time blinking on her alarm clock stopped her in her tracks. It was 11:36PM.

If I'm going, I need to leave now.

Second-guessing herself every step of the way, Rosemary dressed and crept downstairs. Some late-night talk host droned on in the living room—it was probably Dad watching TV since the sound was accompanied by the crinkling of a chips bag. Mom was likely already asleep. Still, Rosemary kept her footsteps as silent as possible as she crept toward the front door.

"Rosemary? Is that you?" Dad called.

She froze. *Don't come check, don't come check...* She started edging toward the kitchen.

Dad appeared in the living room doorway. "What are you doing up so late on a school night?"

"Homework." The lie weighed on her chest. "I came down for a snack."

"All right, just don't drink anything caffeinated." He hesitated. "Your mother and I were discussing the move again."

The pressure in her chest increased. She might as well have been at the bottom of an ocean, being crushed beneath its weight. "Yes?"

"You need to come to a decision by the end of next week." His words had a steely core, but an exterior softened by hope. "Okay, Rosie-Posie?"

He'd probably meant the use of her childhood nickname to be endearing, perhaps soften the blow of his words' finality. It hadn't. She gave a short nod. "Fine."

With a tentative smile, Dad retreated to the living room. Soon, the crinkling of the chips bag started again.

Rosemary breathed a sigh of relief and rattled around in the kitchen for a bit. Then, under the cover of an especially loud burst of laughter from the television, she sneaked down the hall and slipped through the front door.

On a normal night, she might have jogged or even run to Blackwell Pond. She knew the route by heart and could have followed it blindfolded at any time of year. Tonight, though, she moved hesitantly. Each footstep was cautious and planted firmly on the soggy dirt as though she expected it to open up and swallow her. Part of her half-imagined it might. There were definitely supers capable of that.

Rain started to fall again. It had been raining off and on all day. Rosemary usually didn't mind—water was water—but with the droplets pelting off the leafy trees around her, it was difficult to make out any other sounds.

She was soaked by the time she reached the pond. Not that it mattered, other than some minor chafing from her jeans. There were bigger worries. Such as where Biovibe was. A quick scan of the clearing from the forest's edge showed no sign of anyone, though it was hard to make anything out in the dimness. The faint moonlight was filtered through dark clouds and somehow made the shadows even deeper.

The cylinder pressed into her hip as she walked forward, a constant reminder of why she was there. Her heart thumped in her chest. She came to a stop at the edge of the pond.

"Hello?" she ventured, raising her voice a bit over the sound of the rain. Every muscle in her body was tense, ready to sprint back to the trees if something went wrong. *This was a bad idea…what am I doing here?*

A dark shape moved out of the trees on the opposite side of the clearing. Rosemary took a step back as it approached, but a sliver of moonlight cutting through the clouds illuminated Biovibe's face. He looked even more tired than he'd been the night before, dark bags under his eyes accenting his pale skin.

"Do you have it?" His gaze roamed the edges of the clearing, as though expecting something to happen. That did nothing to ease her worries.

"Yes." She reached for her pocket then stopped. "What is it?" *Just give it to him, you idiot!* part of her shouted. Another part whispered, *What if it's dangerous?*

"I don't have time to explain, but it's important that I take it now. Please." He held out his hand with a pleading look that made him look younger, more vulnerable.

What will he do if I refuse? Rosemary's fingers curled around the cylinder but didn't pull it from her pocket yet. "I'm not sure I trust you—"

"A wise decision." The GG officers stepped out of the trees. They held guns trained on both Rosemary and Biovibe. Shaven beckoned with his free hand. "Hand it over now, like a good girl."

"Thank you for your heroic assistance in capturing a dangerous fugitive," Unshaven added with a smirk.

"You were followed!" Biovibe hissed. "You idiot!"

"You're the one who didn't want to just take it last night." Rosemary eyed the gun pointed at her. They weren't actually considering shooting her, were they? *But they tried to drown Biovibe…and I helped him.* Her lungs froze in her chest.

Shaven grinned, looking like a shark that had smelled blood. "Hand it over *now.*"

"We can't let them have it." Biovibe insisted. "It's too dangerous."

"Get away from her." Shaven jerked his gun. "Or I'll shoot you right now."

A smirk twitched the corners of Biovibe's mouth. "Won't do you much good."

"We'll see about that." The officer's finger twitched against the trigger.

Rosemary threw herself backward as the gunshot rang out, twisting midair and using what little momentum she had to do a shallow dive into the pond. With the cylinder clutched in her hand, she swam down to the deepest part of the pond, gulping water so fast her gills almost couldn't keep up. Her body felt like ice.

I could die here. And because of what? This stupid bit of metal? Rosemary wanted to drop the cylinder into the muck of the pond, but part of her held back. It might be her only chance of survival. *What was I thinking?*

Another gunshot rang out, and then there was silence. Was Biovibe dead? Were the GG officers waiting for her to come out of the water?

Something plunged into the pond. Whoever it was, he was swimming about in a search pattern, judging by the water's motion. Looking for her? Rosemary sucked in a breath and moved away from the person more slowly than she wished, not wanting to draw attention.

The person continued to move closer. He was swimming too fast for her to slip by, which meant the amount of pond she had left to hide in was decreasing.

Caught between the choice of confronting the swimmer and returning to dry ground, Rosemary chose the swimmer. She shoved the cylinder deep into her pocket, not wanting to lose it, and with a sharp kick, swam at an angle that would take her in a wide sweep around the man.

He moved faster than she expected, darting through the water with a speed that seemed almost inhuman. A hand closed around Rosemary's ankle, and she kicked. His fingers were like iron bars, squeezing her bones until they ached, but she refused to give up. Still caught, she swam deeper, kicking and twisting so that he had no choice but to follow or release her. *He's going to run out of air eventually, right?*

Another hand closed around her leg, slightly higher up. He was trying to reel her in like a fish.

I don't think so. Gritting her teeth against the pain, Rosemary twisted her body and kicked again, this time with a clear goal in mind. Her abilities meant the water aided rather than hindered her, and she slammed her foot into his body at full force, striking hard muscle and ribs. The impact rattled her, but she kept moving, curling herself about so that her hands could strike next, this time higher up, where she expected his face to be. Her fists slammed into jaw and nose at the same time with a strength born of many hours spent swimming.

The man's grasp on her leg released immediately, and she kicked free. A rush of bubbles followed her as she sped across to the other side of the pond, half-expecting a pursuit. There was none. In fact, the man had begun to struggle in the water, no longer swimming smoothly as he had before. She must have done more damage than she had thought.

Rosemary gulped water. *What should I do? I can't let him drown.*

A small part of her pointed out, *They were going to kill you.*

I don't know if that's true.

They tried to kill Biovibe. Probably did.

A superhero wouldn't let the bad guy drown.

You helped a fugitive super. Technically, that makes you a supervillain.

I can't just stay here…

A second splash rocked the pond as someone else plunged in. He headed straight for the struggling man then dragged him away from Rosemary, toward the shore.

She had to know what was going on above. Sucking in one last breath of water, Rosemary swam to the side of the pond shaded by a large boulder. Slowly, she lifted her head out of the water.

Biovibe was kneeling on the other side of the pond. He had one hand on the throat of an officer—she couldn't make out which one—and the other wrapped around a gun that was pressed to the officer's head. Water dripped from his clothes, and his chest heaved from exertion.

Is he going to kill him? Rosemary looked about for the other officer and saw him lying still. Her lungs squeezed in her chest, making it difficult to breathe. Her gills fluttered uselessly.

"Where is the rest of the machine?" Biovibe shouted.

Machine? What machine? Rosemary sank lower in the water, wondering if she should hide at the bottom of the pond until they had left. *Or could I make a break for it?*

Coughing and choking sounds came from the officer. He wheezed something too low for Rosemary to hear, but Biovibe didn't seem to like the answer. Leaning down on the officer's throat, he growled, "Tell me now or I'll toss you back into the pond."

A faint sound in the distance caught Rosemary's ear. Sirens? This far from town? They had to be coming here. Fear drove her limbs to action, and she flew across the surface of the pond with a few deep strokes.

Biovibe looked up as she rose from the water, dripping wet. "Good, you're alive."

"Someone's coming," she said, gesturing to the woods. "Can't you hear the sirens?"

He tilted his head, frowning. "How far away?"

She shook her head. "I don't know."

A choking laugh came from the officer Biovibe was threatening—Shaven. "You won't get away this time."

"We'll see about that." Biovibe flipped the gun in his hand and slammed the butt against the man's temple, knocking him out. The super then got to his feet and tossed the gun aside. He held out his empty hand to Rosemary. "I need that piece now."

"What is it?" she said again, drawing it from her pocket. "Is it for the machine?"

"That doesn't concern you, kid. Hand it over."

She took a step back. "Or what? You'll beat me up, too?"

Biovibe flinched. "No, of course not! I'm not a monster. Not like these two." He gestured at the unconscious officers. "They work for a branch of the GG that's developing a machine capable of stealing powers from a super and transferring them to someone else. That piece you have is the key to the entire machine; it's irreplaceable. And I have to destroy it."

The sirens were growing louder, and Rosemary could see lights flashing in the trees. Something stirred deep inside her—not quite fear, more like excitement. *Is this what being a superhero feels like?* "I can help. I know these woods better than anyone."

Biovibe raised his eyebrows. "I'd rather not involve you further."

"I'm already involved. These officers, villains, whatever they are, will be after me too now, right? So take me with you."

"You're just a kid—"

"You'll never make it without me." She had to raise her voice to be heard over the sirens now.

Biovibe looked down at the ground, then at her, then at the cylinder she had in her hand. "Fine, but only as far as the edge of the woods. Then you're going home."

Rosemary smiled and held out the cylinder. Once he had pocketed it, she gestured to the trees. "This way."

It was a long, hard run through the trees in the near-darkness. They both stumbled now and then but caught themselves and kept running. Rosemary's ankle ached but she ignored it, as well as her burning leg muscles. The sirens slowly faded into the distance.

All too soon, the edge of the woods approached. Rosemary was starting to limp, but she did her best to hide her pain.

Biovibe grabbed her shoulder as the road came into sight. "You're hurt."

Her heart sank. "It's nothing."

Without responding, he bent and wrapped a gentle hand around her ankle. She winced from the contact to the bruised skin and bone then gasped when a sudden warmth flowed into her injury. As the heat faded away, so did the pain.

"There." Biovibe stood, wobbling a bit on his feet. "Consider it thanks for your help. I have to go now."

She caught his arm. "Wait! Please take me with you. Those GG officers will come after me!"

"Tell them I threatened your family." His teeth flashed in a brief smile. "They'll buy it."

Her mind raced. "You can't find the machine on your own, can you? I could help!"

He looked down at her, his face impassive. "I'm not alone, and you're too young. It would be best if you forgot everything that happened these past few days."

Rosemary gritted her teeth against the unfairness stinging her eyes with tears. Her moment as a hero was gone, crumbled back into the dust that was her reality—no friends and divorcing parents.

Sirens hummed in the distance, a reminder that the hunt was still on.

"You're what? Fifteen? Sixteen?" Biovibe continued.

"Sixteen," she mumbled.

"It's Rosemary, right?"

She nodded.

"And you're a water-breather?"

She nodded again, resisting the urge to scratch the scales on her neck.

"Here." He pressed a small square piece of plastic into her palm. "If I'm still around in two years, contact me. Maybe I'll have a job for you then."

Rosemary closed her fingers around it, feeling the thin edge bite into her skin like a sharp promise. "You better still be around."

He laughed, his expression mixed parts of amusement and some darker emotion. "I'm not planning otherwise. Until then, Rosemary." With a salute, he dashed across the road and into the trees on the other side.

For a moment, she stood there on the road, studying the bit of plastic. It was white and square with only a tiny metal chip imbedded in the center. It looked like any other business card she'd seen, except for the lack of decoration or name. There was no way to know for sure if he was telling the truth.

She preferred to believe he was. Tucking the plastic square safely into her pocket, Rosemary started walking home. Despite her exhaustion and all the worry and fear still tangled up in her chest, a smile started to form on her face. Maybe she didn't know where she'd be two weeks from now, but...

Two years, huh? I'll be ready.

The Fate of Patient Zero

J. E. Klimov

OCTOBER 12th, 2033. 2:30 P.M.

The bitter coffee burned the back of my throat. I have done this every day and somehow never manage to learn my lesson. *And now my tongue is numb.* I tapped the mug then wove my hand through my hair.

"Lucas, are you listening?" A female voice shattered the void in my mind.

Blinking rapidly at the woman in blue in front of me, I stuttered an apology.

"You seemed distracted. Again."

"I'm fine, Dr. Petrova. I just haven't been sleeping much lately. I've been worried about Grayson—I mean, 'Patient Zero'—ever since his reawakening."

Her glasses slid down the bridge of her nose as her green eyes bored into mine. "I told you, call me Lana," she said, tongue rolling with the Russian accent that sent goosebumps up my arms. "You know, I still don't understand this 'reawakening' thing..." She trailed off, scrunching her brows in deep thought.

I stared at my hands, pondering if I should've informed her of the things I witnessed beyond what the clinical documents indicated. There were times I had questioned Dr. Bernard's true intent. He had been manufacturing a plethora of injections before we could prove success with Grayson. I wondered if he was looking for a specific power. As anxiety simmered in my veins, I recalled my therapist's deep breathing technique.

In. Out.

We both sat in a white-washed cafeteria, located in the bowels of Bernard and Sons Corporation.

Lana nestled into her metal chair the best she could and said, "Do you think President Schmitt will repeal the Genetically Modified Infant Bill? I hope so."

Releasing a gruff laugh, I gulped the rest of my coffee. "Lana, that's impossible. There are too many legs to that bill. Some of it prevents a lot of grief for families."

"You know what I mean. The portion that allows parents to select the physical and personality attributes of their future child. I'm not talking about preventing diseases, Lucas!"

A maid mopping the floor stopped to glare at us. Lifting my hands in the air in surrender, I said, "Keep your voice down. You know who we work for. The empire of genetically modified everything."

"But I'm a *medical* professional. Even with the advances in technology, we can't fully eradicate HIV, but everyone is buying into babies with blond hair and blue eyes." She crossed her arms with conviction. "I want to help the sick, but everyone seems to care about creating the perfect child. And eventually enhancing them too. Look at you—a result of a beautiful genetic mix. Blond hair with dark eyes and skin. Your grandmother was—"

"Zimbabwean. Yes, she was. She married a Dutch man and the rest is history." My voice trailed off as I got lost in her eyes. Lana evoked an iron-clad intensity. It was probably why Dr. Bernard hired her in the first place—a geneticist from Russia who had completed residencies in America, with top mentions in health magazines. Her qualifications seemed to fit the mold as my perfect partner, but I had my doubts. She couldn't be heard expressing those kinds of opinions here.

I turned around and scanned the room. A pair of technicians munched on sandwiches, and the maid moved on. No one seemed to be listening to our conversation. The hum of the lights filled the silence. "Listen Lana, you were offered a six-figure paying job, and you accepted it. It would be foolish to throw it away."

Lana stood up with a huff. Her cheeks flushed as she stalked toward the trash to empty her leftovers. After, she marched to the coat hangers and picked out her lab coat.

The whole time, guilt clogged my veins. I couldn't say I disagreed with her. I was just trying to protect her. *If you were wise, you would keep your mouth shut around here.*

I launched my empty cup into the trash and grabbed my lab coat as well. The coffee had done no good. Not only was my tongue still numb, but my body was filled with anxiety instead of well-placed energy. I buttoned up my lab coat one by one, avoiding Lana's gaze. My palms grew sweaty.

After clearing my throat, I said, "Ready to meet Patient Zero?"

OCTOBER 12th, 2033. 2:53 P.M.

I let the keys dangle from my wrist, releasing a pleasant jingle.

"Dr. Pillay? Is that you?" A hopeful voice strained from the other side of an iron barrier.

"Yes, kid. It's me. I brought a friend. We're going to run some tests today."

Silence.

Lana's eyes darted between me and the door. I shrugged and unlocked the four-inch thick door, letting it swing open with a metallic creak. A lanky boy sat crossed-legged in the center of the concrete room.

"My lord," Lana muttered in my ear. "What awful conditions. No bedding, anything."

Raising my brow, I sighed. "It's…so nothing gets burned."

I strolled over to the boy before she could respond and cupped his cheek. "How are you, Grayson?"

"I'm okay. Still groggy from waking up."

His awakening was five days ago. Sadness wrapped its hand around my heart and squeezed. It had pained me to watch over his frozen-state for seven years.

I had signed onto Bernard and Sons research and development team, eager and naïve. Dr. Bernard discussed the results from the initial trials, where a rat developed the ability to camouflage. When the company was given the green light to test human subjects, he assigned me to Grayson. I had to record what power he manifested and how. From there, he wanted me to see if we could alter the molecular structure of the compound to engineer specific powers.

"Let's have a look at you. Come with us to the examination room." I retracted my trembling hand.

"Okay." His large blue orbs fixed on Lana.

"This is Dr. Lana Petrova. She will be my partner from now on. Like a team. A team that caters only to you," I said, raising the pitch of my voice.

"Nice to meet you," she said and stuck out a hand.

Grayson stared at her palm and didn't budge. I pushed his back and guided him out of his room. "It's okay. I understand it takes time to get used to strangers."

"Strangers?" Lana remarked sarcastically behind me.

My smirk faded quickly as we rounded the corner of the concrete hallway and walked into Exam Room One. Two chairs and a metal desk were crammed in one corner next to a medical supply cabinet that hung over the counter. I cleared my throat as I pulled out a checklist. "Dr. Petrova, would you mind taking his vitals? It's three in the afternoon on a Monday. October twelfth."

Within minutes, she had collected his blood pressure, heart rate, and respiratory rate. She worked swiftly as Grayson sat rigidly in his chair, eyes on her at all times.

"Forty beats per minute. Very low," she mumbled, scribbling on her notepad. Flipping the page, her eyes widened. "Blood sample?"

I nodded, observing them both. After our earlier conversation, I wondered how Lana felt examining Grayson. He was the epitome of the GMI Bill. Tall, thick blond locks, crystal blue eyes, clean complexion, and most notably, a "compliance" personality rating of ten out of ten. Supposedly.

When I had first injected Grayson, he developed the power of fire rapidly with minimal adverse events. Every day, we would go through exercises to learn how to summon and control his powers. We developed a good rapport with each other, but once Dr. Bernard wedged himself into the investigation, Grayson unsuccessfully produced anything. And that was when Dr. Bernard deemed the patient uncooperative and modified his protocol to extreme measures. *My patient.*

But by the time I questioned his methods, it was too late. He caught me when I called the ethics line. I remembered him smashing my cell phone before I could utter a single word. His threat constantly haunted me. He told me to follow his orders obediently and silently, or he would make my family "disappear."

I shook my head to dispel my thoughts.

"Dr. Petrova is going to draw your blood while I ask you a few questions. Is that okay with you?"

"Ready to comply," he said, fumbling with his words.

I pulled my chair closer to him and leaned forward. "Depending on your blood results, today may be the day. You've been a patient kid, waiting for five days, not knowing what's going on. So, have you had any allergic reactions since I last saw you?"

"No."

"Any other bothersome physical symptoms? Abdominal pain or chest pain to be specific?"

"No."

"Any thoughts about suicide or harming yourself?"

Grayson shifted in his seat. "I…don't think so."

I etched a question mark on the sheet.

"What thoughts have you been having?"

Silence filled the air. I could feel Lana straining to hear everything. Grayson's lips tightened into a thin line.

"Grayson. Grayson?" I clasped my hand over his and squeezed. He jumped.

"Sorry. Do I have to?" he asked and nodded toward Lana.

"Yes. She is your doctor as much as I am now—"

"Fire," he blurted. Sweat shined on his forehead as strands of golden hair clung to his face.

I motioned for Lana to come forward. "Fire? Please explain. It's okay. We're all friends here."

When Lana arrived at my side, she handed me a thermometer. I twirled the thermometer and slipped it under Grayson's tongue. His crystal blue eyes widened.

"It's okay, Grayson. Just checking to make sure you're healthy." I breathed through each word to avoid the tremor creeping up my throat.

"Fire," Grayson croaked. "I think of fire. A fire that has been burning for seven years, roaring for release."

I scribbled his answer down and tapped the edge of my pen on the last question. "Do you feel safe here?"

Beads of sweat dripped from Grayson's face onto the floor like a leaky faucet. It even began to soak through his shirt. Ripping the thermometer out, I bit my tongue. I had to assess the situation before I set off any alarm bells.

207 degrees.

The thermometer fell to the floor with a clack. "It's time…" I whispered to myself.

"What's happening to me?" Grayson gasped. Sweltering heat emitted from his body.

"It's time, Grayson. Just, just—" I whipped around for the protocol sheet. I couldn't find it. "Lana, get out of here. We need to get out." I stumbled out of my chair and pushed her toward the door.

"Where are you going?" Grayson shouted as he shot up from his chair. "Don't leave me here!"

"We are going to be right outside this door. We won't abandon you," I exclaimed as I pushed my confused colleague out the room. I swung around and slammed the door shut.

A deafening explosion rocked the hallway. I caught Lana around the waist. When she found her balance, I planted my face against the observation window.

"What just happened? Can you *please* explain to me what the hell—"

Fire funneled through the examination room. Grayson's body was but a mere shadow in the center of the room, encapsulated by the flames he generated.

OCTOBER 13th, 2033. 9 A.M.

My hand froze in front of the massive mahogany double doors. While some part of me was relieved Lana had stayed behind to tend to Grayson, maybe our positions should've been swapped.

A chill voice seeped from the other side of the door. "I've been expecting you. No need to dally."

Without hesitating, I stepped inside and flashed a sheepish grin at the man behind a desk. He didn't return the smile. Frown lines highlighted his fish lips and sunken cheeks. None of that could disguise his bulbous nose. There was a yellow tinge to his skin that he didn't have before. I was taken aback by how much his appearance had changed over the years.

"Well?" he asked with a hint of impatience. He stood up and rolled his shoulders. He wore a tasteful navy pin-striped suit, although his stomach protruded ever so slightly. Likely due to a daily feeding of scones and coffee. He leaned forward and spread his fingers on the glass top of his table.

Taking a deep breath, I said, "Patient Zero has manifested his powers."

His eyes bulged. His lips twitched. "In only five days? What a quick recovery!"

Bowing my head slightly, I brought my hands behind my back. I balled them into fists. "Yes," I said through gritted teeth.

It would've been better if there weren't a need for a recovery in the first place, Dr. Bernard.

"Your brilliance never fails to impress me," Dr. Bernard said, pulling out a handkerchief. He hacked into it. Red soaked through the tan silk, but he pocketed it quickly. Clearing his throat, he continued. "And I knew Dr. Petrova would be an excellent addition to the team. Every time I visited, Patient Zero seemed so hopeless."

I relaxed my hands and took a seat. Dr. Bernard strode toward a cabinet in the corner and pulled out a bottle of scotch. He gestured toward me, and I shook my head.

"I would start slow. Maybe write up a different protocol," I said. "I think we made a mistake with the first one. It was wrong to assume physical stress was the only way to trigger his powers." Guilt flooded my chest, leaving me short of breath. "When I worked with him the first few weeks seven years ago, he did just fine, until..."

"Until what?" He growled.

I will make them disappear. You will never see your family again.

I swallowed the lump in my throat. "Nothing," I muttered.

"Exactly," he huffed. "Dr. Pillay, you know I was only approved for one human test subject and power until I can fully document how that power is managed and developed, and I refuse to let this fail. I had hoped putting him to sleep for seven years would allow his body to grow and handle the serum better." He slammed his fist against the wall. "Patient Zero was selected for his compliance profile. He *wasn't supposed* to have any breakdowns to begin with."

"Sir?"

"He had broken down because there was something within him resisting us. Fighting the protocol."

I shook my head. "We need to interview Grayson when he's ready. We can't assume he went rogue on us and wanted to kill us for no reason. We can't confirm his 'resistance.' Maybe it was caused by an external factor. The vaccine itself. Or—"

"I've heard enough." He took a swig from his glass, wincing as he swallowed. "Do you have your SOAP notes?"

Fishing into my large lab coat pockets, I pulled out a wad of paper and handed it over. "Here are my findings from yesterday."

"Perfect. I will review them and let you know when to proceed." He poured himself another drink and smiled. "I can't wait to examine him."

My hands gripped the armrests. "Surely now that you've hired Dr. Petrova, the both of us can handle all the exams and testing."

Dr. Bernard lifted a brow. "Are you telling me how to do my job?"

My mouth ran dry. "No, sir. I am not."

He approached me with a wolfish glint in his eyes. "Do *you* run this company?"

"No, sir." I tugged at my collar.

"Were *you* the one who turned a failed HIV vaccine into a potential human-enhancing drug?" His voice rose, and red blotches appeared over his neck and parts of his face.

Shaking my head, my blond bangs flopped into my eyes. I quickly swept them aside. I sunk into the guest chair as fear multiplied like a virus. "No, sir. You did."

He hurled his glass against the wall, shattering glass everywhere. Before I could react, he shoved his face into mine and shouted, "Then you will do as I tell you! We are following the protocol as I planned it. *I am your boss!*"

The aroma of whiskey filled the air. It dripped from a surface somewhere. As Dr. Bernard stumbled toward a first-aid kit on his shelf, my eyes remained glued to his desk. Like a deer in headlights, shock paralyzed me. My boss had come across as a brilliant and even-tempered man when I signed on to work for his corporation. Since then, I'd witnessed him unraveling piece by piece.

"What exactly are you looking for?" I blurted, immediately regretting my question.

When he turned to face me, hunger blossomed in his eyes. "A world of a stronger, better human race. Imagine—a human that can cure all diseases..." He trailed off and turned back around.

Dr. Bernard opened gauze pads with a crinkle, and all I could do was scan the room aimlessly, trying to form words. An apology, maybe. My eyes landed on the trash bin. Sitting at the top was a box with a prescription label. Leaning forward, I squinted my eyes. In black, bold typing, it ended in *-vir*. I caught my breath. It had to be an antiviral medication. Curiosity itched at my fingertips as I noticed various pill bottles littering the basket.

I didn't realize he was this sick.

He glared at me. "You're dismissed," he barked.

The secretary knocked on the door, and Dr. Bernard shoved me toward the exit. I stumbled toward the lab in a haze. It took two long hallways, an elevator down forty-six floors, through security clearance, and a winding tunnel. Lights hummed above my head like busy bees. I wiped the specks of spit off my face with my sleeve. Whipping my I.D. out, I pressed it against a charcoal pad. It beeped, and I opened the door with a deep sigh.

Lana sat on a chair, typing away at her laptop. Her eyes were glued to the screen, ignoring the chestnut hair unwinding from her bun. The gentle *clack clack clack* of her typing somehow took the edge off my nerves.

When I plopped down beside her, she didn't take her eyes off the screen. "How'd the meeting go?"

My lips seemed glued together. She was still new to the company and naïve to Dr. Bernard's temperament. "Fine," I said.

"Liar. You look like hell," she said, swiveling around to meet my eye.

"No, really. I just had some suggestions about moving forward with the experiment, and I was shot down." I exaggerated a shrug.

Lana pointed her fingers at her screen. "I've been studying the original protocol."

Memories of a ten-year-old Grayson flooded my mind. His parents had signed the consent form after Dr. Bernard offered them a generous lump sum and a flimsy assurance that everything would be fine.

"I also read the clinical documents from 2016," she continued. "The first few weeks were clearly recorded, followed by some extensive testing. There was frequent exposure to physical stressors, but the details of subsequent weeks were not clearly defined." She narrowed her eyes. "That's unusual. What if we were audited?"

I hated myself. Day after day, I had tried to justify my work and stuff it in the back of my mind, but ever since Dr. Petrova joined the team, guilt dogged my steps relentlessly.

"There must be another way." She clasped her hands together.

"I know, Dr. Petrova."

"Lana." She touched my shoulder. "We are colleagues. We both swore an oath to take care of our patients. We need to protect Grayson's rights against those who would seek to harm him for personal gain."

I rubbed my hand against the back of my neck. My cheeks flushed with shame. I cared deeply for Grayson. Too deeply. But I had let him down seven years ago, and his blue eyes staring back at me as he froze up in his pod had broken my heart. "I-I know." My shoulders shook.

"Lucas, what happened? Grayson reacted to the last two exam questions so emotionally."

"He has no memory of seven years ago."

"So, something has been bothering him his first week since re-awakening?"

I blinked in shock. I was so wrapped up in the past, I had neglected to ask why Grayson was acting this way already. Leaning back, I stole a glimpse down the hallway where Grayson was resting.

"You're right. This is worrisome. And I do not want a repeat of what happened. I'm lucky to have you by my side, Lana. Together we will see Grayson through the protocol safely." I paused and looked around. "But we must tread lightly with Dr. Bernard around."

OCTOBER 16th, 2033. 11 A.M.

"Nothing's happening," Grayson strained his voice. "I'm tired. Can we stop?"

I hung my head. I was running out of time. A birch log stood vertically on the table before us, untouched.

"Grayson. You have to try harder. For me, please," I pleaded.

Wires were stuck to his forehead, neck, back, arms, and fingers. He looked like a futuristic marionette doll. A doll that wouldn't perform and the puppet master was about to arrive.

"I don't know how. The last time I produced fire, it just…happened."

"Well, we need to figure out why." I slammed the table with my fist. "How did you feel? What did you think? Do it again!"

Grayson flinched as the log fell on its side.

Running a hand through my hair, I walked out of Exam Room Two. Lana stood watching from the one-way mirror, chewing on a pen.

"Nothing for three days," she said, monotone.

"Three days of ignoring protocol." I paced back and forth. The envelope containing the paperwork lay on the desk. "Grayson hasn't been able to use his powers again."

Her face betrayed her nonchalant voice. "We did our best."

"And Dr. Bernard joins us today. What are we going to do?"

"We report that the first three days of following Dr. Bernard's wishes did not produce results," she said, fiddling with her lab coat. She blended into the white-washed walls. The blue light from the computers made her look like an apparition.

My muscles froze when a buzz erupted in the air. The entrance to the lab swung open behind me. The clicking of shoes sent shivers up my spine.

"Good morning, Dr. Bernard," Lana said.

"Morning, Dr. Petrova," he said in a clipped voice. "Dr. Pillay, I trust things are going as planned?"

Swiveling on the balls of my feet, I faced him and shook his hand. All I could manage was a nod. His face was gaunt, and an irregular red rash peeked beneath his collar. My thoughts traveled to the box of medication I'd seen the other day. I was not his personal doctor, and it was none of my business, but the memory haunted me nonetheless.

Lana cleared her throat. "No success thus far, but the methods we've been using are dated. If we started him slower and avoided tests that physically distress him, maybe we could get your desired results," she said, drawing out her last syllables.

Dr. Bernard's eye twitched, but he managed a smile. As he adjusted his tie, I was hit with a wave of musk. "He's older now. His body should be able to handle everything just fine. Remember, Lana, we are on the verge of discovering a new way of life for people. Super *homo sapiens*. I want you to know that my name is on the line here, and I know what I'm doing."

Lana nodded and reached for the envelope, but he waved his hand. "Dr. Pillay. Let's lower the temperature in there. That seemed to lead to results last time."

I shrunk under Lana's gaze and strode over to the thermostat. My eyes were glued on Grayson as I turned the dial. The boy's head shot up as the vent rumbled to life. The next fifteen minutes were painfully slow. Dr. Bernard ordered a tea, and he sat back, sipping and watching. The cup clattered against the saucer. I never knew he had a slight tremor.

Lana and I stood nervously. I don't think either of us were comfortable sitting. She clutched her clipboard as I chewed on my nails.

A knocking came from the one-sided mirror. Grayson's arms hugged his abdomen, and he trembled from head to toe. Color drained from his face. Even his gold locks seemed faded. "I-I'm c-cold. Can someone turn up the heat please? Dr. Pillay?"

Dr. Bernard swung his head in my direction. He jutted out his fat lip and scrunched his brow. "Not until we see a response. Isn't that correct?"

I nodded.

"And Dr. Petrova, are you taking notes?"

Her mouth opened, but no words escaped. Her eyes traveled to me, and I shook my head.

"Don't say anything," I mouthed.

Without a word, she pulled a pen from her bun and scribbled on her clipboard. It continued this way for another fifteen minutes. Tension clouded the observation room while frost snaked up the mirror. Grayson's breath curled in the air as he stared vacantly at us. The thermostat was down to 32 degrees Fahrenheit.

"Hey, I can't feel my fingers! Cut this out!" Grayson shouted. He pounded the window. His spit froze against the glass. "I can't burn this stupid log, and this isn't helping. Is this some kind of sick joke? What's going on?"

My heart twisted. My fingers twitched.

"Dr. Pillay? Who else is there? Help!" Pounding. He kept pounding.

I can't do this!

I made for the door.

"Get back here, Dr. Pillay!" Dr. Bernard shouted.

As soon as my hand made contact with the knob, it rattled. A reptilian-like hiss filled the air. When I swung the door open, I shielded my eyes as a blaze erupted. Fire jetted from Grayson's throat as the boy screamed. The flames licked the windows hungrily.

"Hey, Grayson!" I waved my hands. "It's okay, I'm here!"

When he turned around, I fell into the line of fire. Dropping, I rolled around, extinguishing the embers. My lungs filled with smoke; I hacked uncontrollably. But he was still screaming. I had to pull myself onto my knees.

Looking up, Grayson aimed at the fallen log and incinerated it. Scrambling to my feet, I lunged at him. I wrapped my arms around his shoulders and took him down.

I gritted my teeth as we slammed onto the concrete floor. An elbow dug into my ribs as he squirmed in my arms.

I shushed him and stroked his hair. "It's okay," I whispered into his ear.

The flames were gone. Grayson rocked in my arms, sobbing.

"I can't control it. I can't!"

Pulling his face to mine, I said, "You can. I'm starting to understand now. I'll take care of you. I failed you once, but I will not fail you again."

Grayson squeezed me as his tears blotted my tattered lab coat. "Promise? You're my only friend."

"I promise," I said, wiping away a tear of my own.

OCTOBER 16th, 2033. 9 P.M.

I stood by my car, staring vacantly into the sky as it opened up. Rained poured on me, but I felt nothing.

Before I left work, Dr. Bernard had pulled me aside with a greasy smile plastered on his face. The rash on his neck had spread to his jaw.

"I have great news. Your report of Patient Zero's recent successes has brought us one step closer to getting approval to test the next batch of vaccines," he had said. "We just need to prove one more event."

"Excuse me?" My stomach had soured upon hearing the news. More Graysons. "Only if he stabilizes," I replied curtly. "There are some mental health concerns I have for him."

"Then prescribe him some mood stabilizers and move on!"

I rubbed my eyes, trying to erase the memory.

"How long have you been standing there? You're getting soaked," said a voice behind me.

Lana appeared and shifted her umbrella over my head.

"You're here late as well," I said.

"I've been preparing some paperwork." She grasped my chin and turned my head to face her. "What's wrong? You haven't said a word since Dr. Bernard left for the day."

I shrugged. "I just think we need to confirm Grayson's well-being before we even *think* about testing more people."

"Ah, yes. He did mention another batch of vaccines. Do we know what powers will be tested?"

"I've tinkered around with the molecules, so I'm expecting the ability to control water, metal, electricity, and I think some sort of telekinesis or teleportation. Oh, and enhanced strength. It was all based on theory, so I won't really know until they are injected into human subjects." I bit my lip. Each raindrop felt like a needle piercing through my clothes.

"You want to save Grayson."

After taking a deep breath, I nodded. "Dr. Bernard has changed over the years. Something's not right," I said, dropping my voice into a whisper.

Emotions filled me to the brim until I couldn't contain them anymore. "Dr. Bernard doesn't care what happens to Grayson! He's just a means to an end. Lana, Dr. Bernard is sick. I don't know with what, but it's clear that conventional medicine is failing him, and I bet he is trying to develop the power of healing. He will go through as many test subjects as possible until we curate the right molecule. The worst part is that I am a part of this terrible process!" I kicked my car, triggering the alarm. The high-pitched beeping couldn't drown out my thoughts. "He threatened my family. He threatened me. But I can't deal with the guilt anymore."

Falling to my knees, I wove my fingers together behind my head and heaved. Lana grabbed the keys and silenced my car. She bent over me and rubbed her hand down my back.

"Lucas. What does your heart tell you to do?"

I let the pitter patter of rain fill the void between us. Thoughts that reeled through my mind like a wild animal slowed to a stop. My heart thundered in my chest. I refused to be a coward anymore. I made up my mind.

"We've got to get him out of here," I said as I stood up.

Lana squared her shoulders and smiled. "Then, that's what we will do. Let's not waste time."

We turned around and made our way back to the building. Red brake lights colored the gray atmosphere. A horn blared in the distance. There was no formal plan, but we agreed to enter the lab and stage a medical emergency for Grayson so I would be able escort him to the hospital. Lana and I would figure out the consequences after that.

The glass building loomed before me. Slamming my I.D. against the scanner, I ripped the door open and made a beeline for the lab. Lana followed close behind.

When I finally entered the observation room, I scanned the area. Everything was filed and neat. That was all Lana's doing.

"He's not in Exam Room Two," Lana cried.

I sped ahead toward Grayson's room. Knocking lightly, I pressed my ear against the door. Nothing.

"Grayson?" I whispered.

Still no answer. Adrenaline rushed through my system. As I sprinted to Exam Room One, I passed a secured medicine cabinet. It was full with syringes. Must be the new "vaccines." I sucked in a deep breath and huffed until I reached the room. Before my hand reached the knob, I heard a voice. Baritone, rumbling.

"You don't want us to try extreme measures again, do you? Do you think I enjoy watching you suffer?" Dr. Bernard's voice filled the air.

I growled under my breath as I balled my hands into fists. Lana cupped her hand on my shoulder and squeezed.

"I thought he had left work already. What now?" she whispered into my ear.

Shrugging my shoulders, I brought my finger to my lips. "Wait for the perfect moment."

"I trust Lucas." Grayson's voice was limited to a whimper.

"I don't understand. Your parents showed me the papers! Compliance ten out of ten! And look at all the problems you caused me!"

"I-I'm sorry. I don't even remember what I did when I was little," he said, sniffling. "I *am* trying to comply with your orders. Dr. Lana and Lucas's orders."

"But, Grayson, sometimes it takes a little pressure to produce something wonderful. Like a phoenix reborn through its own ashes. And I want to make you shine. I want to make sure you're the first 'superhero' the world will come to know. I want you to pave the way for lots of superheroes."

"What are you doing? Stop. Don't touch me!" Grayson shrieked.

I finally peeked into the small framed window. Dr. Bernard struggled with a taller Grayson by grabbing one arm and aiming a syringe with the other. My blood curdled.

"What is that? You aren't even telling me what it is or asking if it was okay with me!"

"This is vercuronium. I want to see if powers can manifest during paralysis."

"WHAT?"

Dr. Bernard flipped him onto the floor and pinned him down. Grayson cycled his legs. My hand remained on the doorknob, shaking uncontrollably.

"No. Stop! Lucas? Where are you? Help me! I don't want this!"

Anger exploded within me as I rammed the door open. "Stop it! Let him go!"

My boss whipped his head and scowled at me. Beads of sweat formed over his dark brows. "I knew you would crack. Just like your little buddy here. And Lana too? I wasn't expecting her to be as weak as *you*." His brown eyes flashed with malice. "Don't take another step, or your careers are over!"

Like lightning, I connected my fist to his jaw. Crunching filled the air as pain exploded in my knuckles. Ignoring the stinging sensation pulsing up my arm, I kicked the syringe from Dr. Bernard's grip. The needle skidded across the floor. Before I could reach for Grayson, all two hundred pounds of Dr. Bernard tackled me. He slammed me against the ground, knocking the wind from my lungs.

Grayson whimpered in the distance, frozen in horror. He was able to raise an arm in our direction, but I shook my head.

"Grayson. Take a deep breath. Take control of your emotions. Don't let the fire take over or we all die."

Dr. Bernard cocked his arm back and formed a fist. Lana dove toward us, wrapping her arms around him, and tried to pry him off me.

"No!" screamed Grayson. "Stop it! STOP—"

A funnel of flames blinded me, covering Dr. Bernard. Lana flew back against the wall.

I tore away from his grip, rolling beneath him to snuff out the flames along my sleeves. He continued to writhe under the maelstrom of fire. I blindly reached back and tugged at Grayson's sleeve.

"Stop it," I commanded. I grabbed his shoulders and shook them.

His gaze flickered, eyes losing their cerulean color. Grayson collapsed in my arms, pulling me down with him. Dead weight.

"Save me," he whispered.

Without hesitation, I wrapped his arms around my shoulders and secured him on my back. Dr. Bernard groaned on the floor. All the fire had been extinguished.

"I resign," I said, loud and clear as I stepped over him and exited the room. I looked to my left, then my right. Everything was quiet. I calculated our escape in my mind.

Lana cleared her throat and pointed to my left.

My eyes landed on a security camera.

"Damn it."

As if I had uttered the magic word, sirens flashed and alarms rang. I cringed at the sound. Waves of vibration shattered my concentration. But Grayson's weight reminded me that I had to move. Somewhere. Somehow.

A pounding on the door to my left signaled that time was up. Lana rolled her chair over and pressed it against the door.

"What now?" Lana exclaimed.

I rushed toward the medicine cabinet. I must've been going mad. Releasing Grayson gently onto the floor, I propped him against the wall. I uttered words of encouragement as I studied the cabinet. There was a padlock that I had no key to.

I slammed my elbow against the glass. Gritting my teeth, I shook off the shards. A dozen syringes stood in lines like miniature soldiers. I tried to read the labels, but my quivering hands knocked the casing onto the floor. Some broke, others remained intact.

"No time, no time," I mumbled.

"Lucas," Grayson said, pointing at the door.

A man in a black uniform kicked it open, slamming Lana in the back of the head. He stepped over her and aimed a pistol at us.

"No time," I shouted as I grabbed the closest syringe. Ripping the cap off, I jammed the needle filled with a purple viscous substance through my clothes and into my deltoid. I bit my tongue as I depressed the plunger. It stung.

It stung all the way down. I swear I could feel it entering my capillaries, then veins…

"Cease and desist or we will shoot!" The officer's voice echoed.

All edges blurred. Colors seeped together. I felt my way to Grayson. When I grabbed his hand, I closed my eyes. "It'll be over soon."

My heart pounded as boots thundered closer. All I could do was wait. Maybe the solution would energize me with super strength. Who knew?

Dr. Pillay, I want you to sit back and close your eyes.

My therapist's voice came out of nowhere. Shoot. I was hallucinating.

Just give it a shot. Imagine a peaceful place. Where is the place you go to seek total and utter peace and relaxation? Can you envision it for me?

Arms grabbed and jerked me away from Grayson, but I wouldn't let go of his hand. Someone else grabbed him and tugged.

"Hold on tightly, Grayson. Don't let go." I barely managed a whisper.

His screaming sounded dull in my ears as some flash of light occurred before me. It was a blur of yellow, orange, and red. Grayson must have unleashed hell again. We were going to die.

Close your eyes. Imagine it to the point where you not just see it, but feel it, smell it, hear it.

My lids felt heavy. I imagined my home in Cape Town. My nostrils filled with a cool salty sea breeze. Beautiful shrubbery surrounded me. I leaned my head back and saw buildings huddled under a majestic mountain. So green.

I squeezed my lids tighter as flames licked at my fingertips. Cape Town was clear as day again. With a gasp, I opened my eyes. Grayson, whose body was aflame, was the only person I saw. Darkness engulfed us. The voices of security muffled. Then, as if yanked by my collar, I flew into the infinite darkness with Grayson still holding onto my hand.

I could barely breathe as wind whipped against my face. A speck of light flickered in the distance, and we approached it rapidly. The searing white light expanded as large as the sun. I covered my eyes with my free arm.

"Hang on, Grayson!"

With a whistle, a gale tossed us through the ball of light, and we both tumbled downward as if the switch for gravity had been turned back on. I slammed onto a grassy surface. The thud beside me had to be Grayson. Rolling onto my elbows, I released a groan. As I blinked, my vision returned to focus.

He lay with his eyes closed. But he seemed unscathed. No burn marks on his skin, but his clothing had disintegrated into tattered threads. I checked his pulse. Sixty beats per minute. Not the best, but he was alive and breathing. I caressed his cheek, hoping to bring him to consciousness without frightening him. "Grayson?" My lips quivered. My eyes grew wet.

I looked away as I blinked my tears out. We were on a patch of land, but before me were miles of beach and sapphire waters. I turned my head slowly and recognized every single building. Table Mountain stood proudly in the distance. The sight stole my breath away. It couldn't be. We couldn't really be in Cape Town...

Grayson broke into hacking coughs. His eyes locked onto mine as I held him. His whole body shook violently. "Where are they?"

I patted his head. "They are far, far away. We're safe. Somewhere no one can bother us."

"But how?" he uttered. The wildness in his eyes faded.

Gesturing toward my shoulder, I said, "The serum worked. I can teleport now." I chuckled; it had worked so quickly. Everything seemed surreal. I promptly cleared my throat and brought his hands to my lips. "Grayson, I'm just like you now. And I promise from this day forward, I will protect you with every ounce of power I have."

My thoughts traveled to Lana. I hoped she was okay. There was no telling what Dr. Bernard would do to her.

When I stared into Grayson's eyes, I noticed red flecks glowing in his irises. Every time he blinked, the blood-red color expanded until there was no blue left.

"Lucas?" His voice was cold and oddly calm.

Startled, I leaned back and swallowed the lump in my throat. "Yes, kid?"

"Revenge." He breathed through each syllable. "I want revenge for what Dr. Bernard has done to me. I want to stop him from doing this to others."

The blood in my veins boiled. Looking him straight in the eye, I said, "I will help you until my dying breath. I promise."

Author Biographies

Sam Waterhouse – Like You

Sam Waterhouse is a reader, writer, husband, and father in Hobart, Tasmania. He spends considerably more time on some of these activities than others. "Like You" is his first published story and fulfills the lifelong goal of legitimately calling himself an author.

"Like You" came from the idea of treating powers like an infectious disease rather than something to be desired. How would people react and what would be done about it? Unfortunately for Jorge, he's found himself in direct confrontation of the source of all unnatural powers.

You can follow Sam on Twitter (@SW_Wordologist) or catch him around town. He'll probably be drinking coffee, so feel free to pull up a seat.

Louise Ross – Super Love

Louise Ross is a writer from the Kansas City area. When she is not crafting or working, she lives in a fantasy world of epic battles and the ordinary person struggling to live in their alternative worlds.

"Super Love" was originally a story challenge through a writers group to craft a story about two disparate love interests in a humorous way.

Check out Louise Ross on Facebook (@alouiseross), Twitter (@A_Louise_Ross), or her blog (83louross.wordpress.com).

LB Garrison – The In-League

Have you ever watched the stars on a warm summer night and wondered if someone was looking back? Thoughts of dinosaurs and aliens dominated LB Garrison's childhood. Adult concerns came later, but never could quite crowd out the wonder.

A microbiologist by profession, and dreamer by choice, LB has always been an avid reader of science fiction and fantasy, and recently a writer of speculative fiction. LB has published two short stories and contributed "The In-League" to this anthology. LB is currently wrestling with a first novel in southeast New Mexico.

Matthew Dewar – Lord Chimera

Matthew's passion for reading and writing developed at a young age. Fascinated by all genres, enthralled by the endless creativity of imagination, and captivated by foreign worlds and intriguing characters, Matthew makes time in his busy schedule to write every day. If he's not reading or writing, you might find Matthew working as a physiotherapist, teaching group fitness classes, entertaining his dog, or dreaming of travelling to an exotic destination.

The idea for "Lord Chimera" came about when Matthew wondered just how far a hero would go to make the world a better place.

In May 2017, Matthew published *Nightmare Stories*, a collection of young adult horror fiction where twelve young teens discover that happily ever afters only exist in fairy tales. He contributed to the first Just-Us League anthology, *From the Stories of Old*, with a retelling of the Ballad of Mulan titled, "The Female Warrior." The *Seven Deadly Sins Anthology: Gluttony* featured the short story, "Hungry, Hungry Henry." He is currently working on two novels and several other ideas that he can't wait to share with the world.

You can connect with Matthew on Twitter (@WriterDewar), Facebook (Matthew Dewar Author), or at his website: matthewdewarauthor.wordpress.com.

J. L. Bernard – The Outlands

What started as a last-minute elective course, transformed into a life-long love for the writing craft. When J.L. Bernard's not fighting his way through video game worlds, he's creating his own one word at a time. While his work naturally falls in with science fiction, he's planning a journey to a place that speaks of a millennium of struggle among supernatural creatures as they survive a world dominated by humans.

J.L. Bernard contributed to the first Just-Us League anthology, *From the Stories of Old: A Collection of Fairytale Retellings* with "The Princess of Alantilus." It's his first published short story and is inspired by his wife's love (obsession) with the Little Mermaid.

"What if a so-called 'monster' saves an entire town?" This question begged to be written about and sparked his interest in crafting a piece for the League's second anthology. Reading and writing about superheroes is like eating candy with a sweet tooth—you just can't stop!

If you would like to see more of J.L. Bernard's work or would like to connect, please visit his website (terraformonline.com) or connect with him on Twitter (@jlbernard88). Comments are always welcome.

Mae Baum – Ice Bonds

Mae Baum grew up among the snow and birch trees of upstate New York, but now makes her home in the urban jungle of Atlanta with her husband, daughter, and two cats. Always to be found with her nose in a book, she enjoyed exploring fantastical worlds and now loves making up her own. She currently has several other short stories out in anthologies and is currently hard at work on a novel series.

She's always been a superhero fan, but has struggled with the idea that a superhero must always be a man alone without friends or family. Her short story, "Ice Bonds," takes issue with both parts of that statement—must the superhero be a man and does he need to be alone?

You can follow Mae on Goodreads (Mae Baum), Twitter (@MaeBaumWriter), her website (maebaum.com), and Facebook.

Renee Frey – Jump Discontinuity

Renee is both an author and the Chief Operating Officer of Authors 4 Authors Publishing. When not writing or publishing, she teaches dance classes and choreographs musicals. She lives in the 'burbs of Philadelphia (Go Eagles!) with her husband and their two-pound puppies: a puggle named Ziggy who may have eaten your lunch, and a chihuahua mix named Megatron who definitely didn't growl at you just now.

She is excited to collaborate with Rowanwood Publishing for this and other anthologies, which spotlight up and coming authors in the fantasy, science fiction, and other speculative fiction genres.

Renee dedicates her story to her late father, Major James Andrew Donald, USAF, retired. Turning her dad into a hero pales in comparison to the real life hero he was. Renee also offers a special thanks to everyone at JL but especially Heather, who made this anthology possible!

Mckayla Eaton – The Tiger of Geminia

Mckayla is an aspiring author of science fiction and fantasy. She's won three honorable mentions for three separate short stories submitted to Writers of the Future, an international science fiction and fantasy short story competition for amateur writers.

She lives in Halifax, Nova Scotia, Canada and is going into the last year of her BA at the University of Kings College.

She's currently working on three fantasy novels, her main project being a young adult fantasy about a young wizard who has to go to Hell and back to defeat a dangerous demon.

You can find her on Instagram as @mckayla_schneider.

Kristy Perkins – Childhood's Last Nemesis

Kristy Perkins is a nanny by day, writer by night (and by naptime). Ever since she could write legibly, she has created stories. She writes fantasy and sci-fi because the fun of designing cultures and planets and languages was too much fun to pass up.

She loves superheroes, and loves seeing what happens when they are presented with relatively ordinary decisions that somehow become bigger when contrasted with their heroism. Her story "Childhood Nemesis" is inspired by those choices that shape the rest of our lives. It is also inspired by a weird daydream, a Netflix binge session, and a long argument about character motivations.

You can follow Kirsty on Twitter (@KristyEPerkins) and Pinterest (perkinswhatif), and check out her blog at nocluewritingplatform.wordpress.com.

Renée Harvey – I Choose

Renée Harvey is a wife and mother, historian, and author in Idaho, USA. Her novels are historical fiction—stories based on the lives of little-known people with messages of their own to share—but "I Choose" gave her the opportunity to stretch her wings in a new genre and writing style.

True to Renée's theme as a writer, this short story has a message within it from a lesser-known individual: her mom. When Renée was a preschooler, her mom told her, "There is a lot of good in the world, and there is also a lot of evil. One day, you're going to have to choose which one you're going to follow." Such counsel left a lasting impression, which nurtured the seeds for "I Choose".

You can follow Renée at PRHarvey6 on both Twitter and Facebook and check out her website: storytellerreneeharvey. wordpress.com.

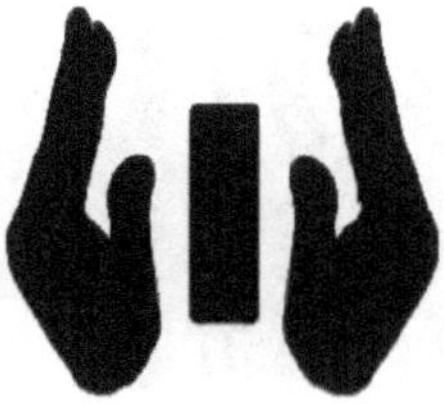

Heather Hayden – In A Breath

Though a part-time editor by day, Heather Hayden's not-so-secret identity is that of a writer—at night she pours heart and soul into science fiction and fantasy novels. In March 2015, she published her first novella, *Augment*, a YA science fiction story filled with excitement, danger, and the strength of friendship. In December 2016, her first published short story, a retelling of the selkie myth titled "Beneath His Skin," was released as part of the Just-Us League's first anthology, *From the Stories of Old*.

When her writer's group decided to compile a second anthology, this time featuring stories about original superheroes, Heather couldn't wait to get started. The idea for "In a Breath" came to her when she considered, "What kind of superhero powers would I want to have?" Flight, teleportation, telekinesis…there are many awesome powers to be had. But what if the heroine had a smaller gift? Something less flashy? From those musings, Rosemary's story was born. Heather dedicates this story to all would-be superheroes, great and small.

You can follow Heather's writing adventures on her blog (hhaydenwriter.com) or on Twitter (@HHaydenWriter).

J. E. Klimov – The Fate of Patient Zero

Ever since J. E. was little, she dreamed of sharing her stories with the world. From scribbling novel ideas instead of taking notes in school, to bringing characters to life through sketches, J. E.'s ideas ranged from fantasy to thriller fiction. And despite a busy career in pharmacy, J. E. has chipped away at her dream. Within this anthology, "The Fate of Patient Zero" is a superhero origin story about a doctor who faces an ethical dilemma. Health care providers are faced with tough decisions daily and are constantly fighting an uphill battle to uphold their pledge to put the patient first.

You can follow J. E. Klimov on Twitter (@klimov_author), Facebook (@klimovauthor), and her blog (jelliotklimov. weebly.com), and stay tuned for her debut novel, *The Aeonians*, which is set to be published late 2017. J. E.'s first published short story, a retelling of an old Japanese fairy tale titled "The Guardian's Secret," is part of the Just-Us League's first anthology, *From the Stories of Old*.

About the Illustrator

Heidi Hayden was raised in the forests of Maine and graduated from the Maine College of Art as an Illustration major. A bookworm by nature, she reads copious amounts of questionable fiction by unpublished authors, in the few moments of spare time when she is not writing and illustrating her own books. She works in gouache, ink, pencil, and fabric, and enjoys repurposing materials for her art.

Heidi has always loved stories about superheroes. She drew inspiration for the anthology's illustrations from her experience in designing logos and her love for the more simplistic forms of comic book art. Hand-drawn sketches were combined with digital vectoring in order to give the images a more modern feel.

You can see more of her work on her website: haydenillustration.com.

About the Just-Us League

Hailing from all corners of the globe, the members of the Just-Us League share a common passion for words and worlds.

The League can be found on Facebook (@jlwriters), Twitter (@JL_writing), and our website (jlwriters.com). Follow us for updates, giveaways, and new releases.

Also by the Just-Us League

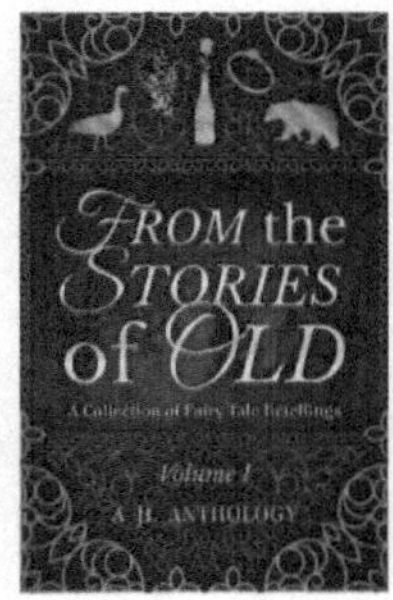